VENUS IN SPARTA

Books by Louis Auchincloss

The Indifferent Children
The Injustice Collectors
Sybil
A Law for the Lion
The Romantic Egoists
The Great World and Timothy Colt
Venus in Sparta

Venus
IN SPARTA

LOUIS AUCHINCLOSS

HOUGHTON MIFFLIN COMPANY BOSTON

The Riverside Press Cambridge

1958

124263

For Adele

VENUS IN SPARTA

BESIDES, it was a great part of that honor they paid their Gods, of whatever sex they were, to adorn them with military weapons and armor, partly out of superstition and an extraordinary reverence they had for the virtue of fortitude, which they preferred to all others, and which they looked upon as an immediate gift of the Gods, as being the greatest lovers and patrons of those who were endued with it, and partly to encourage every one to address his devotions to them for it; insomuch as Venus herself, who in other nations was generally represented naked, had her armor too, as well as her particular altars and worshippers.

PLUTARCH, *Customs of*
the Lacedaemonians

1

THE HUDSON RIVER TRUST COMPANY, at 65 Wall Street, was one of the oldest business structures in the financial area. Designed in 1890, it was among the final works of Richard Morris Hunt, and its dark narrow façade of rough sandstone blocks, broken by row upon row of massive Romanesque arches, tried to express the maximum of solidity in the minimum of space. Happily, its bluff, if bluff it was, had never been called; stripped of its lights and furnishings, with here and there a broken window, like so many of its condemned contemporaries, it would have lacked the dignity of a Roman ruin. Its arches might have seemed only pompous and its beetling cornice an empty boast. But such was not yet its fate. Its interior, on the contrary, had even been renovated, and through the bars on the first story windows the pedestrian on Wall Street could catch a glimpse of white ceilings and fluorescent lights. Everywhere, indeed, the old and the new were uneasily juxtaposed: the long corridor of yellow marble with the busts of the twelve Caesars ran past elevators of gleaming aluminum, and the panel of flashing bulbs that told their whereabouts seemed to pop impertinently at the inclined head of a sleepy Tiberius. The modern note prevailed as one ascended until it triumphed altogether in the third floor, the habitat of Michael Farish, Vice-President and Senior Trust Officer, where all was softened and civilized, all a green smoothness of wall-to-wall carpeting and muffled typewriters and lithographs of Bowling Green and Broadway in the eighteen-twenties and views of Manhattan from the bay.

Michael Farish himself looked to perfection the part of the modern trust officer. There was a marvelous impeccability about him, about the dark hair, combed straight back, greying on the sides, about the immobile, finely chiseled features, the straight nose, the grey, clear, gravely questioning eyes, an impeccability that managed to suggest, along with the dark suit and the claret polish of the shoeshine, the easy strength of the executive: relaxed, assured, well-bred, solely attentive to the problems of his client. Yet Michael, at forty-five, had preserved, despite the impatient grey at his temples, almost too much of the high-cheekboned, thin-faced charm of the boy to fit altogether the role that he was certainly trying to play. To the close observer there was a faintly jarring note in the air of slightness to his general frame, in the hint of conquered timidity in his eyes, in the malaise of his nervous shoulders. But, of course, as the close observer, if fair, might have speculated: was this aspect of still undigested youth not a part of the very essence of the American executive? Was it not visible only because the observer himself was so sharp? And the fact that Michael had selected from the bank's collection, to fill the large green wall space behind his Sheraton desk, a colored print of Peter Stuyvesant expressing his shock at the animated dancing of a young vrouw on the Battery, what was this but the altogether normal desire to appear to customers as one out of the ordinary run, harmlessly but charmingly individual?

Michael was reading his speech for a forthcoming convention of trust officers. He had read it over the night before, expecting that its happy and neat phraseology would provide a pleasant background through which sleep might filter in. But something quite different and also rather disagreeable had happened. Whether it was the second whiskey after dinner or the soufflé, or whether he was simply tired, he could not tell, but the speech had seemed suddenly full of clichés. Well, of course, it *was* full of clichés. Such speeches were meant to be. He had been very careful indeed to put them in. But now they no longer seemed amusing; some of them seemed actually offensive. The good trust officer, he had written, should be a "dynamic planner"; he should understand "human as well as business problems." He had to be "part investment counselor, part tax expert, part Dutch uncle and part plain nurse." Worse still, he had "to relate himself to the life of his community." Michael pushed the manuscript aside and thought with an unaccustomed wryness of the community to which he had related himself, in duck blinds, on golf courses, in sailboats and in shrouded parlors, on wide lawns and on ranches. Oh, yes, he had related himself; he had been bland, agreeable, sympathetic with wives and mothers, hearty and judicious with their men, and prudent, oh so prudent, with the old. He had done it, God knew. And looking up at the large photograph of his beautiful Flora and at the other of his rather sullen son, he tried to dispel the dark little cloud that had hovered so persistently over the top of his mind since his early waking, a sense of damp anticipation uncomfortably different from the mild, hollow, familiar depression that he was apt to feel an hour after lunch and for which he had a compensatory pill. Surely, it was nothing as common as disillusionment. For what illusions, after all, did *he* have?

"Can you sign these now, sir?"

Danny Jones, an assistant trust officer, square jawed and blocky, with thick, black hair and eyes that stared at him with an air of habitual suspicion, stood before his desk.

"Yes." He signed the checks. The signature space below his was for old Mr. Tyson, the co-trustee. "How will you get these to him?"

"Hand delivery."

"No." Michael was patiently emphatic. "I've told you. Take them over yourself and wait till he signs. And remember. Put the big check on top. He'll throw out one of any batch to show who's boss. But it's never the one on top."

"Isn't that a bit queer, sir? I mean, for a trustee?"

Michael sighed. Danny was thorough, even unexpectedly intelligent, but he lacked the very rudiments of imagination. "He *is* queer. All customers are queer. Until proved otherwise."

Each year he reflected when Jones had gone, eccentricity appeared more bewildering to the younger men. They couldn't seem to get it through their heads that people were different from themselves. He hated to be always showing off how well he knew the customers — it was as if he were sticking his head out from behind a curtain in make-up and wig, to show them a world of make-believe — yet they *had* to learn.

"Oh, sir?" Danny was back.

"Yes?" he asked a bit sharply. Danny was a good thirty-four. He had no business calling him "sir."

"I've got to take the Kenny papers to Mineola. Is it all right if I don't come back today?"

"Sure. Play golf." Danny who had married a rich wife, lived near the Farishes on Long Island and belonged to the same club. "Isn't that how we're supposed to build up the bank?"

Danny left, immune to sarcasm, and Amelia Brown appeared in the doorway.

"Mr. Meredith would like to see you." Her tone implied: I know it's a bore, but what can *I* do? She had identified herself with every aspiration of Michael's since he had taken the unprecedented action ten years before of turning her from an accountant into a secretary and convincing her that it was a step up. With him, of course, it was. Amelia at fifty-five, soft of face and tone, silent in her movements like a rather corpulent cat, Amelia, who knew each customer and each file, was worth every penny of her high salary.

"What do you suppose it's about?"

"A new account, maybe. He sounded excited."

Charlie Meredith was talking on the telephone when Michael came in. He was a tall, rangy, angular man of sixty-five who seemed to be smiling as he talked, his head inclined toward his unseen auditor, his eyes looking up over his glasses, questioning, guardedly friendly, worldly-wise. There was a touch of the Cruikshank about him which Michael always felt he should have emphasized, even to the extent of a Prince Albert and a stovepipe hat, but Meredith had no desire to stand out from his fellow bankers and affected instead a series of too light and too youthful colors. It was part of the unhappy effort to fit his fussing and rather old-maidish personality into the story-swapping, baseball loving, downtown world. As senior trust officer, which he had been for two decades before his elevation to the presidency, he had not had to worry about such things, and his greatest comfort was still to call in Michael and discuss nostalgically the affairs of his old department. Yet for all this, as Michael well knew, he had never been a really good trust officer. Unlike Michael, he had never been on social terms with the individuals who benefited from the bank's estates; to him they were the rather shadowy fruit of trees whose sap lay in the stream of cash that passed through the trunks and branches of interlocking wills and trust agreements. He liked to cluck over their antics, purse his lips at their extravagances and frown sternly at their suitors and mates, as if they were marionettes. But he had never really understood them. How could one really understand marionettes?

Today, however, there was to be no philosophizing, no pursing of lips. Old Charlie was clearly disturbed, too disturbed to do more than nod when Michael came in. "I heard something very odd last night at dinner," he began as soon as he put the telephone down. "Perhaps you can explain it to me. I was at Ted Lincoln's. He told me that Mrs. Fred Winters has retained his firm to represent her in our accounting for the Winters trust."

Michael looked at him coolly. "Oh? And since when have we been afraid to have people examine our accounts?"

"Well, it hardly seems friendly of her."

"Since when has Mrs. Winters been friendly? I welcome her lawyers. Let them add up every last figure in the account!"

"Now, now, Michael." Meredith got up and paced to the window. "You know that's no way to talk. Mrs. Winters is an old and valued customer. You brought her in yourself. Aren't we the executor and trustee in her will?"

"We were."

"*Were?* You mean she's changed it?"

"You'd have to ask her lawyers that."

"But have you any cause to think she has?"

"Only what your friend Mr. Lincoln told you."

"Come now, Michael!" Meredith stood facing out the window, his hands clenched behind his back. It was difficult for him to look at people when he was agitated. "You can't expect me not to be upset at the prospect of losing one of our biggest customers!"

"I don't."

"Then tell me. Does she have any reason to be angry with us?"

"Certainly she has a reason. A very good one. In fact, she has two." Michael looked up and down Meredith's back with a faint smile. "Miss Angstron sent one of her statements to Dark Harbor ten days after she'd arrived back in town. And that's not all. There's worse to come." He paused. "The envelope was addressed to 'Mrs. Frederick C. Winters.'"

Meredith spun around. "What's wrong with that?"

"What's wrong? Why, every school child in the trust department knows that Mrs. Winters's business mail is supposed to go to 'Mrs. Harriet F. Winters'!"

Meredith frowned. "I'm sorry, Michael. I can't regard this as a joking matter."

"Who's joking?"

"Do you mean to tell me she'd change her bank for a thing like that?"

"Why not? It shows we weren't thinking of her, doesn't it? And Mrs. Harriet F. Winters is a woman who likes to be thought of."

"But how unreasonable can a woman be?"

"In the trust department we deal with the subtlest particulars of human perversity. As you should well remember."

Meredith actually stamped his foot. "Well, damn it all,

then, why can't your girls learn how to address her statements?"

Michael raised his eyebrows. "Do you suggest I discharge Miss Angstron?"

"Well, no. Of course not. But you might speak to her."

"With your permission, sir, I propose not to say a word." Michael had dropped his smile now, and his manner was firm. "For seven years Miss Angstron has handled Mrs. Winters's correspondence without a single error. A slip was inevitable. Like the fall of a sparrow. If Mrs. Winters takes her business to another bank, they too, will make a slip. In time. Let that be your consolation. It's mostly chance. Victory goes to the one who's in at the death."

"But can't you talk to Mrs. Winters? Can't you tell her it won't happen again?"

"No." Michael was inexorable. "That would be fatal. You see, she hasn't complained. If I let on that I knew the reason for this new attitude, I'd betray that I knew the triviality of her standards. And *that* she'd never forgive."

"Then we take it lying down?"

"Not quite." Michael picked up the ivory paper cutter and squinted along its edge. "Mrs. Winters's lawyers will have to approve our account. Don't worry. It's been checked and double-checked. They will then send her a bill. It will be only mildly padded, but she will still be outraged. She'll remember the last accounting when she had no lawyers and which cost her nothing. With any luck, she'll come to me. I will look at the bill and scream. I will fling my hands in the air. I will go to your friend Ted Lincoln and insinuate that she may not retain him again if the bill is not cut. This will not be strictly true. She'll never retain him again, anyway. But the bill *will* be cut. Slightly. And she'll be as jubilant as if we'd saved her a million dollars!"

"Oh." Meredith sat down again and sighed with relief. Then he smiled cheerfully up at Michael. "I guess you can handle them, Mike. I should know that and not worry. But I can't always help it." He shook his head. "Poor Mrs. Winters. I suppose she means well."

"Who doesn't?"

Returning to his office, Michael congratulated himself that he had handled the matter well. He had raised the old man's anxiety to a fever pitch before applying his drug. Meredith would be in a blissful state of relief for the rest of the day. And bless Michael for it. But why then, he thought, watching the little round pointer above the elevator door, did he feel again the faint foreboding, the small mist over things?

"Mrs. Parr is here," Amelia Brown told him as he got out of the elevator at his floor. "I showed her right in."

"My God, the *whole* family?"

Charlie Meredith's daughter was sitting in the chair by his desk. She had reached the time in life that would best become her, her late thirties. A few years before she had seemed too big; in a few more she might seem so again, but just now her firmness, her strength, her neat blond hair and commanding nose, her wide, penetrating, disconcerting eyes, the opulent plainness of her dress and high heels made up a picture of feminine competence that did not yet repel. She seemed totally at home in his office, but then she was not only Charlie's daughter, she was daughter-in-law of the chairman of the board. When she saw him, she crushed out her cigarette in the ashtray on his desk.

"I came down to pick up Daddy. We've got to go shopping for a present for Mummy. She'll be sixty-five tomorrow. Would you believe it?"

"Never."

Alida Parr chuckled comfortably. "I know. She looks at least five years older. It comes from having no doubts."

"I wish your father had none." He sighed as he sat down and rested his elbows on the desk. "But surely he didn't make you come all the way down here? Couldn't he have met you at the store?"

"Oh? Aren't you glad to see me?"

"Extremely. But it seems such a bother for you."

"What else do I have to do? Don't forget I'm rich, Michael. I'll soon be one of your rich old ladies. I like to keep Daddy out of the subway. He'll never take a cab if I don't come for him. Why do old men cling so to the subway?"

"It must be a symbol of virility."

"Much good it does them!" She crossed her knees now and rested her bag on them. "Tell me, Michael. How is he? Really?"

"Fine. A little fussy, but fine."

"You know I'm counting on you to tell me. I can't bear to have him linger on after the young men start sneering. And why should he? He'll get his pension, anyway."

"Nobody's going to sneer at him, Alida."

"Well, I don't even want them to smirk. Remember that. I can't bear it. You promise to tell me?"

"I promise."

"That's settled, then. I'll go up and get him." She stood up, lingering. "You're looking well."

"I am well."

"I wish we saw more of you and Flora."

He laughed. "Come off it, Alida. You never could abide Flora."

"Perhaps. But that isn't altogether her fault, is it? You never could stand Jimmie."

He stood up too. "Oh, I wouldn't go that far. Jimmie has his points."

She looked at him for a searching moment. There was an odd half-smile in her eyes. "Do you ever think of Baymeath?"

"Often."

"You big fake!"

"I do, Alida. Seriously."

"You know something?" She paused. "I think of it all the time."

"You're the fake now. You have a whole crowded life. Your parents, children, Jimmie — "

"I have nothing," she interrupted sharply. But her eyes, if faintly ominous, were still smiling. "I mean that, Michael. I have nothing." She shrugged and turned to the door. "But don't worry. You're safe, my dear. Quite safe."

He tried to imply, with his sad little smile and nod of farewell, a world of regret. But she was right. He was a fake. He hardly ever thought of Baymeath, the American base on the English Channel, where, briefly, in 1944, eleven years before, they had had an affair. But was it necessary to tell her this? Did honesty require him to hurt her? Particularly when she was so safely married? Of course, the fact that she had the power to bring about the resignation of her father, and that Jimmie's father, Ambrose Parr, had the power to select his successor, might make him seem just a bit of a bastard, but he *knew*, didn't he, that he would have been just as nice had she been a stenographer? Would he? Of course he would! What was it about this day that was stirring up so many morbid doubts? He picked up the Winters account and told Amelia Brown that he would take no calls. Yet at four o'clock precisely his telephone rang. It could only be one of three people: his wife, Charlie Meredith or Ambrose Parr. It was the last.

"If you want a lift down to the island, get off your can! Meet me at the pier in fifteen minutes."

What a day! He had work to do, and he hated that sea plane where he had to shout over the roar of the engines. But Ambrose was chairman of Hudson's board, and twenty minutes later they were taking off on the East River. His host was a tall, powerful man of not more than seventy with a heavy belly, a bald head, a great crooked nose and a red, rough complexion. He was rude and cynical; he was hard and suspicious and selfish, but, at least in Michael's eyes, he had two great virtues: he was neither moralistic nor sentimental. In this he differed from other tycoons. But then Ambrose was not a real tycoon. He had been a famous Yale man of a famous period, football captain and Skull and Bones; he had made a great match to a quiet, loving girl who in dying had bequeathed him the fortune for which he had married her. In the decades that followed he had bought and sold many businesses, with more notoriety than profit; he had fulminated and reorganized and blasphemed his way through hundreds of pages of newsprint. Now, in his old age, the Hudson River Trust Company had the charm of a final toy, and not the least of its assets was his friend Michael Farish, who would go anywhere with him, shoot anything, listen to his stories and match him drink for drink. He talked all the way down to Glenville of the dinner that he was planning at the Waldorf for the convention of trust officers. When Michael objected to the scale of the party, Ambrose shouted him down. He was entirely willing to overpay the piper so long as he could call the tune. The plane was descending, and Michael leaned forward to see the small sailing craft blow up in size, bigger and now formidably bigger, and then he closed his eyes as he felt the swoosh when they hit the water and opened them to find his window drenched in spray.

"We'll have a drink," Ambrose said jumping up. "We'll have a drink, and then I'll drive you home."

At the clubhouse it was still warm enough for them to sit out on the terrace and watch the late golfers finishing in the crisp spring air. "You're very quiet today, Mike," Ambrose observed. "Is there something on your mind?"

"No. I'm just tired, I guess."

"You'd be surprised how much time I spend trying to figure you out."

"Indeed I would. Why?"

"When I bought into Hudson River Trust, I didn't have time to learn all about the banking business. But I had to learn about the officers."

"You certainly ought to know about me. By now."

"I ought to, yes, but *do* I? You and I are very different people, Mike. I've spent my life chasing all over Robin Hood's barn, while you've spent yours in one long, smooth groove." He paused significantly. "A groove aimed straight for the presidency of Hudson River Trust."

If Ambrose was really going to be serious, it behooved Michael to be wary. "Well, I wouldn't say that," he answered with a shrug. "I'd say it was aimed at where I am. Trust officer. I've arrived, Ambrose. I'm out of the groove."

But Ambrose only brushed this aside. "You can be president. Why the hell not? Your grandfather was. Your father would have been if he'd lived. You've got the personality and the background. And the skill, too. As far as I'm concerned, you're one of the reasons I picked up my stock. It certainly wasn't because of old Charlie Meredith!" He paused again, while Michael dropped his eyes. "So there. I've been frank with you. Now be frank with me. Do you want it or don't you?"

Michael looked up at him gravely. It was no time for tricks. "Yes, Ambrose, I want it. It's what I've always wanted. Ever since I was a small boy."

Ambrose continued to stare at him hard, with his mouth half open. "But, damn it, man," he exclaimed suddenly, hitting the table with his heavy palm, "does the idea give you no *thrill?* Do you feel no enthusiasm?" He struck the table again. "If I told you now, 'Okay, Mike, it's yours,' would you kick up your heels and yell?"

Michael felt gathering within him the shadowy forces of a resentment that he should have to beg from this old man what he had once deemed almost a matter of right. It stripped the prize of half its value, and what was the prize, in all simplicity, but his very life? He opened his lips, but had to swallow and then moisten them before he could speak.

"Yes, Ambrose. I'd kick up my heels and yell."

"*Would* you?" The old man shook his head moodily. "Flora wouldn't, of course. Flora doesn't give a damn. Not that I mind that. I can't stand these office wives who push their husbands. But the husbands should care!"

Michael was staring at a couple who were leaving the green and walking toward the stairs that led up to the clubhouse porch. The woman, he could see, was his wife, but who on earth was the young man? When they came to the foot of the stairway he suddenly recognized him and felt a stunned surprise, a surprise unaccompanied at first by any emotion.

"Well, look at Flora," he said in an even tone. "I guess

I've caught her, haven't I? In *flagrante delicto*. Playing golf with Mr. Danny Jones. From the trust company of all places!"

Ambrose glanced indifferently down at them. "She likes them kinda young, doesn't she?"

"Don't we all?"

"All right, Michael, I give up." Ambrose turned away from the green and waved at a friend by the bar. "I guess I'll never get *anything* out of you."

Michael watched Flora as she came slowly up the stairs. At fifty she was still a beautiful woman. At least to him she was. There was serenity in her wide Spanish brow, her black hair parted in the middle, her large calm dark eyes. Flora had always had the danger of plumpness to fight, but the balance of victory was still with her, and her red tweeds were as brilliant as the early spring woods. Danny Jones, who must have been seventeen years her junior, shuffled along behind her, with surly abstracted eyes. But they widened with sudden shock when he saw Michael.

"Why, Michael, what luck!" Flora's eyes did not flicker as they met his when she stepped on the porch. "Thanks, Danny," she said turning back to her companion. "Here are Michael and Ambrose. I can get a lift from them. I can, can't I, Ambrose?" she said, taking a seat at their table.

"If you'll let me buy you a drink."

"How nice."

"And your boy friend? What about him?"

"Oh, my 'boy friend' has to run home to his wife and babies," she said equably, turning to wave again to the rapidly disappearing Jones. "That's strictly be-nice-to-boss's-wife department How good to find you both. I'm dying for a drink."

"I was just trying to crack your husband's glazed front," Ambrose said, signalling to the bartender. "Trying to get him to tell me something about himself. It didn't have to be something big. Something little would have done just as well."

"You think you can succeed in twenty minutes where I haven't succeeded in twenty years?" Flora demanded. "You don't know your Farishes. And speaking of Farishes," she continued, turning to Michael, "you'll have to do something about Seymour. We had a letter from Mr. Fitch this morning. He's the headmaster of Seymour's school," she explained to Ambrose.

"What about?" Michael demanded, immediately tense.

"Well, darling, he didn't say. Only that it was serious, and that you should come up as soon as possible. Tomorrow, even."

"Was there *no* hint?"

"None. He's probably refused to play baseball. Or is imagining himself a pacifist." Flora shrugged and turned to Ambrose as her drink arrived. "I think seventeen's the worst age in the world, don't you? Imagine making a *principle* out of everything!"

Ambrose grunted. "Imagine not wanting to play baseball!"

Michael got up suddenly and went to the bar. His ostensible excuse was to buy cigarettes; actually he was too angry to trust himself to speak. It was always this way when Seymour was in question; he would feel a sudden murderous rage at the world. Wasn't it enough that he should make Charlie Meredith feel like a bank president, that he should make Alida feel she had inspired a great love, that he should make Ambrose feel a sage and Flora a good mother? Why couldn't they let him *be?* Why couldn't they let him have his own son? Now as he carefully removed the wrapper from his package, he composed his features and waited for his blood to calm before returning impassive, joking, detached, to the company of his golf-playing wife and his bank's director. To become head of Hudson might still make up for much. It was a fantasy, anyway, to which he could cling. Perhaps the depression that he had felt all day came from a temporary loosening of his hold on it. He would tighten this hold. It might even help him to cope with the sudden fact of Danny Jones.

2

MICHAEL GOT UP early the next morning, slipping out of the bedroom quietly so as not to awaken his gently snoring wife, and went outside to walk in the woods in the damp dawn. It was the end of May, his favorite time of year, when he and Flora had closed the family brownstone in town and moved out to Glenville, on the north shore of Long Island. There they would stay until the middle of July when they would move to Flora's old shingle cottage in Bradley Bay in the Hamptons for his vacation and a month of beach and ocean air. But the house in Glenville was the only one that Michael regarded as truly their own. New York and Bradley Bay had been inherited, respectively, from his and Flora's families; Glenville they had built themselves. It was a small Georgian octagon of white brick with two square ivy-covered wings, one for the hired couple and one for his study, each separated from the main structure by a glass corridor. The house itself, the long white living room with its black Italian chairs and English flower prints, the tiny, graveled French garden, he had designed as a background for Flora, a further implementation of his general scheme that his very existence should be a frame to set off her beauty, that such was the function of the man whose greatest triumph had occurred at the age of twenty-three when she, the admiration of Bradley Bay, had left the home of her unfaithful husband to seek shelter in his boyish arms.

Oh, he could smile at it now, of course, see it in other
and sharper lights, but hadn't it been, for all that, the great
and dignifying experience of his life? Wasn't it the reason
that he had hardly slept all night, wondering about young
Jones? He turned off into the woods, stamping his feet into
the soft earth as he trudged along, fighting down the erupting, impertinent questions that bubbled up with such mocking cheeriness from the oozy recesses of his suspicions. Why
was he now allowing himself to be jealous, when he had so
resolutely slammed the door against suspicion for twenty
years? Why at *this* point, in the name of God, should he tear
down the sheet that he had spent such ages tucking over the
doorway, to reveal the infinite line of grinning faces, monkeys on the wall of his desperate illusion? Or had he always
been sane and was he only crazy now? He stopped and
stood motionless in a little clearing, his hands plunged deep
in his pockets.

But no, this was no way to face it. It was simply another
problem in a life of problems, a problem such as might be
presented any morning by a client at the bank. Picking up a
fallen branch and stripping it rapidly into a walking stick he
walked resolutely on. If he concentrated carefully on Flora
as she was today — and she was fifty, why disguise it? —
might not the explanation of his bitterness be that he had
assumed she was past this sort of thing, that however naïve
his trust of her in days gone by, his current faith in her was
only sensible? Flora had always been able to combine remarkably the efficient and brusque with the languid and
yieldingly feminine, but of recent years the former had
seemed to predominate. If in her past she had lived for men,
in her present she dressed for women. He usually thought of
her now as sitting at the bridge table, her finger poised on a
card in dummy, then turning it over with a decisive snap

and jangle of her gold bracelets. It was as if Flora, retiring from love, had moved gracefully on to other and milder pleasures whose charm was all the greater for not having been sampled before. She seemed to accept her age as she had accepted her youth and beauty, as she accepted the blend of New York and Spanish blood in her veins and to be quite content to scrape busily away at her card-filled afternoons as though she were scraping ripe melons. But then — and here was Michael's despair, for how could he ever *tell?* — she might glance up from her hand and smile at a young man who was watching the play with a dazzling candor that suddenly suggested her Andalusian mother and the interior life of Moorish ancestresses. At such moments he could even regret the Spanish way of life that might have turned her at fifty into a shrill sharp matron, clad in dirty black, with a hint of a mustache and a key ring rattling at her waist.

Coming into the dining room through the french window, he found his stepdaughter already at breakfast. Ginevra's large, suspicious, rather popping eyes were fixed on the newspaper with that air of seeming concentration that she always adopted when she heard anyone coming.

"Good morning, Ginny."

"Oh, hello." She never bothered to look up. At twenty-six she had the sulky morning manners of sixteen.

"Are you coming into town with me this morning?"

"No. I thought I'd stay out."

"I wish I worked for someone as easygoing as Mrs. Rand."

"I'm no longer working for Mrs. Rand."

"Oh." Michael's heart sank as he faced the project of getting her another job. "When did that happen?"

"It should have happened long ago!" Ginevra looked up at him indignantly. "There was no future in it. Can you see me spending a lifetime buying lampshades?"

"No. Only a few weeks at the most. Was there trouble with Mrs. Rand?"

"Well, what an old bitch she is!" The sudden violence of the word in the dark, damp morning jarred on Michael's nerves. "Just because I happen to be making a luncheon engagement she accuses me of spending all day on the phone. Just because no one calls *her*, the old eavesdropper. Just because *she* hasn't had a man ask her out in thirty years!"

Michael sighed. He knew about Ginny's telephone calls. "What are you thinking of doing now?"

"Well, for heavens' *sake!* Can't a girl take a day off between jobs? What do you think I am, a work horse?"

"I only thought I might be able to help. Sound somebody out." He had developed the habit of mildness years before with Ginny. He knew that the resentment which she showed him was only the resentment that she never dared to show her mother. It was Flora's cardinal sin, in Ginny's eyes, not so much that she was indifferent to Ginny as that she was indifferent to Ginny's resentment. Against the high wall of her mother's independence Ginny could only break her fingernails in vain.

"I think I might go into town tomorrow and see Daddy," she said sulkily. "He's always full of ideas."

Michael was careful to betray no dissent to her jealous scrutiny. "I think that's an excellent idea. What about Flora? Have you discussed it with her?"

"Oh, Mummy. You know how *she* is." Ginny shrugged her shoulders impatiently. "I came home early yesterday to tell her about Mrs. Rand, but she had a date to go golfing with Dannyboy Jones. Naturally, I couldn't expect to compete with *that*."

Michael remained expressionless. He was silent for almost a minute. That she should want so to hurt him was almost worse than the remark itself; the recognition of cruelty always left him feeling a bit giddy and sick. With a sudden intake of breath he recalled that long-ago summer at Bradley Bay and the booming of the late August billows and of the pain that *he* might have caused Ginny. "Do you mean to imply," he asked dryly, "that your mother is so prepossessed with young men in general, or with that young man in particular, that she has no attention to give your problems?"

"Oh, Michael, you are the limit!" she cried, laughing nervously. "It's impossible to get your goat, isn't it?"

"Why should you wish to?"

"Because you're always so balanced. So loyal. To everyone. To Mummy."

"And you think my loyalty is misplaced?"

"Oh, no, of course not. I'm just teasing." Ginny's voice rose again to its accustomed shrillness. "Look, for Pete's sake, can't you let me read my newspaper?"

Michael watched her silently as she leaned dutifully over the society news. If she found the engagement of a friend, there would be a snort followed by a mirthless laugh and the high, dry comment: "Well, really! How desperate can a girl *be?*" Oh, desperate, he half whispered to himself. Desperate.

When he had drunk his coffee he went upstairs to where Flora was having her breakfast in bed.

"It seems Ginny's lost her job again," he said.

"Did you think she wouldn't?"

"Don't you think there's *something* we could do for her? Send her abroad or on a cruise?"

"Again? Let her father do it. The stingy old piker."

"Flora, please!" He turned to close the door to the corridor.

"Do you think I care if she hears me? He *is* stingy. Why shouldn't she know who pays for everything?"

"Because she mustn't. You know perfectly well she mustn't."

"I know no such thing. She's always making a drama of how good he is to her. The best thing that ever happened to her was my divorcing him. As I tell her, too."

"Too much."

"You're too compliant, Michael," she warned him, shaking her head. "Far too compliant. You let her walk all over you. And it's the same thing with Seymour. You'll be putty in his hands when you get up to Averhill tomorrow. That's why I'm not coming with you. I don't want to see it."

Michael felt a bleak little wind in his heart as he watched her resting back so comfortably against the large pillows. "I didn't realize you weren't coming."

"I only decided this morning."

"But, Flora, if the boy's in trouble, the least we can do is show a united front!"

"I disagree," she said firmly. "I'd only make it harder for you. I'd tell Seymour right out that if he can't obey the rules, he'll be taken home and put in public school. *That* would fix him. He's such a precious little snob."

"Flora!"

"He is, dear. Don't forget he's my son, too. But that doesn't blind me to the fact that he's going through an unattractive phase. I only wish I had more assurance that he was ever coming out of it. And I know *you*. You'll go up to Averhill and charm everybody into a compromise that will last two weeks until the next blow-up. But, of course, that's your affair. It's *your* school. You're a trustee. Only don't ask me to go up there and watch! That's too much!"

"Do you have something else to do?"

Flora put down her coffee cup with a click. "Now what sort of a question is that?" she demanded. "I just finished telling you *why* I'm not going."

"I see," he said, turning to the door. But as he stood with one hand on the knob, despair arrested him. "Did you enjoy your golf with Danny Jones yesterday?"

"I did." He took in the surprise of her tone. "Why do you ask?"

"Do you find him attractive?" He turned around now, and their eyes met in sudden, shared embarrassment.

"Not particularly," she replied, looking away. "He's a rather sullen young man. He might be all right with a little polishing. If he ever gets it."

"Yet you play golf with him."

"We happened to meet on the green when we were starting — " she was beginning, but then stopped herself. "Really, Michael, what *has* got into you? Are you trying to make something out of me and Danny? Have you completely taken leave of your senses?"

"Oh, no, no," he murmured quickly. "Nothing like that. I just thought it a bit odd for you to be playing together. I mean, I hadn't known you were such friends."

"I suppose I should be flattered. I daresay he's almost young enough to be my son. But I'm afraid I'm past my days of attracting younger men."

"Oh, Flora, please!" he exclaimed in sudden shame. "Forgive me. I'm such an ass where you're concerned."

"Come here then." When he came over, she gave him a light kiss on the lips and tapped him on the shoulder. "Now. Don't be more of an ass than you absolutely have to be. And remember this. When I start looking around for young men,

I'll expect you to lock me up and keep me from making a fool of myself!"

Michael drove to the station blanketed in the euphoria of a relief that he did not dare examine. But when he came into his office and saw, of all people, Danny Jones sitting by his desk, he could not help starting and turning white.

"I'm sorry, sir." Danny jumped up. "Miss Brown said I could wait in here. I had to talk to you, the first thing."

"About yesterday?"

Danny stared. "What about yesterday?"

Michael recovered himself. "Oh, nothing. Did you enjoy yourself?"

"You didn't mind, I hope? Mrs. Farish and I happened to meet at the first hole."

"Why should I mind?"

"You said I could play, you know."

"Of course, of course. What's on your mind?"

"Something bad, I'm afraid." Danny sat down, his pale aggressive face heavy with the happy, sober concern of a junior who has discovered somebody else's error. "Something I just happened to tumble onto this morning. You remember the limitation on commissions in the Frederick Winters will? That says we're not to get more than one and a half per cent?"

It was Michael's turn to stare. Who was this young man that he could destroy *everything?* "Certainly, I remember."

"Of course, it's been construed to apply only to ordinary commissions. *Not* to commissions for managing real estate. I believe we've taken some three hundred thousand in real estate commissions since Mr. Winters's death in 1939?"

"Approximately."

"Well, in checking our petition on the accounting I

checked the correspondence file all the way back. I found this letter that you wrote Mr. Winters a week before he died." Danny placed the letter in front of Michael who picked it up and read it. Or rather he appeared to read it, for he knew it by heart. He had waited too long to be caught now by anything so foolish as a change of expression.

"I remember the letter," he said calmly. "It simply confirms the commission arrangement in the will."

"Not quite, sir, if I may be so bold. The letter says the 'total' commissions shall not exceed one and a half per cent. The will just says 'commissions.' Wouldn't 'total' include the real estate commissions we've been taking?"

"I think not." Michael shrugged and settled slowly back in his chair. "The word 'total' adds nothing. It simply means total ordinary commissions, and ordinary commissions do not include real estate commissions." Carefully he studied Danny's scowl.

"Can I ask you this, then? Is that your own construction or was the letter ever offered to a court?"

"Let me see." Michael touched his fingers together lightly and appeared to reflect. "No, I think we decided the meaning was too clear to submit to a court."

"But it was considered?"

"Of course, it was considered."

Danny's excitement got the better of him. "And Mrs. Winters went along with that decision? Was she shown the letter?"

Michael's smile contained just the necessary hint of reproof. "Are you cross-examining me, Danny? This is a copy of a letter that was *sent to* Mr. Winters. Presumably it is with his papers. Presumably the family have it."

"Oh." Obviously Danny had to give it up, at least for the

present, or run the risk of being openly insubordinate. He rose slowly to his feet. "I guess it was a false alarm. Sorry to bother you, sir."

"Not at all, Danny. Not at all. I'm glad you take such an interest." As Danny turned to go, Michael called him back. "Oh, Danny. Aren't you forgetting the letter? It should go back in the file, you know."

He sat very quietly for a long time after Danny had left him. It was just sixteen years since he had put that letter in the file. When he had done so, he had been the only person in the world aware of its existence and of its possible effect on the language of the will itself. Nobody had even noticed it before Danny, although the file had been in dozens of hands. Yet he had always known it was there and that ultimately, inevitably perhaps, somebody would read it, as Danny had done, and place a construction upon it, as Danny had done. Through the years the knowledge that this could happen had changed gradually from a fearsome thing to one that had a strange element of comfort. There was actually a queer little relief in the idea that whatever happened to him in Hudson, *here* was always a way out, like the poison capsules that spies wore around their necks in case of capture in enemy lands. But that the capsule should be handed to him in the chubby fingers of Danny Jones was an ironic twist of fate that he could never have anticipated. It made him giddy and a little sick to think that Danny might be his nemesis.

3

HUDSON RIVER TRUST COMPANY, which Michael had so grown to look upon as his natural heritage, was considerably older than the building which it occupied. It had survived for more than a century and through several changes of title, always retaining, however, the name of the great river, viewable from its upper windows, so reassuringly evocative, like the Christmas calendars of the trust department, of New Amsterdam and the cautious Dutch, of merchants trading peacefully with pipe-smoking Indians while fat little nutshell vessels rode cozily at anchor in the background. The Hudson Company Limited had been founded by Howlands and Aspinwalls to finance their China trading; its successor, Hudson Bank of Commerce, had been an organ of credit for Secretary Chase in Civil War years; its offspring, in turn, the Hudson Life Insurance and Trust Company, had closed its doors in the panic of 1907. Resuscitated by Mr. Morgan himself, it might have lived out a pale and uneventful life as an obedient cog in that empire, subsisting on a just adequate backlog of stock transfers, had it not been for the gradual burgeoning of its family trusts in the loving hands of Maury Farish. This great gentleman, whose photograph in *King's Notable New Yorkers*, wide-faced, smiling, bland-eyed, with silken white sideburns, helps somewhat to explain the almost legendary confidence that he inspired, had developed to a high art the knack of inducing the newly rich, quite simply, to hand over their money to him. Once in his plump white matronly hands they must have visualized it as being neatly assorted, with many busy shuffles and pats, and then reassembled into sober little packs of trusts that would give an old varnish to the newest bills. By the mid nineteen-twenties, when old Maury died, the trust business, formerly a sleek and unobstrusive tail, was wagging the large and rather bony dog of mercantile loans.

His son, Maury, Jr., had died before him, and the mantle of the trust officer, followed ultimately by the mantle of the presidency, fell upon the nervous shoulders of Charlie Mere-dith, a former accountant whom old Maury had originally trained to be a loyal helper to his attractive but less than brilliant son. Meredith, finding himself a lord where he had only dreamed of being a steward, had always been a touch uneasy in his new job and tended ultimately to regard young Michael, when he came to work in the bank, with the mingled respect and jealousy of an old regent who has occu-pied the throne beyond the minority of its lawful heir. It was a feeling that young Michael had done nothing to dis-courage.

The acquisition of the Winters family by Hudson in 1939 had greatly strengthened Michael's position, making him an assistant trust officer at the early age of twenty-nine. The business came in, oddly enough, not from the Farishes, but from Michael's maternal grandfather, Dr. Lear, the rather dandyish veteran of a more decorous age whose medical prac-tice had dwindled as the fortunes of his patients had increased and had finally disappeared altogether with the passing of a small group of titans in whose yachts the sporty doctor had passed whole seasons on end. Bereft by the market crash of the fruits of all his carefully garnered tips, he lived on in Paris, appearing once a winter to visit his daughters in New York, a thin, wiry, tweeded figure with a goatee and a drooping left eyelid that had found its mention in the memoirs of several famous ladies. It was like him to cast the Winterses at Michael's feet like a pair of dead fish.

"I'm sending Fred and Harriet Winters to you," he told him. "She was old Nathan Fellows's daughter, you know."

"Grandpa!"

"I don't like them. Never have. But I liked Mr. Fellows, and the old boy liked me. Harriet makes a fetish of everything her father cared about. When I die, Mike, I want you to bury me quick before she has me stuffed and stuck up in that wing of the Fellows Museum with all the fake Tintorettos and Veroneses."

"*Are* they fake?"

"Of course they are. And Harriet knows it, too. But she thinks people only care who bought them, not who painted them. Anyhow, Fred's had a row with his bank, and she told me he was going to Hudson River Trust. I told her to make him do it through you so you'd get the credit."

"Gosh! How can I thank you?"

"Don't. Things have come to a pretty pass when a young man in the prime of life is grateful for a pair like that."

"I'd better start learning. Like what?"

"Like two dried-up old caretakers."

"But I thought they were old New York!"

"That's it, my boy!" The doctor slapped his knee with a loud laugh. "That *is* old New York. Mean. Moralistic. Servant-distrusting." He almost spat the word. "Middle class."

Negotiations opened the following week. Michael found

himself called for the first time into the office of the president of the bank to meet him and Mr. Meredith, then trust officer, and the lawyers who represented Mr. and Mrs. Winters. He found that he was treated with a new respect, but neither he nor Mr. Meredith, nor even the president, for that matter, was allowed to see the Winters will. The lawyers were very firm about this. When Michael was finally summoned up-town to meet the august testator, it was presumably after the execution of the document that was to name his trust company executor and trustee. He waited fifteen minutes in the library and had ample opportunity to examine the black boule cabinets, the ebony chairs, the dusky, gold-framed landscapes, the oriental bazaars by Jerome and the huge bronze groups ranged over the glassed-in bookcases: a charging elephant, a stag torn by hounds, a dying gladiator, athletes wrestling. It was remarkable that amidst so many depictions of violence the prevailing impression should have been one of such utter stillness. When Mr. Winters came slowly in and sat down, Michael saw that his eyes were pale blue, like a baby's, his face brown and wasted, and that the silver paper cutter with which his long fingers played was no sharper than the crease in his black trousers.

He proceeded, at once, rather to Michael's surprise, to out-line his testamentary scheme. He did this slowly and gravely, pausing for short periods between his sentences. To him it was manifestly a high duty to provide for the posthumous safeguarding of the property that he had nursed so devotedly in his lifetime. Trusts were the pyramids of his horizon; every dollar was to be buried under one of them for the maximum time permitted by statute. Michael saw the whole plan rise before his eyes like an embattled fortress, sullenly defiant of the surrounding countryside, a last stronghold against the invasion of taxes and indigence. When the old man had finished, he seemed to regard Michael for the first time.

"Your grandfather speaks highly of you, young man."

"My grandfather is very loyal."

"It is necessary in these matters to be entirely frank. Dr. Lear is a gentleman who has, I believe, lost the greater part of his heritage and savings. He is charming and talented, conceded. But you will understand me when I ask if you revere him as a grandparent or as a financial adviser?"

"I revere him."

"That's all?"

"That's all."

"Well, I suppose I must consider that a good answer. At any rate, I shall accept it. You must bear with my suspicions. It sometimes seems as if the modern world were a conspiracy to take bites out of property in its natural passage from the dead to the living. The tax collector, the court guardian, the lawyer. Even the trust company. Perhaps I should say, *especially* the trust company. You will wish to see my will, Mr. Farish?"

"No, sir. That is entirely your affair."

Mr. Winters just raised his eyebrows. "Perhaps your grandfather is right. Perhaps you *will* be a good trust officer."

"I shall try, anyway."

"There's one thing I should tell you. Your bank will *not* receive the commissions allowed by statute."

"Oh?"

"One and one half per cent of income and principal." Mr. Winters was very definite now. "And no commissions on principal until the end of the trust. Until Mrs. Winters's death."

Michael calculated feverishly in his mind. Then he closed his eyes and took a chance. "That'll be fine, sir."

Mr. Winters regarded him gravely for a moment. "You're right again, Mr. Farish. I never bargain. Will you write me a letter to that effect?"

"If it's in the will, sir, is it necessary?"

"Perhaps not." Mr. Winters pulled a bell rope. "But I should prefer it." An elderly woman in black with a pad came hurriedly in, breathing heavily, and sat down. "Miss Furman, will you take this, please? 'Confirming our agreement of October 9th, 1939, I hereby instruct you that our *total* commissions as trustee under your last will and testament will not exceed one and one half per cent of principal or income and that no principal commissions will be payable until the termination of the trust.'" When he had finished and Miss Furman had typed it, she tore two sheets out of her machine and handed them to Mr. Winters. He tossed them on the table before Michael. "Will you sign, please, Mr. Farish?"

"Of course." Michael signed both copies. "But wouldn't you rather have it on the bank's stationery?"

Mr. Winters thought for a moment and then nodded. "I would," he agreed and turned away with a dismissing gesture. "Have it done over and mail it to me. Good day, Mr. Farish. And please remember me to your grandfather."

Michael and Flora had just moved into his mother's brownstone house in the east sixties, which she had given them, and everything there was in a commotion. It was not surprising that he should have left behind his briefcase with the letter and copy the next morning when he went downtown. It was a Friday, and he did not go to the office again until the following Monday morning when he remembered it only as he was descending the stairs to the subway. Cursing silently, he returned home, but when he stood again at the door of his and Flora's bedroom, the domestic scene before him seemed fully worth the delay of his coming back. Flora, radiant in a Chinese robe, was nursing little Seymour, her eyes on the social page of the *Herald Tribune* spread out on the bed before her. Seymour's nurse was taking a message on the telephone. Little Ginny was playing with bottles of perfume at her mother's dressing table, and two French poodles were playing on the floor. Michael had always admired Ruth Draper's sketch, "The Italian Lesson," showing the start of a New York society lady's day with her busy court of children, tutors and servants. The scene before him struck him as the Draper sketch in miniature, and he was proud to be even the ignored spectator of this busy home that he had created. Going over to Flora's table beside which he had left his briefcase, he gave Ginny a friendly pinch.

"Don't!" she cried, and her angry little face puckered up. "Don't!" She ran over to her mother. "Mummy, make him stop!"

"Make who stop what?" Flora looked up from her paper. "Oh, hello, dear. Back already?"

"I forgot my briefcase."

"Mummy, he pinched me!"

"Well, what of it?" She pushed Ginny away from her. "Don't fuss, child." She handed Seymour back to his nurse and adjusted her robe. "Did you see that old Mr. What-you-ma-call-it died? The one you've been chattering about so?"

"Who?" Michael stared at her. He never saw the morning paper till he bought the *Times* on the subway.

"That Mr. Summers."

"*Winters?*"

"Yes, that's it."

Michael ran to her bed and turned the pages of the *Tribune* with trembling hands. And there it was, beside a picture of the old man taken some years before: "F. E. Winters, philanthropist, succumbs at home. Son-in-law of Nathan Fellows victim of heart attack."

"Darling!" he cried. "Do you know what this *means?*"

"What?"

"It's my first estate. My very first!"

Flora wrinkled her nose in distate. "What do you have to do? Embalm him?"

"That's probably done already," he mused as he read down the column. "I see he died on Saturday. Funny that Mr. Meredith didn't telephone me."

"Maybe he did. We were in the country."

"Oh! So we were."

He took a taxi down to the office where the doorman greeted him with the message that he was to go straight to Mr. Meredith's office. The latter was smiling broadly.

"Couldn't reach you yesterday, my dear fellow, but it's all right! We've seen the will, and we're named as executor *and* trustee. There's a limitation on commissions to one and a half per cent, but I got an opinion last night from our counsel that it doesn't cover real estate commissions."

Michael had a sense of sudden lightning in the halcyon sky. "Real estate commissions?"

"Well, of course, my dear boy. The estate's almost ten million, but seven of it's tied up in real estate. With the extra five per cent for management we'll do very nicely. Very nicely indeed. I don't mind telling you I had a bad turn when I saw that limitation clause in the will. But the lawyers say it applies only to ordinary commissions. Thank God!"

"And if it didn't?"

"If it *didn't!*"

Michael paused to moisten his lips. "Suppose it applied to *all* commissions?"

"But it doesn't!"

"But *suppose*."

Mr. Meredith shrugged. "I suppose we might break even. By careful planning."

"We could always refuse to qualify, couldn't we?"

"And lose Mrs. Winters? She's the one with the *real* pile. No, we'd have to go through with it. But don't worry, Mike. I tell you, it's all right!"

"Could I see a copy of the will?"

"Here. Go read it, my boy. It's your estate. Go study it."

Michael went back to his desk with the copy of the will and studied it in a distant, dazed way. He did not have his own office, then, but he heard nothing in the big room around him, no bells, no voices, no general clatter. When he came to the commissions clause he reached for his briefcase and took out the fatal letter. The worst, of course, was true. The word "total," absent from the will, glared at him from the page in his trembling hand. When his secretary came up and talked to him about the day's appointments, it gave him a sweetly sickening sense of danger and of suicidal power to think of what he held in his hand, unconcealed, in a room full of dozens of the curious.

"I can't see anyone," he told her. "I shall have to plan the setup for the Winters estate."

As she turned away, he took a deep breath and resolved to control his panic. However bad, the situation had to be assessed. In the first place, there was no other copy of the letter but the two in his hand. Had Mr. Winters mentioned its existence to anyone? To Mrs. Winters, for example? He could always say that he had been told to write a letter confirming the commission rates in the will, but that Mr. Winters had died before he could do so. But Mr. Winters's secretary, would she remember typing it? If she did, he could say that he had torn it up preparatory to dictating another on the trust company's stationery. Would she remember the word "total"? Most unlikely. Anyway, it would be his word against hers. "Oh, there was a letter," he could always say. "Simply a formality confirming the will."

Then why not destroy it and put an end to the whole foolish crisis? Why not get on with the ascending process that seemed to be the business of life, the singling out of one's own sure seat in the game of musical chairs? He was already half assured in the special game which he was playing that he might one day occupy the chair at the head of the table, that he would sit in his grandfather's seat, the seat that had been destined for his father had he lived. And there he would sit, Michael Farish, a bank president, a married man, a father and the trustee of many trusts. And *then* could he relax? Then would he have finished the task that he used to fancy he had undertaken that early morning of his boyhood when a white, thin-lipped mother had awakened him to say, traditionally, "We must help each other now"? And all the anticipated excitement of a world of inky cloaks and hushed voices, of high, envied sadness and swelling organ tones had collapsed suddenly before the reality of a wasted corpse that he had not even been allowed to see.

But would he ever finish? Wouldn't there always be the sly, sneering voices in the background to suggest that he was only pretending, like the little girl who covers her cheeks with Daddy's shaving cream and cries out that she's a man? And *if* he ever finished, if he ever attained the protective coloration of success, if the sly voices were ever muffled, would there be anything left but the dullness of heaven and its eternity of harping? No, there had to be a way out, an escape; there had to remain the possibility of relief, of sur-render, of conviction. He could at least be a sportsman with the shade of Mr. Winters. He even smiled at his own quixoti-cism as he now placed the letters carefully in his center drawer, just where anyone would look if they ever did look. When the Winters file was thick enough, he would insert them in it. Getting up, he went back to Mr. Meredith's office with his copy of the will.

"You're right, sir," he said cheerfully. "Everything's fine. How soon do you think it'll be admitted to probate?"

4

AS MICHAEL'S TAXI took him from the station to Averhill School, the morning after his conversation with Danny Jones about the commissions, he looked ahead for the first sight of the Gothic chapel. Monolithically, as it appeared around a bend, it rose incongruously and dominatingly over a school of red brick and white columns, a giant phallic symbol to remind one that duty is never done. With a sobriety that was immediately reflected in the stiffened lines around his lips Michael thought of Mr. Minturn, the late headmaster, the small, brisk, simple, silver-haired man who had oscillated between the extremes of a chuckling benevolence and a terrifying wrath and who represented God to two generations of Averhill graduates whenever in their atrophied religious consciousness they thought of a deity. He could be thankful, at any rate, that he did not have Mr. Minturn to cope with. It was bad enough to have Seymour at a school over which the great headmaster's spirit so vividly brooded.

He had always known in his own boyhood that he was destined for Averhill. There had never been any evading of it. It had waited for him with the deceptive beauty of which family friends in their undiscerning fashion always spoke when they mentioned it, but which he knew from the beginning could have nothing to do with the real character of the place. Averhill he still thought of as in the early fall of his first vision of it, with the smell of fresh white paint on the gleaming columns of Minturn Hall and the red and yellow leaves blowing across the broad green of the campus. "A beautiful school," he could hear his mother saying indifferently, "the most beautiful, I daresay, in all New England." It had hung before him like a cluster of autumn fruit with the cold of a dark winter locked inside, as cold as the tower of the chapel, bursting up like a great grey warning monk in the midst of the stately revels of colonial housing, as cold as the newly chiseled grey of his father's tombstone. He remembered his first day there, gazing down from the varnished stairway to where his mother was standing to wave him goodbye, and the sight of her, looking so small and pathetic in her widow's mourning, had almost broken his heart. Yet it had been quite as sad for him as her, for she would turn in a moment and leave and go back to New York and her friends and her bridge and the busy, gossiping, non-violent female world of his truncated childhood from which he was now forever excluded, leaving him to the reality behind the false front of the beautiful columns, behind the friendly smiles of the welcoming masters, leaving him to the wide grey hell of cellars and lockerrooms echoing to the piercing cries of unimpeded boys. But there was to be no turning back; there was never any turning back. There was not to be even the surrender to the impulse to run down the stairs and throw himself into her arms and kiss the startled, shocked look from her face. No, it would never do; she would be cross with him, as much for breaking her down as for breaking himself down; it would be messy; it would be careless. As long as one knew what the other felt, what need for demonstration beyond the public peck on the cheek, the quick, sympathetic nod, maybe just a flutter of a hand wave? And she was gone.

But, of course, he had survived at Averhill. In the first long blurred two years with the cluttered schedule of study and exercise, exercise and study, with feverish interruptions for chapel, for changing into stiff collars and blue suits, for sacred studies, for being hazed and hazing, he had been like a member of a dance chorus, carefully, self-consciously, at times agonizingly in step. Only on a few occasions did he stumble and fall out of line, and the memory of the sudden whoop of jeers was enough to prove — if proof had been necessary — that the nervous monotony of the dance was a hundred times preferable to the icy panic of such defection. Yet it was most significant of all that when he thought back now on those early sleepwalking years, there was a sweetness in the very midst of the dull pain, a rather heady sweetness, for it was in Averhill, the very Averhill which trained his sex to do its fighting, where he had first become aware that there was hidden color amid the whites and greys of a dreary universe, that there was music even in a chapel organ, poetry in an English class and something like affection, something like what the poets spoke of as love, even among boys.

Mr. Minturn, of course, had done all he could to stamp it out. He had rumbled dark warnings from the pulpit about "sentimentality." But there were still the boys who disappeared to the cellar, on long walks; there were still the noises in the dormitory at night, the scaring knowledge that others were being franker in their experimentation. Michael never went to the cellar or on such a walk; there was already the fear in him that what to the others might be permissible was to him denied, that with him it might be something more than promiscuity. Anything that was stripped of feeling belonged to the Averhill world of reality: the smutty joke, the leer, the sermon, the grace before meals, the football victory, the unthinkable thing in the cellar. But if there was something in one's blood that tinged the crisp clear New England air with golddust, if one could look beyond that grey chapel tower at the sunset over the playing fields and feel the tears welling in one's eyes, it was a thing to be kept to oneself. It was no part of becoming a man.

He had arrived and stood now in the lobby outside the assembly hall, listening to the bell and watching the boys pour in. The bell seemed to summon them out of the very walls. The dark varnished stillness in which he had been standing, with the shadowy lithographs, survivals of his own day, of the Forum, the Colosseum, the Maison Carré, was in a few moments teeming with boys walking and running, boys shouting, pushing each other, the older ones coming last, refusing to hurry, scorning the bell but mindful of it. And suddenly he saw Seymour, tall, gangling, striding along abstractedly in clothes that seemed to have been slept in, pulling a comb from his pocket and jerking back the long black hair that seemed about to inundate his sallow, oblong, intelligent face. As he passed Michael he saw him and stopped.

"Oh," he said. "Oh, it's you."

Michael put a hand on his shoulder. "I'm going to see Mr. Fitch. I'll be around to your study after supper. You'll be in?"

"What do you think? I *have* to be in!"

Later, on his way to the headmaster's house, Michael speculated more closely as to the nature of Seymour's offense. Whatever it was, it was by no means the first. Seymour and his friend, Rex Webb, had been in fairly constant trouble ever since they had formed, a year ago, what had appeared to Michael as nothing less than an alliance against society. As Catholics in a Protestant school (Seymour had been raised in Flora's faith), they had expressed their spirit of dissent by gluing together the pages of all the prayer books in the chapel. As individualists they had refused to play football and as intellectuals they had picketed the headmaster's study because of his reduction of Latin to the status of a voluntary course. On each occasion Michael had journeyed up from New York to straighten things out. Happily, he had been one of the committee of three which had nominated the present headmaster to his post. But his influence was beginning to wear thin, and Flora, a strong advocate of the sink-or-swim school, now openly criticized him for shielding Seymour from the consequences of an independence that she accused him of having fostered. But there it was. He was trapped in his own habit. Whenever the world seemed to threaten this sarcastic and cold-blooded child, Michael felt compelled to stand defiantly between him and his aggressors, to take on his own shoulders the sins of a boy who was saying things that he had never dared to say, that he had never even wanted to say

Mr. Fitch occupied the study that had formerly been Mr. Minturn's, but very little of the old atmosphere remained. Gone were the photographs that had covered the walls to the ceiling, of classes, of crews, of teams, of glee clubs; gone was the multitude of memorabilia that had littered the big desk and tables. All was now as bare and spare as Mr. Fitch himself, a balding, rangy, big-nosed man with a glittering smile and a firm handshake, who proclaimed his patience and his liberalism with every tolerant shake of his Roman head. The only picture on the walls was a reproduction of a Rouault Christ.

"I won't beat around the bush, Michael," Fitch began briskly. "I owe you the facts, both as a parent and a trustee.

As you know, we took in a colored boy in the third form this year. We also have several Jewish boys. We've never had the slightest trouble, nor did we anticipate any. But in the last two weeks we got it."

Michael's heart sank. "Tell me."

Fitch picked up a file of printed documents and handed them across the desk. "These pamphlets were found in each pew of the chapel. They were also discovered in the desks of some of the classrooms. They were printed on our own press."

Michael in the silence that followed read through the first of these. It was a clever little diatribe on the evils of desegregation, emphasizing the cruelty to a Negro in being brought up with white boys who would not accept him socially when they grew up. There was the usual business about the "sisters" whom he could never hope to marry. It was Seymour's style. He glanced up at Fitch and simply nodded.

"Worse was to come," Fitch continued gravely. "A ball of tar with feathers stuck on it was found on our colored boy's pillow last week. A sign reading 'Niggers and Jews keep out' was discovered over the door to the library. And last Sunday night as the boys were walking back from evening chapel a large burning cross, made of wood and paper, suddenly flamed up in the middle of the campus. One of the masters caught sight of a boy running away behind it and took off after him. It was Rex Webb. He confessed immediately to the whole thing. Defiantly, of course. As he and your son are inseparable it did not take very much cross-examination to implicate Seymour. Now he, too, has admitted it."

"I see."

"I suppose some drastic steps are necessary," Fitch concluded, closing the folder before him. "Before I acted, however, I wanted to talk to you." He paused to concentrate the expression of sympathy in his large grey eyes. "Believe me, Michael, I feel more for you in this than for anyone else."

"I'll talk to the boys," Michael said, standing up. "I'll talk to them now."

"Of course. But I thought you'd first like to hear more about the background of this thing. I — "

"What more is there to say?" Michael cut him short. "I should have foreseen it myself. Like a typical fatuous parent I failed. Where are they?"

"They share a study, as you know. I told them to be there all evening if necessary. To wait till you came."

"Thank you. I know where it is."

As Michael recrossed the campus and traversed the long corridor to his son's study, the fingers of the hand that clutched his left lapel scratched at his chest, as if to hem into his very heart the escaping image of the pathetic, gawky boy whom he had so desperately tried to love. But he was already aware from a hard, growing chill deep within him that whatever hurdles love could surmount, and there were many such — Seymour's egotism, his irritability, his coldness — there was one, that of cruelty, which would always bring it down in a tumbling heap. For how could anyone love a boy who had done what Fitch had described? Standing now before Seymour's door, he paused to acknowledge with a bitter nod the shrewdness of this new fury that seemed to be dogging his steps. Then he rapped sharply on the panel and heard Rex Webb's cheerful cry: "Come in, Mr. Farish!" When he entered, Seymour only looked sullenly away, but Rex came briskly forward to shake his hand.

"We've been waiting for you, sir. With what anticipation you can imagine."

Rex was a marked contrast to Seymour; he was as small and compact and organized as the latter was tall and unco-ordinated. He had neat, curled blond hair and smooth white skin, and had it not been for the air of foxy intelligence in his bright blue eyes he would have seemed of an almost cherubic innocence. He made Michael feel like a family lawyer who had been summoned to get him out of a jam, a useful retainer, tried and loyal, who had to be humored with a jocose friendliness.

"Good of you to come, sir," Rex went on, "awfully good." He smiled as if to include Michael in the tiny club of Averhill's adults. "I suppose you had quite a do with Fitch. The good soul takes things hard, doesn't he?"

"I had a talk with the headmaster," Michael corrected him gravely. "I certainly found him upset."

"Facts, facts." Rex shook his head and sighed. "Naturally they're nasty things to face. Particularly if one has spent a lifetime avoiding them."

"Are you referring to Mr. Fitch?"

"Who else?"

"And are you and Seymour the facts that he has spent a lifetime avoiding?"

"Not quite." Nothing could dim the luster of Rex's small smile. "Your son and I, Mr. Farish, are simply a means to an end. We hold up our little mirror before the headmaster's bemused eye."

"And what does he see in it? The face of one scared colored boy?"

"Exactly!" Rex almost clapped his hands. "How well you put it, sir!"

"I'm glad I'm able to 'put' it, for I certainly don't understand it. What is the great merit in terrifying this boy?"

"Oh, Daddy, the colored boy had nothing to do with it," Seymour broke in, in his dryest, most impatient tone. "Any more than the Jew boys did. Try not to make the waters any muddier than Fitch has already made them!"

"I think we'll refer to him as *Mr.* Fitch," Michael said sharply. He paused for a moment to regain his calm and looked away from his son. There was a slow cold feeling moving out from his stomach, a heavy, dead feeling, a sense of hopelessness in the room around him. "Why am I muddying the waters?"

"Because the real issue has nothing to do with Negroes or Jews! It has to do with self-deception!"

"On whose part?"

"On Mr. Fitch's." Rex was now answering for Seymour. "Let me explain it to your father, Sy. You see, Mr. Farish, we've done a bit of research in the threat of Communism. Seymour and I simply believe, in common with many of our leading citizens, that the biggest hole in the dike today is the attitude of easy optimism of the liberal gentleman. The old-fashioned F.D.R. attitude that the left can still be placated."

"The same attitude that disapproves of putting glue on prayer books?"

Rex paused for a second, but then smiled even more broadly. "That, I confess, sir, was a prank."

"But the burning cross? That wasn't?"

"Oh no. That goes to the essence of things. You see, sir, the headmaster doesn't dare call this school what it obviously is." Rex bestowed the little frown of the practiced lecturer on his visitor. "It's obviously a private academy for sons of the rich, the well-born and the wise. I've borrowed the phrase from Mr. Hamilton, but I think it fits. This, however, will never do for the reverent Fitch. Oh, dear no. To him we must be an American school, a democratic school, a liberal school. Geographically representational and totally desegregated. Except — " Here Rex raised a warning finger. "Oh, always that 'except.' *Except* we must still be the same old school! So we pick the whitest Negroes and the blondest Jews, a Hindu who's been reared in England and a Eurasian missionary's son, and presto! We're liberal! As liberal as a fancy dress party!"

Michael paused to keep his temper. "And what *should* Mr. Fitch do?"

"Let him take *all* applicants! If he must be liberal!"

"You would prefer that?"

"It's not a question of what *I* prefer, Mr. Farish," Rex responded with a smiling headshake. "It's a question, as I say, of wishful thinking. A very dangerous kind of wishful thinking, too. The same kind that made people see an idealist in Alger Hiss and a crusty, lovable old curmudgeon in Joe Stalin. That was what Seymour and I were striking at. If Fitch had his game, we had to have ours."

"Even at the expense of hurting that boy? Hurting him, perhaps, for his whole life?"

"I knew we'd get to that!" Seymour cried suddenly, turning to his friend. "That's Daddy's whole morality! That you mustn't *hurt* people. Just the way his God is only a licker of wounds. It's the ultimate dilution of the Protestant ethic. Finally there's nothing left but pity. And is it pity? Of course not! It's self-pity. Read Graham Greene!"

"Oh, Seymour, shut up!"

Both boys looked at Michael in astonishment. Rex was the first to recover.

"You *were* laying it on a bit thick, I must say, Sy," he reproved his friend and turned his back, smiling once more, to Michael. "You must forgive us, sir. We're so used to having these discussions alone, we forget when we have a visitor. It's just speculation, you know. No offense."

Michael sighed. However detestable, Rex was at least attractive. "What does *your* father think of all this, Rex?"

"Well, he said it might be better if he didn't come up." Rex now actually winked at Michael. "He pointed out that you were a trustee and could handle it if anyone could."

"Handle what?"

"Why, our not getting kicked out, of course!"

For the first time since Fitch had told him the news Michael realized that he was dealing with boys. He could make out at last the apprehension behind the studied indifference of their expressions. Rex had obviously underestimated his own father's disapproval. Michael knew Mr. Webb, a leading investment banker on the street, shrewd, attractive, cordial, an isolationist in wartime and an imperialist in peace. But Mr. Webb was not a violent man; he would never have sanctioned the vulgarity of that cross of fire.

"So your father wants you to finish up with school?" Michael asked dryly. "He fails to see the value of your efforts to broaden the headmaster's vision?"

Rex decided that it was time for a sheepish grin. "Daddy thinks we've jumped the gun a bit. He says that tags are tags, and that a diploma from Averhill is not to be sneezed at."

"Even at the sacrifice of your beliefs?"

"Well, he says we won't sacrifice them by being quiet for another few weeks."

"In other words, he gave you hell."

Rex repeated the sheepish grin. "That's right, sir," he admitted. "That's about the score."

Michael sat for several seconds thinking. Then he got up. "I think I need some air. I want to think things over. I'll take a walk."

"Shall we go with you, sir?"

"No. I think you'd better not."

He knew where he wanted to go, and he had to go there alone. Leaving the building, he crossed the empty campus in the chilly air of the New England spring. When he came to the gymnasium he turned off toward the football field and climbed a small grass mound on the top of which stood a circular marble bench half enclosing a drinking fountain and the statue of an angel with spreading wings. He looked down for a moment over the empty field and then turned to read the carved inscription that ran along the back of the marble bench: "In Memoriam. Peter Teriot. 1909 – 1929. 'I asked for life, and Thou gavest me life: life everlasting.' "

"I envy you, Peter," he murmered aloud. "I envy you with all my heart."

5

PETER TERIOT had been a form ahead of Michael which in the Averhill of their day was an almost impassable social barrier. The upperclassman who condescended was considered a person who could not get on with his formmates, and the junior aspirant was branded as one who felt himself too good for his. But Peter was above such rules; he was simply no part of the Averhill scheme of things. While Michael struggled hard to fit himself into a picture that he felt to be intrinsically alien, Peter did not even seem to care. He was a tall, rather ill-made boy of surprising physical agility (he could cross his feet behind his neck and frequently did), whose small blue eyes, large nose, oval chin and crew cut gave him an expression of almost comic arrogance that in no way belied his true character. For Peter, the last of a famous New York family which had not been in trade since the eighteen-forties and which had produced several men of letters and artists, more renowned, however for their lofty eccentricities than their minor if undoubted talents, condescended magnificently to the school. His winters in Averhill were but the pale shadows of summers spent in climbing the Himalayas with his stepfather or hunting bear in Rumania with his Uncle Herbert. How much of this Peter actually did and how much was the product of a perfervid imagination the other boys never knew, but it was incontestable that he spoke German and Italian, and that Uncle Herbert, lecturing at the school on the dragon lizards of Komodo, had publicly regretted that Averhill's schedule prevented his taking "old Peter" on the forthcoming expedition. Peter was not popular, for he tried too hard to impress, but the rather stunning effect of his total irreverence for school standards together with a reputation for half-crazy violence as a pugilist won him a certain grudging respect and kept him from being the object of any persecution that he could not afford to ignore. He strode about the school, squinting shortsightedly at the occasional thing that struck his fancy, laughing loudly to himself, his clothes darkened with the smudge of scientific experiments, unabashed in his unacceptable enthusiasms, yet with the soul of a Roman hero in a novel by Marion Crawford.

Michael and Peter became friends in the spring of the latter's next-to-last year. It came about during a production of the annual school play, a version of *The Hunchback of Notre Dame* in which Peter made a tremendous and unexpected hit in the role of Quasimodo which he played in a stumping, eye-rolling, chuckling fashion reminiscent of Lionel Barrymore, then at the height of his stage career. Michael, as assistant stage manager, found himself constantly coached by Peter who had an astonishing knowledge of lights and scenery. "My great-uncle, Albert Teriot, was married to Clara Tinetti, you know," he explained. "Briefly, but still married. She always said she was at the mercy of the man on the switch panel." Michael assumed that their brief intimacy would not survive the play, particularly after Peter's success which made him, for two whole days, the talk of the school. But Peter seemed as little conscious of his new popularity as he had been of his comparative isolation, and taking no advantage of better social opportunities, proposed to Michael that they take a canoe trip on the school birthday. They brought a box lunch which they ate on an island in the river while Peter, to Michael's horror, for it was a capital offense, casually smoked cigarette after cigarette. Turkish ones, too.

"Don't worry," he said at the sight of Michael's bulging eyes, "I'm not even going to offer you one. If we're caught, your breath will be as pure as snow."

"I'm only worried about you."

"Don't. All guilt will fade before a peppermint. How few things in life is *that* true of." Peter inhaled deeply. "Tell me, Michael. Why did you want to be a stage manager? Such a dreary job."

"Someone has to do it."

"Yes, but why you? It's barely respectable. By Averhill standards. And I always think of you as such an Averhillian. Am I wrong? Soul as well as body. Though it's only the body, of course, that Mr. Minturn asks for."

"What would be more respectable?"

Peter flung his cigarette in the water and reached for another. "Oh, football," he said, shrugging. "Or glee club. Or masturbation."

Michael laughed. "I'll be frank," he confessed. "Only don't tell anyone. I need it for the yearbook. You know, that list of things after your name."

Peter stared at him blankly for a moment and then let out a whoop of laughter. He had a high, jarring laugh, and Michael felt very foolish. Yet the prospect of a blank space under his picture in the graduating class book was a nightmare that he felt even Peter must share. "So that's your secret!" Peter cried. "How long must the list be? But of course! A *respectable* length! Not too long, not too bristling with honors. That might be showy, perhaps? Or too bare, too sorry a record of the busy competing years? How many lines? Six? Ten?"

Michael stirred uncomfortably. "Well, what's so wrong with that? How would *you* like to see your name with nothing under it at all?"

"But I'd adore it!" Peter lay back on the ground and clapped his hands. "Think of it! Peter Teriot, class of 1925. And then nothing. A filmy white blank of that expensive paper they use. All milky and pregnant with meaning."

"Meaning what?"

"Meaning they'd given me my life back! All for my very own. Don't you see what you're letting them do to you, Michael? You spend your time at school worrying about one idiotic list. You'll spend your life worrying about what will be on your tombstone. And what *will* be, poor boy? Your dates of birth and death, quite the most important things about you, the name of the woman who may have been your spouse and perhaps a Latin inscription that no one will understand. When will you learn that all you have is *now?* This very moment? This Tiepolo sky?" Peter suddenly threw his arms up toward it.

But Michael was thinking of his father's inscription: "Beloved husband of Gertrude Lear Farish." There had not even been a Latin phrase. The idea that his father might be of less significance, simply because he was buried, or that the free blueness of the sky should bear any relation to the restricted life beneath it, was disturbing. "Don't you believe in anything, Peter?" he asked.

"I tell you, you goon, I believe in *everything!*" his friend cried, sitting up. "It's you who believe in nothing. Because you believe in the school. You believe in the whole black academy of moon-faced little snobs. You believe in that wily old fanatic who's always telling us in biblical phrases to keep our hands out of our pockets!"

"Oh, Peter! Mr. Minturn!"

"Well, I grant him style," Peter admitted. "He's genuine, I concede. In another century he might have been a Savonarola. But today what is he? A hopeless anachronism, running a pasteurized version of an English public school. With all the zip gone, the empire, the dukes, the horse guards. Even the snobbery gone, the *real* snobbery. Nothing left but a petty middle-class money snobbery about who belongs to what country club!"

There was a long pause. "I don't agree with you," Michael said judiciously. "There may be some truth in what you say, but I think Mr. M is a good man."

"And you, too, can be a good man," Peter sneered. "You've taken the first step by being a conformist. Except a conformist who believes in nothing. That may redeem you yet. Maybe that's what I like about you, Mike. That sense of nihilism beneath the glazed surface."

Michael was moved. He rarely thought of people as liking him. "What do you want to be, Peter? I mean afterwards?"

"Oh, a buccaneer, a king, a collector of pornographic pictures." Peter plucked up a handful of grass and threw it in the river. "A dentist, a beachcomber, who cares? As long as it's not fit to print in the chaste pages of the Averhill *Alumni Journal*. And you?"

"Oh, I thought you knew," Michael said, getting up to go back to the canoe. He smiled down at Peter. "I'm going to be an inscription on a tombstone."

Later in the spring, just before commencement, an extra-

ordinary thing happened. Peter was elected one of the five
school prefects for the following year. Now prefects were
exalted creatures, being intermediaries between the student
body and the faculty, and Michael was dazzled. Upon anal-
ysis, however, it began to make sense. The prefects were
elected by the outgoing sixth form and the masters, and it
was well known that Mr. Minturn, for all his probity, was
not above dictating to the convention. Peter had attracted the
attention of the faculty with his high marks, his playing of
the organ in chapel, his eccentric brilliance. There was
no question but that from an adult point of view he must
have seemed quite the most remarkable member of his form,
and no adult, it was safe to assume, had heard the excoriating
terms in which he was wont to denounce the school. The
sixth formers, on the other hand, had been grudgingly impressed by his performance in the play and less grudgingly
so by his rather violent ability on the hockey rink, the one
organized sport that he seemed not to despise. And then, too,
unrebuffable like all people who are insensible to petty criticism, he had a certain disarming camaraderie of manner that
it seemed churlish to resist. It was almost flattering — that
was the amazing thing — even for an older boy to be taken
up by Peter. Although he never would have had the mandate
of the lower school, or even that of his own form, the outgoing sixth, with their eyes turned to the approaching pleasures of Harvard and Yale, could pause, with their new air
of maturity, to reappraise a boy like Peter.

It was little surprise to Michael that he saw less of Peter
the following year. The sixth formers were the gods of the
school and the prefects super-gods. They were admitted to
the masters' houses as almost social equals and shared with
them the responsibility of running the school. Mr. Minturn

loved to quote Arnold of Rugby's: "If the sixth form is in sympathy with the school and with me, there is no position in England that I would exchange for this." And Peter, Michael observed a bit wryly, seemed to be loving it. His high voice could be heard reading "Tamberlane" with Mr. Cotton, the English teacher, in the latter's study long after lights were out for the rest of the dormitory. The school play, *Cyrano*, he not only directed but starred in, and the *Averhill Magazine* devoted pages to his Browningesque dramatic monologues about Pizarro and Cortez. As captain of the hockey team he was victorious over St. Lawrence's, the time-honored adversary of the school, and beat them also in a debate on "Should Prohibition Be Repealed?" It seemed, indeed, to be Peter's year, and Michael wondered if he wasn't at last developing a sentiment about the school. Walking back with him one night from a glee club meeting where Peter had happily harmonized with boys whom he would have formerly described as moonfaces, Michael asked him if he hadn't changed his views.

"Oh, you know how it is," Peter retorted, kicking a pebble ahead of him rather viciously. "They get you a bit. With the whole little fantasy of pretending that we're big, brave men. They hand out medals and sing songs and make you a bit dewy-eyed, before you stop to think it over. They almost carry it off. It's like what Daddy says about Ramsay MacDonald being taken in by the glitter of the Court of St. James's. But it is just glitter, after all. It has nothing to do with life." His mood suddenly changed, and he gripped Michael on the shoulder. "Oh, Mike, we'll have fun at Harvard. Just you see. That will be living, boy!"

His words made Michael uneasy. At each of its turns life seemed fairly to bristle with thickets of new pleasures on which one had to seem glad to be torn. Was Averhill itself only a kindergarten? Had he used too much of his energy in a mock battle, and would he find himself at a disadvantage when the tips came off the foils?

Peter graduated in a blaze of glory, carrying off a quarter of the upper class prizes and shining as author of the class poem which he read aloud at Commencement in a high, shrill tone that made its elaborate classical references seem designed to show up the ignorance of the audience of rather dazed parents. And Michael, in the following fall of his own sixth form year, confessed to a feeling of faint relief that Peter was away at Harvard. For he found that he, too, enjoyed being a sixth former, and he did not want Peter around to sneer. He was beginning at last to emerge from the cautious reserve of his earlier years and to see that it might be an asset to be good-looking and even-tempered. He found to his surprise that other boys enjoyed his sense of humor and that it was not impossible to be popular. Of course, he could never be *really* popular like Harrison Duer who was captain of the football team or Sam Hazard who was senior prefect, but he could be known as someone who had done his best with what he had, who had played on the football team although a bit underweight and who might have been captain of the debating society but for a tendency to stutter in public. Michael had never made any enemies, but now he began to make friends. Averhill's teeth had been drawn, and it was only his lurking sense that it must be time to move on to the next hurdle, that kept him from getting the full pleasure of it.

The next time that he saw Peter was in Cambridge after the Harvard-Yale football game. The whole sixth form was allowed to attend on the alternate years when the game was at Cambridge; they drove in with masters and were allowed to stay on afterwards and visit their friends in the college provided they caught a train back to school no later than nine o'clock. That any violation of this privilege, such as drinking or smoking in the rooms of undergraduates, would result in expulsion, was gravely emphasized by Mr. Minturn himself prior to each biennial departure. Michael formed a group with four others: Fisher, Emmons, Solbright, and Drew Van Nest. The last named was a recent friend of Michael's; he had been too prominent in the form to be an intimate in the days of the latter's shyness. He was a fat, strong boy with a habit of violent laughter and an obsessive but self-conscious curiosity about the great world that lay beyond the boundaries of Averhill. It was a curiosity that made his final year there, despite a prefecture, seem a rather flat waiting period. Michael soon discovered why Drew had asked him to be one of the party.

"I understand Peter Teriot's giving a party after the game," he said to Michael in the car on the way in. "Did he ask you?" Michael nodded doubtfully, for he had not been planning to go. "How about taking us along? They say Peter really knows how to do it." He lowered his voice so the master driving the car would not hear. "Beautiful girls. Champagne. I hear even seniors and law students come!"

There was no refusing that eager round countenance. Besides, it was gratifying to be able to do a favor for such a group. Michael felt elated, and his elation was accentuated by the general excitement when Harvard won the game. He and Drew and the others made their way slowly back to Brattle Street, waving streamers and singing, to the house where Peter, who would never have condescended to live in freshman quarters, had rented rooms. These were already crowded when they got there, and Michael felt his heart sink when he saw the mass of flushed faces, heard the loud gramophone and the cacophony of voices. But Drew pushed him forward, and he found himself behind Peter, who just then turned around, a drink in each hand, and faced him with a glittering eye.

"Why, Mike!" he cried. "You've come to Cambridge at last! How are you, boy! Didn't I tell you? Isn't this living?" And he laughed in his sudden shrill, mocking manner, so that Michael, appalled, wondered if he were not already making fun of his new life. Then he hurried off with his drinks, leaving Michael to glance anxiously around the room and reflect that Drew had been right, that there *were* seniors and law students at the party. Directly across the room, and obviously tight, was Freddy Lassiter who had been senior prefect of Averhill five years before and with him was Flora Cameron, the beautiful postdebutante from Bradley Bay. She was smiling, but she looked the way she looked at the beach club, placidly, even contentedly bored, but still bored. To Michael it was as if Peter had attained a whole new generation of sophistication. If he laughed at *that*, well, was there anything he wouldn't laugh at? And what did his laughter mean? Peter was back now and being the good host.

"What'll it be, boys? Can you handle this stuff?" Michael saw they were all taking scotch. "A peppermint before you go back, remember that, Michael?"

"No, thanks, Peter," he said with a firmness that surprised them all. "Just some soda water. That's all." Averhill was all that he had in that room; Averhill he would cling to. Peter took him and Drew over to meet Flora Cameron and Freddy Lassiter. Drew stared at Flora's white immobile face and her dark, distant, not unkindly eyes and began almost crazily trying to entertain her. Peter smiled as if he were showing off a monkey.

"Thank God it's our last year!" Drew almost shouted at Lassiter. "And then watch out, all of you, here comes Drew! The little boys grow up, Freddy." It was astonishing how rapidly the whiskey reacted on him. "I bet you hardly remember us. We were only second formers when you were senior prefect. And now, next year, we'll be up here, too! Getting royally drunk every night. Except maybe Michael. He can feel Mr. M's radiating waves. Even at a distance of forty miles and through how many smoked-filled rooms. It dashes the cup from his hand!"

Drew went on interminably in this strain, and the others laughed mildly. Flora asked Michael if it was against the rules to drink, and when he told her it was she seemed quite shocked at Drew. Michael immediately warmed toward her; it was as if this beautiful girl had suddenly aligned herself with the "real" adults. But, even so, standing with his soda water he felt conspicuous and different, and Averhill with its red brick and white columns and the Gothic tower standing high against the sunset over the playing fields seemed as much a home as had his mother's face on that first day when she had turned to look back at him on the varnished stairway. But that is life, he told himself grimly. When you begin to enjoy things, it's time to move on.

Peter had rejoined the group and was suddenly angry with Drew. "Why should Mike drink if he doesn't want to! Can't you have a drink, Drew, without sneering at someone who doesn't?" He laughed again his mocking laugh "How true it is that virtue is stronger than vice! Virtue can bear it alone, but vice can't. Virtue seeks the monastic cell, and vice is lost without a party!"

It was not long after this that Bertie Emmons came up to Michael and whispered that Drew Van Nest was obviously getting drunk. "The son of a bitch will get us all in dutch," he hissed. "Let's get him out of here." Emmons was a sallow, bitter boy who resented the least demonstration of pleasure in others. "There's always one in every crowd. It never fails." They alerted Solbright and Fisher who immediately understood and nodded. Peter looked vaguely concerned, but then he shrugged his shoulders, and as Michael left he saw that he was sitting on the floor crossing his legs behind his neck to amuse Flora Cameron. He heard the latter's little cry of incredulity.

Outside it was at once apparent that Drew was going to be a real problem. He kept resisting when they tried to get him into a taxi and wanted to appeal to every passer-by, making elaborate bows. Finally they got some coffee down his throat, and on the train for Averhill he subsided into a rather brooding silence. Aroused at the school station, for a minute he did not seem to know where he was, but he obeyed Emmons meekly. Fortunately they were in the same dormitory, and Michael watched with misgivings the larger figure lumbering after the smaller into the darkness across the lawn.

The next morning Michael noticed that Drew was not at breakfast. Emmons, tight-lipped and inscrutable, simply remarked that he had been taken to the infirmary in the early morning. When the others prodded him for more information, he only shrugged his shoulders angrily, and Michael knew grimly that they faced disaster. Yet breakfast went by, and chapel, and the long Sunday morning. It was not until just before lunch that he felt a hand on his shoulder, and, starting, looked up into the grave features of Sam Hazard, the senior prefect.

"Let's go into my study, Mike, shall we?"

Sam in his study sat back in his swivel chair and touched the fingers of each hand together as Mr. Minturn did.

"I'm not going to play cat and mouse with you, Mike," he

began. "The matter is far too grave. I'll put my cards on the table. Drew Van Nest was sick to his stomach in the infirmary this morning. He was obviously stewed to the gills. Mr. M is determined to get to the bottom of this if he has to hire a squad of detectives from Boston. This isn't a time to worry about snitching on people; it's a question for the school, the masters, even the trustees. I've left you to the last because I trust you. But I'll tell you what the others told me first." He looked at Michael squarely in the eye for several seconds. "Drew says he was the only one of you who had a drink at Peter Teriot's. That's like Drew, but no one believes it. Fisher, however, confirms Drew. Solbright, on the other hand, says all of you drank. Emmons says that only he and Drew did."

"I did not drink at Peter's," Michael said after a pause. "Or anywhere else."

"And the others?"

"That's something you'll have to find out for yourself. You have no right to ask me."

"But this is big stuff, I'm telling you!" Sam cried, striking the desk. "We're way beyond the little boys' game of who can't tell on who."

"Some of us are. Some of us aren't."

"You've told me more than you think, already."

"How?"

"Because you wouldn't let anyone be expelled who *hadn't* been drinking. If any of them, besides yourself, hadn't, you'd have told me."

Michael paused, but only for a moment. His wits were about him. "It was a big party at Peter's, and we weren't all together. I couldn't say positively that anyone but myself had *not* been drinking."

Sam looked at him a moment with what Michael took to

be a rather grudging approval. "I'm sorry, Mike. You'll have to go in and see Mr. M. Right away."

Mr. Minturn shook his head sadly when Michael repeated the same story that he had told Sam. It was as if he regretted now, almost irritably, the very sense of schoolboy honor that he himself had done so much to build up. "You have to understand, Michael," he pointed out, "that there are moments when a headmaster, when a whole school, for that matter, must get to the truth. When it becomes the duty of everyone concerned to rise above the prejudice against a tattletale and be man enough to come forward publicly and tell what he knows. At whatever cost. To himself or others. You'd have to do it in a court of law, my boy. You must do it now. You'll be doing your duty to the school if you tell me just what happened in Teriot's rooms."

Michael found to his own stunned surprise that he was contemplating the small, now silent old gentleman with something like detachment. "I'm sorry, sir. I have to follow my own conscience. I can only speak for myself. I had nothing to drink in Teriot's rooms."

"I would like to believe you, Michael. I always have. But how can I be convinced of a part of the truth if you won't tell me the whole? Others have professed to tell the whole, you know. It has even been said that all *five* of you were seen drinking. Who am I to believe, Michael, if you won't confide in me?"

Michael bowed his head. "I'm sorry, sir."

"That will be all, then."

It was odd that he should feel, walking away from the headmaster's study, a kind of dry and melancholy elation. It was as if it were all now over, the future, all the futures, with their demanding vistas, opening one after the other like room upon larger room, each filled with Peter's chattering, mocking friends. Now he could stop and stop without disgrace, for even Mr. Minturn in his heart knew that Michael was playing by the rules. There was not the empty exhaustion of victory or the bitter reality of defeat; if he were expelled now, it would simply be that he had been excused from the game.

But it was not over so easily. Mr. Minturn sent two masters into Cambridge that afternoon to make private inquiries. Freddy Lassiter's cooperation was secured and various persons, including Miss Cameron herself, were discreetly interviewed. It was established beyond question that of the five sixth formers attending the party only Michael Farish had refused a drink. And Mr. Minturn, with the terrible consistency that was his weakness as well as his greatest quality, his ears deafened to the entreaties of parents and trustees, proceeded to expel the guilty four.

It created a sensation that was to be talked about among friends and enemies of Averhill for years to come. For every champion of Mr. Minturn who insisted that only thus could he run a school along the moral lines that he professed, there were at least two, often strangers to the school, who cried shrilly about the rigidity of his age and generation. The Boston newspapers, never fond of a headmaster who permitted no reporters on his sacred campus, played up the incident mockingly. A group of Harvard undergraduates, intoxicated, drove down one night from Cambridge and dragged the cross from the altar to throw it in the river. But all this was later. At the time the school was simply stunned, and Michael found himself, the solitary survivor of the famous group, regarded with a kind of awe. It was known that he had refused to tell on the others, and this was considered, even eventually by Mr. Minturn himself, as a good thing, but the combination of his proper conduct at the party with his proper conduct at the disciplinary aftermath gave him the reputation of one who was just a little too good to be true. He was admired, but he was not admired with envy. For the time being he was destined to walk alone.

Peter Teriot came down from Harvard for a long dark scene in the headmaster's study. It was even rumored that Mr. Minturn had telephoned President Lowell, but unsuccessfully, to have him expelled. But it was only a rumor. Such, of course, was not Mr. Minturn's way. Peter told Michael about the interview that afternoon as they walked together down to the river before Peter drove back to college. He was smiling, and he maintained his note of cool detachment, but it was not convincing.

"Do you remember my once saying he should have been a Savonarola?" he demanded. "Well, he should! If you could have heard him, Mike! It was magnificent. '*I* can forgive you, Peter. I only pray that God will.' It almost gets you, that humility. Because he *means* it. He's the only one on this benighted campus who does. 'If *you* can forgive me, Mr. M,' I told him, 'I'm sure God can.' "

Michael rebelled. "Peter, do you have to be smart about *everything?*" They walked on in silence through the red and brown of the late fall woods, and when he glanced again at Peter, he was appalled to see that he was crying. "Oh, Peter," he murmured. "What a dope I am."

"No, no, you're right, you're right, old man." Peter stopped and turned away until he had got control of himself. "Of course, I'm desperate. How could I not be? How can I fight them all?"

Michael stared. "Who?"

"Mr. M, of course! And his whole band of angels. There's no winning against them, don't you see? Because they won't play *fair*. They never do anything to the real offender, like me. They simply cut the throats of their own sheep. And then toss the bloody carcasses at *my* feet and howl: 'Look what he's done!' And it's true in a strange, perverted way. Because the sheep would be alive but for me. Mr. M can look me in the eye and smear me with his own crime and make it stick. What can I do but expire like the Emperor Julian crying: 'You have won, O Galilean!' " Peter stopped short and closed his eyes and shook both fists suddenly in the air in what seemed to be a fit of passion. "But if they'd only fight fair! Oh, God, if they'd only fight fair!"

He went back to Harvard after their walk, and Michael was summoned to Mr. Minturn's study. He wondered, a bit blankly and quite without apprehension, if he was to be reprimanded for his bad associations. He had a sympathy for Peter's suffering that was deeper than anything that he had ever felt in his school career, and he knew now with a quiet conviction, irrational as it seemed even to himself, on which side of any line he would have to take his stand. But his new loyalties were not to be tested. There was a vacant prefectship with the expulsion of Drew Van Nest, and what the little man with the grey head and piercing eyes was now doing was offering it to him.

He was also not to suffer any test of his future relations with Peter. The latter died of spinal meningitis while on an expedition with Uncle Herbert that very next summer up the Amazon. It was impossible for Michael not to see in this the retribution of an angry God called down upon Peter's offending brow by the outraged headmaster of Averhill. After a while he ceased even to try to see it in any other way. It was an interesting if depressing revelation of how the conflict of values between any friend of his and Mr. Minturn might be resolved. Yet he continued to feel in his own way, and without any apparent contradiction, that it behooved him to be like both of them, that they represented a forking of the path to adult achievement at a point at which he had not even arrived. And one's leaders, of course, were always potentially reconcilable, if over nothing else than their joint discouragement with one's own ineptitude at following them. Michael's feelings seemed to receive their ultimate justification in the fountain at Averhill that was erected in Peter's honor and consecrated by Mr. Minturn himself. The angel with great brooding wings, designed by a sculpting Teriot, was considered a masterpiece, and the memorial itself, commanding a noble view over the football field and the blue and green woods beyond, was powerfully evocative of the tragedy of great promise struck down at the threshold. If it was the apotheosis of Peter Teriot, no priest could have consecrated it with more humility than Mr. Minturn. It was observed at the outdoor service, as the latter turned in his blowing vestments to bless the bowed heads behind him, that his eyes were filled with tears.

6

BUT PETER SEEMED LESS DEAD, that chilly spring evening by his fountain, than he had seemed for a quarter of a century. The dazzling vision of manhood that he had once offered to his friend's cautious gaze, so dangerously and temptingly individual, no longer seemed to have been wholly extinguished by the heavy muffled grasp of what Michael had deemed to be the truer male world, the world to which Peter's early disaster and death had so abruptly reconsigned him. As he stared up now at the brooding angel in the fading twilight he could almost see Peter, sprawled on the marble bench of his own memorial, raising one long leg idly in the air, could almost hear his mocking laugh and voice: "Isn't that just the sort of angel my family *would* have put up? Like something of William Wetmore Storey's in the Protestant Cemetery in Rome. And don't you adore the inscription? Can't you see me asking for life and getting it good: life everlasting? Just the kind of trick Mr. M's God *would* play!" Michael shuddered, and Peter disappeared. But in a minute he seemed to hear the high voice from his other side: "And what are you doing back at school, Michael? Oh, but I forgot. Of course. You're a trustee! How like you, dear Michael. You *would* be a trustee. You've turned out well, I'm sure. Getting ahead nicely, though not at the top. But then there's something a bit vulgar about getting to the top too soon, isn't there? Let's have a look at you. The right clothes, yes. Except those cufflinks are a bit too big and a bit too golden. You got them at Alfeoni's, didn't you? Not *quite* a gentleman's store. And the right tweeds, too. And I'm sure you belong to the right clubs. It all fits nicely into my picture of your home life. And a big, bosomy wife with an eye for the boys!"

"No!" Michael cried aloud, jumping up. "No!" But when he saw he was alone, he sank back on the bench, resting his suddenly tear-filled eyes against his arm.

"No?" the mocking voice continued. "What do you mean 'No'? She had an eye for the boys even in *my* time. How like you to marry a girl of that kind, Michael. How *very* like you. But then that was always the thing about you: your predictability." Michael clenched his fists. "For example, this trouble about Seymour. You've always encouraged his friendship with Rex, haven't you?"

"But Seymour had no friends!"

"Naturally not," the voice by the fountain answered. "How should a boy like Seymour find friends? But was that the reason? The real reason? Oh, think, Michael. *Think!* Wasn't it just possible that the real reason — the *true* reason — was that you thought Rex was like *me?*" Michael started, and his ears rang with Peter's imagined yelp of triumph. "So that *was* it! I thought so! Oh, Michael, how could you so degrade me? As dear old Browning would have said — do they still read *him*, by the way? — 'What had *I* to do on earth with the slothful, with the mawkish, the unmanly?' So Rex was to make Seymour what you had not been? Ah, well, again, it could have been predicted. Because you were a goody-goody, Seymour had to be an ass!"

Again Michael rose and shuddered. It was almost dark now. "Please, Peter!" he whispered.

"Does it make you happy to think I'm Peter?" the voice

sneered. "If I were Peter, do you think I'd be in Averhill? Wouldn't I be in New York, perched on a window sill, to watch old Flora and her muscle-bound boy friend make love?"

"No!" Michael exclaimed. "No, there's nothing in it!"

"Oh, no! Of course not! And Ginny didn't tell you that her mother had a date with Dannyboy, did she? Right after Flora told you she met him by chance on the golf course?" Michael clapped his hands to his ears. "But that's not the real clincher, is it?" the voice went on remorselessly. "You and I both know the real clincher, don't we? Don't we remember how Flora answered your impertinent question yesterday morning? Don't we remember how she kissed you? And how false it was? Now let me tell you how she would have answered if she had *not* been having an affair with Danny. You know, don't you?" Michael nodded slowly as he listened to Flora's tone, rough, bantering, quick to resent the least intrusion on her independence. " 'You ask me if I find Danny Jones attractive? Damn right, I find him attractive! And I warn you right now you'd better be sweet as sugar to me this summer, Michael. Because I'm contemplating a perfectly shameless affair!' "

Michael hurried away from the fountain and across the deserted campus to the headmaster's house. He went into the hall without ringing and burst unannounced into Fitch's study.

"I've thought it all over! There's only one answer. Fire them!"

Fitch rose quickly to his feet. "Michael!"

"They're no good. They're rotten. I ought to know, don't you think? I brought one of them up, didn't I?"

"Michael, for heaven's sake, sit down. You look distracted. Let's talk this over."

"What's there to talk over?" He slumped heavily in the chair opposite Fitch's and leaned forward, covering his face with his hands. "Oh, my God, I'm so ashamed!" he murmured. As if from far away he heard the balanced rhythm of Fitch's sentences, sympathetic, composed, judicial. There had been, he vaguely learned, no idea of expulsion from the beginning. Graduation was only a few weeks off. Michael had been summoned only to help impress upon the boys the gravity of their misbehavior. They would be on probation, of course, but if they would give their word to the headmaster —

"Their word, their word!" Michael looked up suddenly. "What do you think *that's* worth?"

Fitch looked at him sternly. "I'm afraid I have to caution you, Michael, about the parental fallacy. Seymour is a human being quite independently of his relationship to you."

"I know, I know." But *did* he? If he could ever think of Seymour as not his son, might he not actually dislike him? And if he disliked Seymour — well, he did not know. It was a void.

"I've never agreed with the old Minturn policy of getting rid of boys who have the 'wrong attitude,' " the headmaster continued. "It always seemed to me that that way the school was shirking its responsibilities. Your son is just as much my problem as the colored boy. It's all part of the same problem, in fact. Only now we have both sides."

Michael listened submissively as Fitch discoursed on the problems of the liberal headmaster. When he rose to go the latter escorted him to the door, gripping him firmly by the elbow.

"You'll give my best to Flora, won't you? I know how distressed she'll be by all this."

"Oh, yes. Yes."

"And one thing more, Michael. I wouldn't tell Seymour, if I were you, that you thought he should be expelled."

"Why not? Don't you think he deserves even that?"

"A boy likes to think his father's behind him. No matter what."

"He doesn't show it."

Again Michael traversed the long corridor to the boys' study. He found them in waiting for the assembly bell for supper. They both jumped up as he came in.

"It's all right," he said tersely. "He'll give you another chance."

For just a moment the pleasure on each face was unmistakable. Then both boys scrambled back behind their usual masks.

"May I congratulate you, sir?" Rex stepped forward with a broad smile to take Michael's hand. "Even *I* didn't think you could pull this one off. I guess Daddy was right when he said that the Farish touch could do anything. What did you do? Drop some telling hints about the headmaster's pension? Point out that the board of trustees, unlike the school, had not yet been desegregated?"

"I behaved, I suppose you'd say, like a typical trustee," Michael murmured, turning away to the window to avoid the proffered hand. "I hope that you will behave for the rest of the term like typical sixth formers."

"Never fear," Rex said, laughing. "Seymour and I will go underground. Our outward conduct will be beyond reproach."

"That's all I care about," Michael said quietly. "Your outward conduct." He nodded at his own reflection in the window. "Yes, that's really all I care about now."

"Oh, Daddy, how wonderful!" Seymour exploded with his mocking, gasping laugh. "I never thought you'd actually express it! It could be the motto of Hudson River Trust, couldn't it, Rex? The *outward* conduct? Daddy, you're priceless! Would you like to see the farce Rex and I are writing? It's called 'Baby Billions and the Friendly Trustee'!"

Michael turned and walked to the door. "Be careful, Seymour," he said as he looked back at them. "The terrible day may come when you actually feel the pinch of gratitude. When you're tempted for once not to kick your benefactor in the teeth. But be brave, my boy. Resist it. The moment will pass. And then you can go back forever to your old ways!" He closed the door behind him, and Seymour's high laugh followed him down the corridor. But he did not hear Rex's laugh. Perhaps there was still hope for Rex.

7

MICHAEL DID very little sleeping in the train that night. He kept reviewing in his mind the times that he had seen Danny Jones and Flora together. These had been fairly frequent, for although the Joneses were younger, Danny's wife, who was pretty and popular and whose parents were well known in Glenville, was asked to many of the same parties with the Farishes. He remembered Flora sitting next to Danny at dinner on two occasions; he remembered her describing him as a "friendly thug"; he even remembered her expressing surprise that he should have chosen a career in a bank, a remark that he now interpreted more as a reflection on banks than on Danny. But when had they met alone? Was it likely? What would a man that age with a young wife want with a woman of fifty? His mind swung back and forth, between the extremes of conviction and reassurance, until he gave up even trying to sleep and sat up in the early morning to watch the long suburbs of New York slide in grey lines past his window.

When he thought of the day that lay before him and the great Romanesque arch over Hudson's main door, it was no longer with the hope: I *will* be president. Before, he had always allowed himself to enjoy the illusion that when he had reached the pinnacle, he would be safe from the observers at last left behind and would be able to put his feet up and enjoy the panorama of the view. But now all was changed; it was as if he had arrived within sight of the peak only to find the chunky figure of Danny Jones squatting on it, puffing away at a pipe as coolly as if he owned the whole mountainside. The top, instead of being beyond the crowd, would only more expose the climber to the hard glare of its prying eyes and he, Michael, would stand naked before a staring world, all his worlds, past and present. And yet if he failed to take the final step, if his hand slipped at the final boulder, would he not tumble back past the steep grey into the hopeless anonymity of the downtown world, dissolving slowly in his fall like a descending cinder? He could never see Wall Street except through the eyes of a small boy, shepherded by a large and benevolent father through a narrow lane of monstrous edifices toward a tall black steeple, shut in, cramped, not even defiant, having become, through decades of soot and ticker tape, almost another, a grimmer office building. And he remembered the sad sense of companionship that he had felt for this captive parent, who so longed to be using his great muscular frame in one of the ball games at which he excelled, knowing that he, his son, was also doomed, as men were doomed, after the incredible liberty of childhood at the knees of happy, telephoning women, to go down to the narrow streets and the tall, dark buildings and to come home, such hours later, with a damp stiff collar, to reach down a sweaty and bristling cheek for a dry and pampered small boy to kiss.

But what was this devil of sex that it could turn his life to ashes? Why could he only sit now and stare dismally out the window at suburban stations, seeing nothing but his own picture of Flora meeting Jones in the house in town and the violence of their lust intensified by the very stillness of the white summer wrappings, the rugless floors, the green baize on the pictures? Why should that act which they had the discretion to hide away, which would not have existed for him but for a guess, perhaps a suspicion, be enough to disintegrate the whole fabric of his existence, his bank, his family, the gold cufflinks from Alfeoni's, Mrs. Winters, even Seymour himself?

When the train got in, he went uptown to Sixty-first Street to leave his bag and bathe before going to the office. On the sidewalk he met Alberto, the Sicilian watchman employed by several of the house owners in the block, and a thought struck him.

"I've always treated you right, Alberto, haven't I?" he asked, reaching a hand into his pocket. "If you knew something I ought to be told, you'd tell me, wouldn't you?"

"Oh, yes, sir, Mr. Farish. Yes, sir!" A hint of worry flickered across the cheerful demeanor that even thirty years in his occupation had not destroyed. He became positively grave as his fist closed on the ten-dollar bill that Michael handed him.

"I want you to tell me something." Michael listened to his own voice and thought it sounded controlled. "I know Mrs. Farish has been coming into town during the day. Has she been going to the house?"

Alberto's face became inscrutable. "I think she did, yes."

"Did you ever see a young man go in with her? A blocky, dark-haired young man?"

"Oh, Mr. Farish, whatya mean asking questions like that?" Alberto shook his head sadly. "Mrs. Farish lovely lady. Don't go asking questions like that."

"I'm going to ask the questions I want to ask, Alberto."

"Mrs. Farish one lovely lady," insisted Alberto, still shaking his head. "One lovely lady. Always good to everyone."

"I'm not going to do any harm to Mrs. Farish," Michael reassured him sharply. "I have reasons of my own for finding out. I take it, anyway, that you *did* see the man I describe come in. Is that right, Alberto?"

"I think maybe he come to see about painting the hall," Alberto mumbled. "Yes, I think she tell me that. He wasn't in there long."

Michael turned to go into the house. "Thank you, Alberto," he managed to articulate. "Thank you very much. Yes, I'm sure it was about the painting."

By that evening, when Flora met him at the train in Glenville, he was able to describe the details of his interview with Mr. Fitch as though Seymour had been his only concern on the trip to Averhill. He omitted from his recital his own recommendation that Seymour be expelled. Flora listened attentively at first, but before he had finished she was looking out the window, half stifling a yawn.

"Well, I'm glad I let you handle it alone," she said. "You're so much better at that sort of thing without me."

"How about you?" he asked, suddenly tense as he looked fixedly down the road ahead. "Have you been better off without *me?*"

"Whatever are you talking about?" She turned and stared at him. "I've been fine. I played eighteen holes of golf yesterday afternoon. It was the *most* beautiful day."

8

THINGS IN THE OFFICE that Michael had always taken in his stride began now to exasperate him unbearably. Worst of all was Charlie Meredith's fussiness. In the past he had rather enjoyed the old man's increasing dependence on himself as a harbinger of his own ultimate promotion. But now he could see only the fraud, the loss of nerve; he analyzed savagely the widening discrepancy between his superior's demeanor and capacity. If Meredith could still pose to clients, with his broad, silent grin, with the charming backward tilt of his white head, as the benign, wise family counselor, Michael knew how tenaciously he clung to office routine as his armor against the discovery of incompetence. When he came in one morning in the week after his return from Averhill and found that Meredith, as usual, wanted to see him "right away," he marched into his office, smarting with anticipatory irritation.

"Yes, sir?"

Meredith, looking up from his desk, smiled his nicest smile. "Ah, Michael, my dear boy," he said blandly, "sit down, sit down. I have something to ask you."

"I have a meeting at eleven," Michael said a bit peevishly.

"Oh, but this will only take a few minutes. Tell me, Michael." The long, red-veined fingers were slowly folded on the spotless blotter. "I know how patient you always are even with the most difficult clients. That's why I'm so sure there were some special circumstances in the matter I wish to discuss."

"What matter, sir?" Michael asked shortly. "Has there been a complaint?"

Meredith maintained his determinedly cheerful smile. "You can't guess?"

"I'm afraid I left my crystal ball at home this morning."

"I see." The smile faded a bit. "Very well, Michael. It was Mrs. Winters. She said she called you the other day and that you were busy on the telephone. She left word for you to call back, and you never did."

Michael rubbed his brow slowly and then remembered. Of course, it was true. Good God, what *was* happening to him? "I'm sorry, sir," he said, deflated. "I must have forgotten."

"Forgotten? With a woman like Mrs. Winters? But, Michael, you *don't* forget. Tell me, are you quite sure you're feeling all right?"

"Yes, sure. Why?"

"I think you're looking tired. Do you have something on your mind? What about Seymour? Was it bad news that took you up to his school last week?"

"It's all right now."

"Michael, I can't help you if I don't know."

"It's all right, sir, please." He tried desperately to keep the quiver of exasperation out of his voice.

"Very well, then." Meredith shook his head. "My wife just telephoned me," he continued, changing his tone briskly to one of more cheer. "She says she and Flora are going shopping this afternoon. To buy a new coat. So sweet of Flora to help her pick one. We all know what wonderful taste she has."

Michael looked up in sudden shock. "Flora? But Flora's in Glenville. She told me she wouldn't be in town all week!"

"That's what she told *you*, my dear boy. But we know what women are about shopping. When Alice called her, she said she was coming in this morning and would meet her after lunch. So there we are. We husbands know nothing!"

"So it would appear." Michael rose to leave. "Would you excuse me, sir?"

He had to find out if Danny was going uptown. The idea of even trying to concentrate on anything else was absurd. Standing in the passageway by the elevators he stared through the glass partition into the big room where the junior trust men worked. Then an idea struck him, and he picked up one of the telephones on the counter.

"Give me Mr. Jones's extension."

"Yes, Mr. Farish."

He watched as Danny, across the room, unconscious of his supervision, picked up the telephone.

"Jones speaking."

"Oh, Danny," he said casually, studying the latter's profile. "Michael Farish. Are you by any chance free for lunch today?" He saw Danny's head turn quickly toward the door of his own office. Fortunately, it was closed.

"Gosh, Mr. Farish, I'm awfully sorry. Could I take a rain check on that? I've got a safe deposit opening uptown."

"Oh, have you?" Michael paused to keep the curiosity out of his tone. "Which estate?"

"Willoughby."

"I thought that was Jack Earl's."

"It is." Michael saw Danny's lips tighten and one hand move nervously up the back of his head to scratch his hair. "But I told him I'd cover the box opening. He's got a lunch meeting of his tax committee."

"I don't mean to be stuffy about it, Danny," Michael said in a sharper tone, "but you know I don't like this swapping of jobs. There may be another will in that box. It's Jack Earl's matter, and I want him to be there." He watched intently while Danny, like a small boy, turned and half stuck his tongue out at the closed door of Michael's office. "Will you tell him that?"

"Yes, sir." Danny's tone was almost surly.

"Then maybe we'll be able to lunch, after all?"

"Huh?" There was a pause as Danny recollected himself. "Oh, yes. Fine. Any special time?"

When Michael hung up, he kept his hand on the telephone and continued to watch Danny. The latter had slumped down in his chair with an expression of sullen disappointment. After a few moments Michael again asked the operator for his extension and saw Danny snap around to pick up the receiver.

"Jones speaking."

"Oh, Danny," he resumed blandly, "Miss Brown has just reminded me I have an appointment in Newark. I'll have to be over there for lunch and the afternoon. Sorry. But you go ahead to Jack Earl's box opening if you want. I just remembered that you may be helping him on that estate, so you'd better be familiar with it."

There was a marked distinction between Danny's expression and the tone of his voice. Over the wire Michael simply heard his noncommittal "All right, sir, thanks," but through the glass he could see the sudden broad smile and the gleeful snap of his fingers. On his way to the elevator Michael passed Amelia Brown.

"I won't be back today," he told her. "I'm going to Newark."

"You'll be at Standard Trust?"

"Yes."

"With Mr. Jamison?"

"Yes. I mean no." He hurried on, suddenly impatient with his own nerves. "Never mind. I can't be reached. I'll be in conference."

The taxi that took him uptown deposited him on the corner of his street, and he peered cautiously down both sides before approaching the house. There was no sign of Flora. Of course she might have already gone in, but he could always say that he had come up to get some papers. He walked briskly down the sidewalk and let himself into the small dark hall with its chairs and mirror wrapped in green summer plastic. Going to the bottom of the spiral stairway he paused and looked up. The house was absolutely still.

"Flora!" he called. "Oh, Flora, are you in?"

Silence. He went upstairs and into the front living room on the third story from which he planned to peer out and wait for her arrival. The bedroom was on the same floor in back; he could get to it in plenty of time from the moment he spotted her on the sidewalk below. But after he had stood for a few minutes peering down through the curtains he was overcome with restlessness and went to inspect his hiding place.

Flora's bedroom had formerly been his mother's, but it was as different now as Flora was from Gertrude. Gone were the mahogany bedsteads and the faded prints of the seasons and his mother's solid, unfeminine chest of drawers; in their place was a vast double bed with a Venetian headboard, two posters by Toulouse-Lautrec and a skirted bureau, with a triple mirror, covered with small bottles. Indeed the wanton, the faintly blowsy air of the chamber, combined with Flora's failure in any habit of neatness, had driven Michael to the chaster simplicity of the small dressing room in back. There he had put up a cot when Flora had complained of his snoring, and, more recently, he had come to sleep there altogether. The door between this room and Flora's was locked in summer because of the safe in Michael's closet, but over it there was a shuttered transom window. As Michael now confirmed, by pulling over his bureau to stand on it, he could command a partial view of the bedroom by peering down through the slats.

Satisfied, he returned to the front room and gazed up the almost empty street to find no view of Flora. He was about to get a chair when, happening to glance down, his heart bounded. There was Flora actually fitting her key in the front door! Frantically he hurried back to his dressing room, closed and locked the door and got up on the bureau. In a few moments he heard her step on the stairway and saw her walk briskly into the room and sit down on the bed by the telephone. The complete normalcy of her demeanor, the easy way that she stretched out one foot to admire a new shoe before dialing, the utter lack of expression of her features when she terrifyingly looked up and at the transom — he could not help but duck — gave him an odd feeling of not being there at all.

"Is that you, Claude?" she was saying. "Is four o'clock all right for my permanent? Oh, good. I'll be there."

He felt a fool for thinking she would call Danny. Obviously, he was already on his way uptown. Nor would she risk it; the girls at the switchboard knew her voice. There was silence now, and he tried to see what she was doing. One of the slats concealed her head. Then he heard a match struck and felt reproved by the innocence of her smoking. Several minutes went by while she thumbed through the mail that he had seen on the hall table, and suddenly the telephone rang loudly, almost indecently. She caught it up at the first ring.

"Hello?" Her voice was sharp, tense, irritated. "Hello? Oh, Danny." He could hear the sigh of her relief. "Where are you, darling?" There was a pause. "Oh, just at the corner? Oh, good, sweetie. Yes, come *right* now. The coast is clear. I'll come down and let you in."

When she had hung up and hurried from the room Michael got down from the bureau and surveyed his own blank face in the mirror. The puzzled eyes stared back at him, intensifying his sense of unreality, and then his lips shaped into a leering, semi-idiotic smile. "Was that what you wanted to know, boy?" he asked. "Congratulations!" But could there be any *real* shame, while he was alone, unbenownst to the world, all alone with a mirror in his own dressing room? Who was Michael Farish, after all? Wasn't he down at the bank? He heard footsteps now in the next room, hurried footsteps, and he scrambled back excitedly on top of his bureau.

What he saw transfixed him. Danny was already stark naked except for his socks. He must have torn his clothes off as he ran upstairs. He stood in the middle of the room, staring at Flora with a sullen, almost hostile expression as she sat on the bed pulling her slip over her head. It was as if he grudged her even the few moments it took her to undress before he could satisfy his desire. When her slip came off, Flora looked up at him adoringly. Michael had never seen such a look of submission on her face before. He felt suddenly suffocated by their physical intimacy; everything combined to intensify his sense of it: the darkened room, the June heat outside, oppressively hovering, and those large nude figures. As Danny moved forward and pushed her back on the bed, Michael closed his eyes.

When he was nine years old, he had wanted to see his mother without her clothes on and had stolen into her bedroom to hide behind the couch from where he could peek into her bathroom. He had never seen a naked woman, only his younger sisters, and his curiosity had been excited by the descriptions that he had heard from the more knowledgeable boys at school. Apparently the pictures of nude goddesses and models in the art books in the family library did not tell the whole story. Apparently there were other things. He waited in the hall until he heard his mother go to her bathroom and then slipped in and ducked behind the couch. She had left the door open, and he could hear the splashing. But when he peered cautiously over the top of the couch it was to stare directly into her startled eyes.

"Michael!" she cried. "Michael, what are you doing there?"

He fled. He fled to his own room in panic, though he heard her voice calling after him. He huddled in his bed, shaking with shame. There had been a sternness in her eyes that made him disgusting to himself. Irredeemably disgusting. Peggy, his big Irish nurse, came blustering in and told him that he was wanted and led him firmly downstairs by the hand. They found his mother sitting at her bureau in a dressing gown.

"All right, Peggy," she said. "I'll talk to him alone." And when the door closed behind Peggy she turned to him gravely but without anger. "What did you want, Michael?"

"Nothing."

"Was that why you hid behind the couch? Because you wanted nothing?"

"Yes. I mean, no." He stared at the floor, unutterably wretched.

"Wasn't it because you wanted to see me undressed?"

He shook his head.

"Wasn't it?"

"Please, Mummy!"

"But there's nothing wrong with that. It's only doing it in that sneaky way that's wrong. There's nothing shameful about our bodies. If you want to see me, you should come and ask me." His eyes were still fixed to the floor. "Would you like to see me now, Michael?" He shook his head passionately. "It's perfectly all right."

"No, no!"

"Now you're being silly. It's perfectly natural for your mother to have a body. And perfectly natural that it should be different from yours." He was aware now that she was standing up, and he heard the thump of her dressing gown as it fell to the chair. It might have been the thump of a belt across his shoulders. "Now look at me, Michael. Come on, look at me." He tried for a moment to raise his eyes, but he couldn't. He couldn't! "Michael! It's all right, dear, I'm not going to be in the least offended with you. I want you to see me. I *want* you to see what a woman is like. Michael, where are you going? Come back here!"

But he had fled, fled back to his own room and from there to Peggy's room where he fell on his knees by the bed and sobbed in the anguish of fear and shame.

When he finally opened his eyes he was suddenly aware that there had been complete silence from the next room for the last several minutes. Turning around he raised his head stealthily to the transom shutters and after a brief pause forced himself to look down at the bed. For a moment he could not understand what he was seeing; then he made out that the broad white expanse was Danny's back and the thing moving on it Flora's arm. Danny was sitting on the side of the bed, slumped over, and Flora was lying beside him, running a finger idly up and down his backbone.

"Do you want a drink, darling?" she asked.

"I never drink before lunch."

"Oh, of course. Your little rules. How could I forget them? Still, there are some things you do before lunch, aren't there?"

"Don't be coarse. I know I'm nothing but an animal to you." Danny's voice was sullen. "When you're back at the bridge table with your pals, you never give me a thought. I don't exist for you, really. You have your hairdresser and your masseur and me. For different reasons. If they *are* different reasons!"

"Oh, darling, if you only *knew* how wrong you were. I think of you all the time!"

"Not of me, you don't. Of what you do with me."

"But, sweetheart, what's the difference?"

"Exactly! There you are! Exactly!" He stood up. "I'd better be getting back."

"Oh, Danny, already?"

"I have a job, you know."

"But surely we could have lunch. Don't they let you have lunch?"

"And be seen with you at a restaurant? No, thanks! I give *some* thought to how things look. Even if you don't give a damn."

"But we could go to that little omelet place around the corner," she protested, sitting up. "No one would ever see us there."

"You can take the chance, sure," he retorted. "What do you risk? Michael would swallow it. But can you imagine what Sandra would do? Why, she and her old man would kick me right out in the street! Right back where I came from! That's the difference between you and me. There's no place Michael can kick you back to."

Michael was surprised at his own objectivity. He could even see that Flora had made a fatal mistake in allowing Danny to discover how infatuated she really was. For Danny was the kind who would despise anything that he entirely possessed; his satisfaction would lie only in scaling the ramparts of the contempt that he attributed to others. He would never be able to forget that he was the son of a superintendent of a country estate, and Flora lacked the subtlety to detect in the surliness of his attitude his need to possess and dominate the chatelaine of his childhood acres.

But his speculations were interrupted by hearing his own name. Danny must have previously told her something about the commissions in the Winters will, for she was trying to persuade him to drop the whole matter. Michael was surprised at her perspicacity.

"It won't do you any good at the bank," she was saying. "Really, it won't."

"But why should your husband object to my pointing out a perfectly honest mistake?" Danny demanded irritably. "What's wrong with that?"

"Nobody likes to admit a mistake. Besides, he doesn't like you," she added flatly. "Difficult as that may be for you to believe, he doesn't."

"Why not?" Danny's tone became nasty. "Aren't I good enough for him? Does one have to be a Farish and the president of Hudson River Trust to talk to him?"

"Oh, Danny, don't be silly. Can't you take my word for *anything?* He just doesn't like you, that's all!"

"Well, I don't like him! And the whole thing begins to make me wonder how honest a mistake it was!"

"Oh, Danny. Everyone knows Michael's honest as the day is long!"

"Sure, stand up for him!" Danny sneered. "He's more of a gentleman than your despised lover!"

Michael could sense Flora's immediate panic. "It's not that Michael dislikes you personally, darling," she protested. "It's only that you and I are so friendly."

"You and I! But you told me he didn't know anything about that!"

"Oh, he doesn't, really. But you can never be sure what people suspect, can you?"

"You mean, he *does* suspect?"

"I just mean he's sniffing around," she said impatiently. "That's only natural, isn't it? Besides, he's terribly jumpy these days. Maybe it's this Winters business. When I asked him how long it would be before you'd make vice-president, he got all huffy."

"Why did you ask him that? That doesn't sound like your usual tact."

"But it was the most natural thing in the world! After all, you and Sandra are friends and neighbors. It would be artificial of me to show *no* interest in your career."

But Danny was no longer listening to her. "Michael jealous!" he exploded. "That's all I need, isn't it? Dear God, it's perfect! To be suspected of sleeping with his wife by the future president of the bank! Oh, boy!" His tone rose almost to a shout. There was a recklessness in his self-pity that transcended caution, an obsession with the very disaster that he feared. "Can't you see it? It's not only my wife and children I'd lose. I'd wind up on a blacklist! Local boy makes really good!"

"Danny, don't yell," she warned him sharply. "And you're not making any sense. Michael doesn't know anything, and he isn't going to do anything. If you'll only just not keep bothering him — "

"Of course!" he cried. "Why should *you* care? He *expects* it of you. I can just hear him: 'Poor Flora. She has her little weakness. After all, she can't help it, can she? She inherits it from her mother.' "

Flora put her hands over her eyes. "Oh, you bastard," she murmured.

"Do you think I don't know about your mother?" he sneered. "*Everyone* knows about your mother! But what does it matter? You're a Cameron, aren't you? One of the charmed circle? People close their eyes to your little foibles. But young Jones, who cares about him? He'll get the axe, of course, but in the usual tactful way. A word from Michael to Mr. Meredith. The bank doesn't find young Jones 'congenial.' No raise for Jones next Christmas. No bonus. The handwriting on the wall!"

When Flora uncovered her eyes, her expression was at once calm and bitter. She got up and went to her dressing table. "You're not really afraid of losing your job," she said as she brushed her hair. "Or even of having people find out. You're ashamed, that's the thing. You're ashamed of me."

"Why do you say that?"

"Because I understand you, Danny. You wouldn't be ashamed of having an affair. All your little friends do that. You're ashamed of having an affair with a woman who's older. That's the whole thing."

"It is not!"

"Ah, but it is, dear." Flora sighed deeply. "That's why you always abuse me afterwards. But then you come back." She turned around to smile timidly at him. "At least you have so far." The note of pleading came back in her voice, and Michael winced at her mistake. "Haven't you, darling?"

Danny was getting into his underdrawers which he had found by the door. "Sure," he said. "Sure, I have."

"And you will again, darling?"

"I suppose."

"If I promise to be careful? If I promise never to mention your name to Michael?"

"I'll phone you, Flora. But don't you call me. It's not safe."

"You'll call me soon?"

"Oh, sure."

"Oh, Danny, promise!"

"Look, I've got to get back downtown."

Flora had to be satisfied with this, and she said no more. When Michael looked again, Danny was gone, and she was sitting alone on the bed, puffing listlessly at a cigarette. He even felt a certain sympathy for her, so entirely was he now the spectator. He had ceased to be himself in reserving a front seat for the tragi-comedy of Michael Farish.

When Flora finally dressed and left the room, he came out and peered over the landing to hear the hall front door close behind her. Then he carefully made her bed which she had characteristically left untouched. He wondered with a dry amusement if she would even notice. Anyway, it was over. All his life he had looked forward to the end of things, even of things that were meant to be pleasures. His mind had been fixed on the swim after the eighteen holes of golf, the picnic after the fishing, the whiskey by the fire after the day's shoot. Perhaps even the charm of the presidency of Hudson Trust had been in its very aspect of finality. But when things were over, he wondered dully as he left the house and headed for the park, what then? After the swim and the picnic and the whiskey, what?

Later that afternoon, in the dark, almost deserted bar of the Hone Club, under its huge faded American landscapes, there was no sound besides the bartender's discreet shaking of Michael's martini and from the adjoining room the rattle of dice where two elderly and wax-faced members whiled away the remnant of the day and a bottle of whiskey at the back-gammon table. Michael raised his glass half in irony to them, and they stared back with brief nods. He did not know them; they were club "regulars," the little group of old bachelors and widowers, unobtrusively alcoholic, who huddled behind the big, dark walls from daylight, from the market place, from women, and consoled themselves in their dusky male solitude with salacious tales and sports events.

"Mike Farish! What brings *you* uptown at this hour?"

It was Ambrose Parr, magnificent in a red velvet jacket, buttoned tightly over his round paunch. He had a cigar in one hand, a whiskey in the other, ready for one of his long club evenings, where he could hold forth unchallenged at the bar, shouting dead-pan insults at his cronies and laughing his violent mirthless laugh.

"I had to see a client uptown," Michael murmured. "It hardly seemed worth it to go back to the office."

"It's not. Of course it's not." The big, gnarled hand gripped Michael's shoulder painfully. "You'll stay and dine with me here. Yes, you will. I insist." When Michael continued to shake his head, he suddenly shouted: "Who do you think is chairman of your board, I'd like to know? You're dining with me, and that's an order!" And turning to the impassive bartender he snapped: "Well, you ring-tailed blockhead, do you think you've learned to mix a martini that doesn't look like a doctor's specimen?" The man smiled perfunctorily and reached for a glass filled with cracked ice. "This is the only time of year to dine at the club. When the wives move out of town and the husbands stay. In the winter the place is full of dried-up old pansies who have no place else to go." He watched severely as the bartender mixed his drink and then nodded grudgingly as it was handed to him. "Mike, my boy," he continued, squeezing his shoulder again, "you don't know what a relief it can be when June rolls around. Thank your lucky stars you're not a widower. You wouldn't believe what some of these blue-haired old gals stoop to to catch a husband. I tell you, Mike, I need a gun at times. Honest to God, I need a gun."

Michael bristled. Who was Ambrose to sneer at old women? Did he ever stop to think what *he* looked like, with his square bald head and sagging jaw and the incongruous finery of his red coat and tie? Like a turtle in a shop window with a painted shell.

"I could write a book about it, Michael," Ambrose went on. "I really could. 'Memoirs of a Widower.' It would sell like hot cakes, too. But there's something else I have to discuss with you tonight." Taking his drink and holding it carefully before him, he directed Michael by the elbow to two leather chairs in the corner of the bar. "Tell me, Mike," he said as they seated themselves, "what do you think of Charlie Meredith's work these days? Frankly. There's no such thing as personal loyalty when you're talking to the chairman of the board. I want to know if he's slipping."

Michael had long ago prepared his answer for this question: "I think Mr. Meredith can slip a long way before he meets the first man who's good enough to succeed him." This was to prove his own loyalty and to admit at the same time that the president *had* been slipping. But now his defense was prompt and spontaneous. "I don't think so at all," he said firmly. "I think Mr. Meredith's never been in better shape."

"Do you?" Ambrose eyed him beadily. "Well, I don't. I think he's skidding fast. I think it's got to the point where we may want to retire him next fall. And if we do that, I think you may have some inkling of who my candidate for his successor is likely to be."

So here it was again. Michael looked down to avoid Ambrose's inquiring glance into the darkness of the old carpet. It was as if he were peering into brackish water, making out nothing but a vaguely moving shadow, growing now, growing enormously, until he saw it was moving upward toward him, swiftly and ominously, about to break the surface with the shocking reality of splashing jaws. "I don't see any need for Mr. Meredith to retire!" he cried suddenly. "If a man's doing a good job, why not let him go on doing it?"

"Let's keep our voices down, shall we?" Ambrose whispered sharply, looking apprehensively about the room. "I don't want anyone here to get the idea I'm easing Charlie Meredith out of any job. After all, his daughter's married to my own son. Damn it, man, we have the same grandchildren!"

"I'm quite aware of that."

"All right, then," Ambrose said testily. "You and I won't talk any more about *when* Charlie retires. But there's no reason we shouldn't discuss his successor, is there? After all, he's got to go some day, hasn't he? Who would you put in his place?"

"Someone from outside."

"Why? What's wrong with our own men? What the hell have we trained them for?"

"Jim Rand, then."

Ambrose blinked at him, debating whether such modesty could be genuine. "Rand's not a bad man," he conceded with a shrug. "He might do if we didn't have a better. But he lacks the polish, the finesse. That special knack with people. You know who's got that, Mike."

"Who?"

"All right, Michael, we'll play it your way. We'll talk in riddles."

But Michael, staring at the floor again, was only conscious of the teeth in the foam. "I'm sorry, Ambrose. I don't get you."

Ambrose snorted with exasperation. "I've spoken about this habit of yours before," he said roughly. "This goddam reserve. People don't feel they know you. You may be a damn good listener, and I'm sure you could pry the secret out of the Sphinx, but nobody knows what makes you tick. You keep it all locked up inside you. What are you trying to hide, Mike?"

Looking up over Ambrose's head, Michael seemed lost in contemplating the great dusty canvas of a sea battle in the war of 1812. Once again, as by the transom shutter, he had the sensation of stepping out of himself and walking about to contemplate the oddity of Michael Farish. He suddenly closed his eyes. "What is it, Mike?" he heard Ambrose say. "What are you thinking?" And then he was back at Averhill, a second former, in the dark semi-privacy of his cubicle, huddled up under the covers and pantingly intent on his solitary pleasure, until he heard again the sharp rip of his curtain rings thrust aside, and they were around him, all of them, the demons, tearing off his blankets, and there was the throbbing shame and relief, the muffled pleasure, the abysmal despair of exposure.

"I'm a cuckold, Ambrose!" he cried, snapping his head around at his startled companion. "That's what I've been trying to hide! I'm a cuckold, and I deserve to be one! Why not? Flora's a healthy woman and what am I? A cuckold! Of course! A cuckold!" There was even satisfaction in repeating the word, in letting it explode in that murky air, in defying the unforgiving with the unforgivable. Ambrose glanced quickly around.

"Keep your voice down, old man, for Pete's sake, will you!" he hissed. "It's not the kind of thing you want to spread around, is it?"

"Why not? You say I never tell people anything!"

"Shut up, I say!" Ambrose's tone was a bark, and Michael was silenced. But, incredibly, the sternness that he now saw gathering in the old man's eyes was not intended for him. Ambrose went on in a hushed, tense voice: "So she's cheating on you, is she? Well, I'm not surprised. Never mind, fella, they're all alike. Damn them. Damn them all!" He reached over to grip Michael's shoulder again. "Keep your chin up, boy. We'll teach that hussy a lesson that she won't forget!"

"It's my fault," Michael insisted. "What have I ever given her?"

"Don't kid yourself. You've given her plenty. These big gals get frantic when they hit fifty. Just can't have enough of it. It's a disease, really — "

"Ambrose!" Michael stood up suddenly. "I don't want to hear what it is! And I'm afraid I can't dine with you tonight."

He saw the relief of Ambrose's expression. The latter rose hastily and guided him to the door. "That's all right, fella," he murmured paternally. "Don't give it a thought. Much better for you to be quiet somewhere. Have a few drinks and take in a show. Don't be in the dumps. It happens to more people than you think. Many more. You're quite right. It's no time for club dinners and tall stories."

Michael allowed himself to be conducted down the stairs and out to the front door. It would not have surprised him to hear it locked behind him, so apprehensive was Ambrose at the possibility of a club evening being dampened by the gloom of his younger friend. Danny Jones, with his ribald tales of conquest, would have been welcome enough, but who wanted to hear the wailing of a cuckold? As he hurried away down the darkening street he reflected grimly that the twenty years of his marriage to Flora had shrunk already to the dimensions of the story that Ambrose was now telling to the small guffawing group of club regulars at the bar.

9

MICHAEL AND FLORA had first become friends in the summer of Michael's first year with Hudson River Trust. It had happened at Bradley Bay in the Hamptons where her family, the Camerons, and his mother's, the Lears, had been summer residents for several decades. Michael, twenty-two and earning a slender salary, had been glad enough to spend his weekends free with his mother and younger sisters in the big, damp shingle house on the dunes that had been withered and darkened by fifty years of exposure to winter seas. Bradley Bay was a more expensive summer place and the house a bigger one than Gertrude Farish could really afford, but it had been the iron resolution of her widowhood that her children should at least be exposed to all the things that had been more easily available in their father's lifetime. That such things might not necessarily have been the best things, it was too late, after Maury's death, for her to admit, or if the idea ever occurred to her, she would dismiss it with a brief: "Well, let them learn to cope with Bradley Bay first." For that community was more than a family to her, more than its social reputation, more even than the symbol of carrying out her maternal duties; Bradley Bay was her childhood; it was the muffled roar of the Atlantic on a hot August day; it was romance. She still saw it as it had been in the nineties with its great shingle cottages rising up so starkly new in the dunes and its wide, flat fields of blue hydrangeas and goldenglow. She thought of the tall, trim figures of her mother and aunts moving about the croquet lawn, with barège veils and parasols, half confused now in her mind with the darkened snapshots in her own scrapbooks; she saw herself in a runabout with a bay, the end of her whip just flicking a fly from his ear, driving to the tennis club to watch Maury Farish in the semi-finals. And if the younger generation didn't see that, she would reflect with a little wrinkle of her long straight nose, if Michael and Gwen and Susan couldn't be expected to remember the joy of sitting with Maury on the porch of a Sunday afternoon, well, why didn't they work up their own romances? Couldn't they do *anything* for themselves?

Michael's difficulty that summer was precisely that he couldn't. He had developed a certain self-confidence, but not in romantic fields. His first year at the bank had gone off very well, and he had earned a substantial raise. He was always neat and well turned out, and he was frequently asked out for dinner by older and even distinguished persons. His mother was delighted with his progress and came close to showing it; she would leave the dinner table when she saw him in the hall, dressed to go out, and straighten his black tie with nervous, accurate fingers while she poured forth, from the well of her knowledge of Bradley Bay, instructive comments on the history of his evening's hosts. Even Gwen and Susan, absorbed respectively in their postdebutante and debutante careers, found him kind and helpful at parties and were inclined to spare him in the sharp give and take of family arguments. It was not fun, it was hardly sporting to kid someone of so equitable a disposition. But in spite of his raise and the warmth of family approval, in spite of the general question among Bradley Bay mothers: "Why can't *my* boy be like Michael Farish?" Michael was far from being satisfied with himself. In sober truth, he was almost desperate. The simple fact was that he didn't have a girl, and what was a good deal worse, had never had one. Oh, of course, there had been the cousins with whom he had danced at parties — he was known as an almost comically assiduous cousin — and the serious, plain, rather blue-stocking girls whom he took sailing or to the movies and to whom he professed feelings of guarded friendship, but he never even attempted to persuade himself that this was the same thing. He knew that he had not done badly in the various particulars of preparing himself for life, but he felt with a growing despair that if he couldn't find a girl, the whole essence of what he was attempting was missing, that he would have created nothing of himself but a plaster cast of a man that anyone more than a casual observer would take for just that. Worse still, he was even beginning to suspect that his own good looks were a kind of fraud that well merited the sneers that he could already anticipate.

It was a problem, too, that he had to face alone, for he had a conviction that his virginity was a shameful thing, more shameful, indeed, than any sexual deviation or depravity. To hold his head up in a world that had lost faith in everything but sex meant to be always on guard, to have no true intimates, to be able to imply with a smile or a wink to his boasting friends that he, too, had his reasons for going to this or that place on a certain weekend. Yet it was not, heaven knew, that all was pale and still within him. His mind, like most minds, was a mine of erotic fantasy. If there was very little that had happened to his body in actuality, there was very little that had not happened to it in his imagination. The fastest and most sophisticated girls at the Beach Club, the kind whom Michael was apt to shun for their less disturbing sisters, occupied relations with him in his daydreams that would have certainly surprised them. Like an early puritan, he almost resented them for the emotional havoc that they created. But unhappily for his peace of mind, he lacked the puritan's smugness. He had no sense that right was with him. On the contrary, he had a melancholy sense that the deity, if he existed at all, would be enthusiastically on the side of all that went on in the dark behind the dunes on the nights of club dances. He had only intensified his mood of despair by two visits to brothels where the girls, symbolizing the aggressive and to him justified demands of their outraged sex, had panicked him into impotence. Women, he decided gloomily, would always charm in inverse ratio to their proximity. At times, when alone, the bitter tears of self-pity would well up in his eyes. It was too ironic a twist that after taking all those hurdles of his adolescence, after clearing each and every one, he should fail with the last and then discover that it was the only one that counted, that, failing it, he might as well have saved the energy that had carried him over the others. Unlike the hero of legend who had to undertake a series of tasks to earn the hand of the princess, he found the lady herself, instead of his reward, the greatest task of all.

His mother, suspecting that he had an inner concern, asked him once, just a bit too casually, if he would care to see Dr. Jennison. The latter was one of the first psychiatrists to be considered respectable by her conservative set. This might have been because he didn't seem like a psychiatrist; he was a big, hearty, well-bred man who never used the jargon of his trade and appeared to practise with the "horse sense" of the old family practitioner.

"Why do you say that?" Michael asked, defensively. "What would I go to him for?"

"Oh, problems," she said vaguely.

"Do I strike you as having so many problems?"

"No, dear, of course not. But all young men have problems, don't they? That's what Jennison's for. Don't worry about the bill. I'll blow you to it."

Michael let the matter drop, but he thought it over carefully and finally made an appointment with Dr. Jennison, but without telling his mother and at his own expense. He found it astonishingly easy to talk about things that he had never mentioned to anyone. The doctor listened with a friendly and comprehending sympathy, nodding his head briefly from time to time, his massive hands folded and still on the blotter before him. He did not seem in the least surprised about Michael's predicament or to feel that it was in any way either ridiculous or unusual.

"You'd be interested to know," he said when the problem had been identified and placed, as it were, on the desk between them, "how many people come to me with troubles that are largely matters of nomenclature. They suffer the tortures of the damned at the idea that a particular label may fit them or that it may not fit them. Am I a man? Am I a coward? Am I a failure? Am I an invert? Sometimes, simply, am I a lunatic? If you could ever get it through your head, that it's you, only you, who's pinning the label on, or taking it off, you'd have your problem half licked. Now, tell me, young man, what it is that you want. What you want more than anything in the world?"

Michael was taken aback at the promptness of his own reply. "I want to be married," he said. "I want to have a family."

"Well, then you'll get married," the doctor stated with an assured nod. "It may be as simple as that."

When Michael came out of his office the sky over Park

Avenue, as Peter Teriot would have put it, was a Tiepolo blue. His heart was so full of hope and gratitude that he thought it would burst. On subsequent visits the progress was slower, but it always seemed to him that there *was* progress. The doctor's simple and plausible theory was that his father's death, coming when it did, had paralyzed him with a sense of overwhelming responsibility. At the age of twelve he had imagined himself to be the head of the family, and an acute sense of inadequacy had been the obvious result. If he could learn to concentrate on his accomplishments and not his failures, he would begin to see that he had not done badly at all. With the growth of self-respect his fears of the opposite sex might be expected to decline. Michael had six sessions with Dr. Jennison before the latter's vacation. It was agreed that they would have another series in the fall, but as it turned out Michael never went back. For that was the summer of Flora Dexter.

He had met her, strictly speaking, on many other occasions. Everyone in Bradley Bay knew Flora Cameron, and, of course, she had been present at the famous party in Cambridge at Peter Teriot's rooms. But she was six years older than Michael and married to Bobbie Dexter who was at least that much older than she; at twenty-nine she was hardly a member of the junior set. Michael for several summers had admired her fervently in his own inhibited fashion; he was entirely convinced that she was the most beautiful woman in Bradley Bay. It was astonishing to him that the whole community did not agree with his estimate. Yet it didn't. For despite her glistening and raven hair, parted in the middle over her wide brow, despite the whiteness of her skin, despite those large black eyes and that tiny, distinguished hook in her nose, so oddly Cameron in the very center of Andalusian sensuousness, despite the firm briskness of her walk over the flagstones of the beach club in the highest heels to the audible clink of her gold bracelets, Flora was admired by few as intensely as Michael admired her. She was liked, of course, well liked; it would have been unthinkable not to like anyone as amiable as Flora. Admiration, however, was another thing. Bradley Bay tended to take her for granted, to answer, with a faint surprise, to any comment on her beauty: "Who? Flora? Good old Flora?" It might have stemmed from nothing more than that everyone remembered her as a stout little girl, or from Flora's own apparent unawareness of her charm, or even from the fact that her Spanish mother's low birth and postmarital career had made her, at least as a child, a kind of second-class Cameron. Flora, at any rate, showed no yearning to be more highly considered. She simply wanted to be on good terms with the world, and indubitably she was. She liked cards; she liked gossip; she liked humor of the childish and fantastical variety favored by the smart set, and, most importantly of all, she had no wish, even for a moment, to raise her eyes above these simple goals.

If there was a tendency in Bradley Bay to appreciate Flora somewhat less than she deserved, it was nowhere more apparent than in her husband. Bobbie Dexter was a large, red-faced, choleric man who played games very hard and took his pleasures with the querulous and never smiling gravity of a small, spoiled child. He ran half the club events and complained bitterly about the running of those which he didn't; his wide, exasperated countenance, looming like a fiery sun over the deep blue of his silk polo shirts, aroused the timid respect of the members and the detestation of the employees. One would have thought that the club was a business corporation, so grimly did he occupy himself with its problems of management. Even his extramarital love life was conducted like a new investment venture; he made no secret of his interest in Lola Shea which had become, after a couple of seasons, one of the more accepted, the more respectable affairs of Bradley Bay. As Flora had not identified herself with any other man, her continued attachment to her husband was taken for granted, and it was even said by the sentimentalists that she "adored" her Bobbie. Yet the most determined of this school had to admit that the suffering which they attributed to her seemed in no way to mar her outward placidity.

Michael had for more than a year felt a conflict between his anger with Dexter for such treatment of his wife and a reluctant gratitude to him for having thus rendered her, at least in Michael's fantasies, a subject of sympathy. A Flora betrayed was at least a Flora approachable. Not, of course, that he approached her. It was enough to be paralyzed by girls of his own age without seeking to be turned to stone by one who was older and married and even a mother. But such inaccessability only added fuel to the flames of his imagination, and he used to wait to watch her, across the pool at the beach club, as she arrived every Saturday and Sunday at noon. Nothing would have induced him to forego this satisfaction of his weekly anticipation of what she would do. She would go to the shallow end of the pool and call several times to her little daughter, Ginevra, that it was time to get dressed. When Ginevra finally obeyed, she would take a cigarette from her bag and close it with a sharp click, putting it back under her arm. She would then stand for a few moments with the cigarette unlit while she scanned the patio for one of her friends. There always seemed to be one. She would then join the friend for a game of backgammon and a martini until Ginevra was ready. Sometimes Ginevra would have to wait while her mother had a second martini. Ginevra sulked, Michael observed and Flora shook her dice.

It was inevitable that at a club where everyone more or less knew everyone the morning would eventually come when Flora would fail to find a backgammon opponent and might even ask him to play. Yet Michael, before it happened, never actually imagined that it could. Besides, did he really want it to? What, for example, would he call her? Flora? Mrs. Dexter? He was thus completely tongue-tied on the rainy Saturday in July when the patio was deserted and Flora, having ordered Ginevra to dress, suddenly altered her course to where he was standing under the awning and asked, pointing at the backgammon table: "How about a game?"

He followed her dumbly over to the table and sat there as her efficient fingers arranged the men. Too late he realized that he should be helping and did so, with sudden clumsiness. Flora lit her cigarette.

"You're a Farish, I know," she said, sitting back and taking him in. "Is it Bill?"

"Michael."

"Michael it is. I'm Flora. Ten cents a game?"

He shrugged manfully, as if any sum were acceptable. She beat him four games straight with a good deal of doubling during which very little was said. Then she sat back and smiled at him. It was an easy, good-natured smile, the kind he had seen her give to members of her own group.

"You need practice," she said. "Winner buys the drink." She ordered the martinis with her regular signal to the bartender, simply by turning her head and raising two fingers.

"Isn't it funny how you and I can come to the same club day after day without ever meeting till now?"

"Oh, but we have met," he protested. "Years ago at Harvard. After a game."

"Really? And do you say *years* ago? My dear Michael, years ago you must have been a baby!" But there was no sting in her words; she acted as if there was easily a generation between them.

"I was still at Averhill. In my sixth form year. We came in for the Yale game and went to a party at Peter Teriot's. You were there with Fred Lassiter."

She stared for a moment in obvious surprise. Then suddenly she nodded. "But I *do* remember! Good old Fred. Fancy your remembering that." An expression of polite concern came over her face as she recalled Peter. "And that poor Teriot boy, he died, didn't he? Yes, of course. I think he was some sort of cousin of mine. Was he a great friend of yours?"

"Well, a friend. He was a form above me at school."

"But, oh wait!" she exclaimed suddenly. "There was something else about that party! Wasn't there trouble about the Averhill boys drinking?"

Michael was ready now even to admire a detachment that could view a tragedy of such dimensions as "trouble." "Four boys were expelled," he answered in a voice that he could not succeed in making anything but sepulchral.

"Oh, dear. I shouldn't joke about it, should I? Were you one?"

He laughed aloud at such a misconception of himself. "Oh, no. I was much too goody-goody for that."

"I doubt it," she said with gratifying conviction. "I doubt it very much." The waiter arrived with their cocktails and

despite Michael's protest she signed the check. Then they
talked about schools and rules, and Flora said that she could
never have put up with the discipline of such a place as
Averhill, that she was a creature of impulse. The subject
suddenly died, and in a flurry of nervousness he inquired
about the health of Miss Cameron, her grim old maiden
aunt.

"Oh, Aunt Stella's quite wonderful," she said with perfunctory zeal. "I think it must be disapproving of others that
keeps her alive. But I do love her, you know. She's been
such a duck to me."

Michael suddenly remembered that Miss Cameron had
notoriously disapproved of Flora's mother and was known to
be nasty about Flora. He was ashamed of himself for oblig-
ing her to be a hypocrite. What had she to do with ancient
aunts? "How tiresome of me to pester you with chitchat
about relatives!" he exclaimed with more violence than he
had meant. "Why is it that we're all so afraid of silence?"

"What a funny boy you are!" she exclaimed, laughing in
surprise. "You haven't been pestering me in the least. As a
matter of fact, you've entertained me extremely. And now I
see Ginny. I'd better find Bobbie and take them both home
to lunch."

"Are you coming to the dance tonight?"

"I suppose we might. Will it be fun, do you think?"

"It will if you come!"

"Aren't you nice?" she responded easily, without surprise,
taking his compliment, he was both relieved and sorry to see,
as another club banality. "We're dining at Mabel Farquhar's
to play bridge. But we might look in later. Except it's not
much fun for us wives, you know, with our husbands glued
to the bar, talking about the stock market."

"Doesn't your husband like dancing?"

"Oh, with some people, yes. But 'some people' is away this weekend. I think she's in Maine."

He was elated that she should take him so into her confidence. Or even, he reasoned quickly, if it was only the reflex of her sophistication, to include him in such sophistication. "I'll pick you up at your dinner and take you to the dance, if you like," he suggested boldly. "Then your husband won't have to go if he doesn't want. And I'll dance with you all evening, too. I won't go near the bar."

"Well, you might not have to dance with me *all* evening," she said, laughing again. "It's just possible that someone might cut in. Or maybe we could bribe one." He was starting to explain, hotly blushing, wretched to have been so gauche and by his gaucheness to have given her an excuse to pass off his suggestion as a joke, when he was interrupted by Bobbie Dexter. The latter appeared suddenly at their table and, ignoring Michael completely, suggested tersely to Flora that it was time to go. She seemed quite unaffected by his gruffness.

"Here's a young man who wants to take me to the dance tonight," she said. "And what's more, he promises not to stay glued to the bar. What do you think of that, Bobbie?"

Dexter just glanced at Michael and then back at his wife. "Well, isn't that dandy?" he snapped in tones that made Michael tingle with shame and anger. "Come on, Flora. It's time for lunch. Shake a leg, will you?"

"Don't forget now, Michael," she said, getting up. "I'll be expecting you at Mabel's. About eleven-thirty, don't you think?" And leaving him too excited and bewildered to speak, she followed her husband whose broad retreating back only too vividly expressed his feeling that Michael was not even worth a parting nod. But what did it matter? As he sat alone at the table he had to clench his fists to make himself realize that she had actually accepted.

Of course, it was awful that night at the Farquhars'. He had known that it would be. They were all playing bridge when he arrived, and Flora was too much absorbed to do more than wave to him. He mixed himself a drink and sat by himself on a sofa for almost an hour, miserable and ignored, until Flora, finishing a rubber, glanced at her watch and exclaimed: "Heavens, if I'm going to the club, I'd better go. Look how I've kept this poor boy waiting. Anyone coming?" Nobody was, and she rose. Her friends seemed to take it entirely for granted that she should go to the dance with Michael. Dexter barely glanced up from his cards when she said good night to him.

At the club he danced with no one but Flora. When she joined a group at the bar and told him to go and dance with "one of those nice young things," he stubbornly remained at her side. That he was hardly included in her friends' conversation did not matter to him in the least, for he burned inwardly with the excitement of knowing that Flora was with *him*. His own friends, of course, had noticed this; he could tell that easily enough from the nods and glances that he got. On the dance floor he was too conscious of this not to be somewhat distrait, and Flora's interpretation of this as his ennui at being stuck with her was the only painful point of the evening. "Look," he told her finally, with a vehemence that effectively surprised and silenced her, "this is the first time I've ever enjoyed a club dance. Can't you understand that?" When he took her home, however, there was nothing but the most formal of leavetakings under the porch light.

"I've had a wonderful evening," he said a bit pompously. "Do you think I might take you to a dance again?"

"I can't imagine why not," she said, one hand on the doorknob. "I can think of nothing nicer than to be picked up and taken to the club and danced with and seen home. You revive my faith in gentlemen, Michael." She turned and with an easy deliberation gave him a kiss on the cheek. "There. I think you're a sweetie. Good night."

For the rest of that summer he spent the better part of every weekend with Flora. He played backgammon with her at the club before lunch and in the afternoon he would walk down the long beach from his mother's place, past the weather-stained piles of shingle that eyed him with a flattering disapproval, to sit with Flora on her own strip of sand and gaze at the sea through dark glasses. On Saturday nights he took her to the movies or to dances at the club. Their conversations, as mild in quality as they were lengthy in duration, dealt largely with Flora and her various problems: could she afford a larger apartment in New York? Was Ginevra old enough for dancing school? How often did he think she really had to call on Aunt Stella? She accepted his interest in the details of her living as if it was the most natural thing in the world. She failed to show, it was true, a corresponding interest in his, but Michael would have been ashamed to have her do so, and was as grateful for indifference as if it had been tact. She never discussed her husband, except for a few casual references to his "flame," and Michael had an uneasy suspicion which he tried to stifle that so long as this large, irritable and irritating man performed his marital duties with a certain degree of regularity, she could regard his unfaithfulness with something like calm. He was impelled, however, to such considerations by the inescapable fact that although she found his own company diverting and his person not unappealing, she was making no effort, direct or indirect, to intensify their relationship. And he was quite sure that if she had wanted to, she would have. There was nothing of the flirt about Flora. When he had summoned up the courage one night to lean over in the car as they stopped before her house to kiss her on the lips, she had simply murmured: "Good night, pet. You really are rather a pet, you know."

That he was Flora's pet seemed to cause a commotion in inverse ratio to the proximity of the observer. Bobbie Dexter, for example, seemed to regard him, if at all, as a mere convenience in keeping his wife distracted. Michael even resentfully wondered if Bobbie did not despise him for *not* being his wife's lover. Flora's set, on the other hand, obviously took it for granted that he was, but without any particular interest. Flora to them would have been a fool not to divert herself as much as her husband did. This, however, was by no means the attitude of Miss Stella Cameron and her contemporaries. They were thoroughly scandalized at what Flora was doing to that "nice Farish boy" and gathered together under the umbrella tables at the club to murmur bitter things about her Spanish mother and how blood "told." As for Michael's own friends, they showed much the same resentment which boys at Averhill had shown to classmates who associated with boys in upper forms. They didn't want him to think that *they* thought he was bettering himself, and he found himself excluded from various parties by girls who took the trouble to tell him, with humorless laughs: "I suppose, of course, you'll be going to the Dexters'." Yet Michael found it all exhilarating. To have people disapprove of what they took to be his love life was a thousand times better than

living with the haunting fear that they might have guessed
he didn't have one. There was no more dizzying compliment
to his untutored ears than: "Are you *still* hanging around
with Flora Dexter?"

It was difficult, however, for even Michael to find a compliment in the attitude of his family. His sisters were disgusted with his failure to dance with them at the club or to
take part in any of the activities of the junior crowd. He
could have been pardoned for devoting himself to one of
their friends, but not to Flora. They professed to find it
unnatural of him to be attracted to a woman who was almost
thirty and made venomous and faintly veiled references to
her age, her potential plumpness and her husband's infidelities. Michael retorted to these with a new heat, which further
embittered their relations. Only Gertrude Farish, on one of
these occasions, kept him from leaving the house. Yet she
herself was deeply concerned about his new friendship. She
knew that it was customary, even appropriate, for young
men to have their first affairs with older women, but, unlike
her daughters, she knew that Flora was not *that* much older.
Nor did she like the way the thing was becoming talked
about. It was all very well for a young man to be temporarily
associated with another man's wife, but a continued and glaring liaison in the very heart of a small and observant community was quite another thing. Gertrude had always suspected that she would have trouble with Michael, from the
simple fact that he was too good. Very well, here it was.

"I'll be frank, Michael," she told him one morning when
they were sitting together on the porch. "I don't like this
thing between you and Flora Dexter. I don't like it at all.
In the first place, I don't like her."

"Oh, Mother! You don't even know her!"

"I've seen her enough," Gertrude retorted, looking up from her sewing with penetrating blue eyes, eyes that had the unexpected hard beauty of stained glass in the darkened interior of old churches. Gertrude had a long, clear, rather worn face and prematurely grey hair, and she always dressed during summer in spotless white. But her eyes were her main feature; their color made up for all her plainness. "I've known her most of her life, for that matter. She'll be sloppy when she's older, mark my words. Just the way her mother was. You don't remember Inez Cameron, of course. But she got fat and used to loll around the clubhouse eating caramels." Gertrude's straight nose wrinkled in distaste. "You knew she ruined Sandy Cameron's career in the State Department, didn't you? He married her when he was first secretary in Madrid. That was *that*, of course. I remember his poor old mother trying to put a good face on it. And *then* what do you think Inez did? Up and left him! Catholic, caramels and all, she up and left him for the tennis pro at the club. A man years younger than herself, too!"

"I don't see what that has to do with Flora," Michael said with dignity. "You're so obsessively genealogical. Can't people ever be just what they are?"

"Wait till you've seen more than one generation grow up, my boy," she said, biting a thread. "They always repeat themselves. Except sometimes they get worse. Particularly with mixed blood." She shook her head. "The Cameron moodiness with a Spanish temper. No, thank you. Not for *me*, anyway."

"Flora's not moody."

"Let's wait and see about that. Why have second-class friends when you could have first?"

"Really, Mother! How can you say Flora is second class?"

"She's married, isn't she?"

"What on earth has that to do with it?"

"I think it has everything to do with it. Ask Bobbie Dexter, why don't you?"

Michael simply threw his arms up at this. Yet when Flora came to lunch with him and his mother only a few days later, she and Gertrude seemed to get on well enough. His mother talked volubly about the early Bradley Bay and the dominating role then played by Flora's Cameron uncles, and Flora, amused and responsive, quite willing to exchange her own vague childhood recollections for Gertrude's more specific ones, showed none of the boredom that she had shown on the one occasion when Michael himself, who knew all his mother's stories, had ventured into these same waters. Women were certainly different with each other, he could only reflect, as he smothered the sudden warm little thought, as exciting as it was presumptuous, that maybe they were different just then because they were fighting over *him*.

There seemed to be no reason that matters should not go on indefinitely as they were going. Everyone but himself seemed quite satisfied with the status quo. Yet, as it turned out, it was not he who changed it. One Saturday evening, late in August, when he called for Flora, he found her alone in the living room with the cocktail things already out. She had not waited for him to start. Bobbie was off sailing, and she seemed in a bad mood.

"He says he can't go to Philippa's over Labor Day," she told him right off. "It's the limit! He knows perfectly well I've been looking forward to it all summer. After all, Philippa's my oldest friend, and now I *never* see her."

"Why won't he go?"

"He says he can't get away from the office early enough.

He says he may have to work on Saturday. But, of course, it's just that he's signed up for the mixed doubles with Lola. I know *that*."

"Why can't you go without him?"

"Well, exactly!" she said petulantly. "Why not? Because he says it's too expensive. That if we have a house here for the summer we ought to stay in it."

"But can he decide that?" Michael demanded, as though any problem of Flora's could be solved by logic. "Don't you have your own money?"

"Yes, but he takes care of it."

"Well, that's the limit! You mean he makes you an allowance out of your own income?"

"No, not exactly. We have a joint bank account. Oh, I don't know," she said impatiently, dismissing such details with a wave of her hand. "All I know is that there never seems to be anything in it."

"I'll give you the money. I'd be proud to!" Even in the stoutness of his gesture he wondered, a bit feverishly, how much she would require. But no matter. He would find it.

"Ah, that *is* cute of you," she said, taking his hand and suddenly smiling. "But of course I couldn't go alone," she said, sitting back again and letting his hand drop. "I can't be a single girlie at a houseparty. Not *that* houseparty, anyway." She sighed. "And to think I've been cooped up here every weekend all summer!"

Following her eyes about the room he seemed to take it in for the first time, with its matted floor, its white wicker furniture, the engravings of sheep going to pasture, returning, its dark, damp, seaside look. Yet it had been all enchantment to him before, and he was hurt that it should be only a place where she had been "cooped up."

"I can't bear that he should treat you this way!" he exploded suddenly. "He's utterly outrageous!"

She looked up in surprise. "Bobbie, you mean?"

"Who else? It's inconceivable! Here he is, married to the most beautiful and wonderful girl in Bradley Bay and he carries on brazenly with that mangy trollop! How do you *stand* it!" If he had been afraid of going too far, he quickly realized that his fears were ungrounded. Flora was clearly delighted. She poured herself another cocktail and settled back comfortably on the cushions. She seemed to have quite lost her pique at the prospect of missing the Cape Cod weekend.

"Mangy trollop is rather good," she murmured between sips. "I'm sick and tired of being told that she's leonine."

"It's all very well for *you* to take it so calmly," he continued in the same violent tone. "*You* have the patience of an angel. But what about all of us who love you? Do you think it's easy for *me* to stand by and watch it going on?"

"Why, Michael." She was smiling, but she looked at him curiously. "Are you trying to tell me that you *care* for me?"

"Of course I am!"

After a moment her eyes flickered away from his, and she faintly shrugged. "I suppose Bobbie is rather a beast," she said. "But what does one do about it? I never heard that those things were improved by scenes."

"You could leave him!"

"Oh, sweetie, you're so drastic. One doesn't go about leaving husbands like that. They're not that easily come by."

"They would be! For you!"

"For that you get a kiss." Flora leaned over, and he kissed her hard on the lips, but when he tried to put his arms around her, she sat back again. "That will do for now," she said in a kind, definite voice. "So you really like old Flora, do you?"

"Old!"

"Well, sweetie, I must be seven years older than you."

"Six. I *know*."

"You mean you've looked me up?" Her eyes were amused. "Then you *must* care. Tell me about yourself. About your love life, I mean. Have you been having affairs with all the little debutantes at the beach club?"

He flushed uneasily. "Not all."

"With any?"

"Maybe one or two."

"Who?"

"Really, Flora! Men don't tell that sort of thing."

"It's just what they do, dear. *Just* what they do. You don't have to listen to the catalogue of Bobbie's exploits. But I'll tell you one thing. If you haven't been having affairs, there are plenty of little girls who've been disappointed."

"If I've caused any disappointment this summer," he said stoutly, "it's been all your fault!"

"You know you're a little bit nuts," she said, laughing. "But in a nice way. Oh, yes. In a very nice way."

They had more drinks and then went out to a restaurant and on to the club dance. At dinner she told him all about Bobbie. How he had been unfaithful to her even on their honeymoon with a night club singer in Nassau. How he always insisted on telling her about his infidelities, comparing her own performance minutely with that of her rivals. How he had seduced little Ginny's nurse the summer before and was not even currently faithful to Lola. Michael had never heard of such promiscuity among people at Bradley Bay and marveled with a discouraged jealousy that such fire could lurk behind the sullen temperament of Flora's husband. But

what made him even more uncomfortable was his uneasy
suspicion that Flora had no basic disapproval of her man, but
instead only a resigned disgruntlement that she should have
to share him with others. Michael could hardly believe that
she actually loved Bobbie, but it was obvious that she disliked
him less than she should have. At the dance, however, she
fortunately seemed to forget all about her erring husband.
She had two more drinks and became very gay, rather gayer
than Michael thought was entirely fitting. She leaned way
back as they waltzed and closed her eyes and led him round
and round until he was seriously dizzy and feared that they
would both go crashing to the floor. He was well aware that
his friends were watching and felt for the first time, even as he
despised himself for feeling it, that it might not *always* be a
social advantage to be bracketed with Flora. But then the
music stopped, and she opened her eyes and told him with
sudden sobriety that she wanted to go home.

What would happen when they got there had never been
out of his mind that evening. He had been in a state of re-
pressed frenzy the whole time. How it would actually happen, how he would measure up, how she would look on him
afterwards, were questions that flashed about in the limpid
darkness of his tumultuous imagination, back and forth, like
crazy beacons. On the drive to her house he could not even
speak, but stared ahead down the road while she chattered
about the dance and who had been there. The only thing
that he had not anticipated was that when they got there, *she*
would be the one to do everything.

"Come on, get out," she told him when he had stopped the
car before her door. "I'll give you a drink."

He was almost as silent in the living room as he had been
in the car. Before he had finished his drink, Flora, showing
in her smile the hopelessness of their conversation, rose.

"I think we'd better go upstairs now, Michael," she said. "Don't you?"

"Will your husband be coming back?" he asked without looking up at her.

"I doubt it. And I doubt if I care."

Upstairs in her bedroom he sat on the edge of the bed, staring at the floor while she undressed. When she sat down beside him and he saw her legs, his throat was too dry to speak, and he turned away as if blinded. But Flora was ready for anything.

"Come now," she said gently putting her hands on his shoulders and turning him around. "This will never do. Not if you want to be a true member of Bradley Bay's smart set." And he let himself be managed, even undressed; he let her turn the lights off and take him in her arms. And when in the dark he felt his fears fall away, when he came alive again and held her tightly, it suddenly seemed as if he had gone mad, as if his very body were erupting, as if he had lived his twenty-three years for no other reason than to arrive at this very moment.

When he woke up he stared into the darkness and wondered blankly where he was. Then he suddenly sat up and saw Flora's sleeping figure in the moonlight. There was something infinitely reassuring in the soundness, the naturalness of her sleeping, and watching her Michael thought that his heart would never hold together to contain the sudden throbbing surge of his joy. "I'm a man, I'm a man!" rang the cry in his brain. Getting up and slipping quickly into his clothes which he found on the floor, leaving the socks that he could not find, stuffing his tie into his pocket, he tiptoed out of her room and down the corridor to the stairway. The stairs led directly to the living room which he could see was lighted, but as he remembered that he and Flora had left the lights on and as he heard no voices, he ventured quickly down. It was not until he reached the landing that he saw that he was not alone. Bobbie, in a red shirt and blue jeans, was sitting on the sofa by the fireplace, staring into his drink. Similarly dressed, but lying asleep on the sofa, her tawny head in his lap, was Lola. Bobbie looked up, and his eyes met Michael's. The look of astonishment gradually faded into a sneer.

"Well, if it isn't young Lochinvar!" he exclaimed in a loud surly tone. He was evidently very drunk. "How are you doing, kid? Has Flora taught you her little bag of tricks? Quite a bag, isn't she?"

"I don't have to take that from you, Dexter!" Michael heard his voice, just a bit too shrill, retort. "You gave up your right to complain about Flora years ago. Everyone knows *that!*"

"My, *my!* Aren't we the little man! Has Flora been watering the down on your chest?"

Michael found that he was suddenly trembling. But it was a tingling, satisfactory kind of trembling; it came from an anger that he could not control. "You have no right even to mention her name!" he cried. "When you don't mind bringing your women into her house!"

"Why, you snot-nosed kid!" Bobbie lurched to his feet, and Lola, her head falling back against the sofa, woke up with a cry. "Come to think of it, you've been a bad taste in my mouth too long. Like a hair in my egg! You'd better scram and *quick.* Or do you want me to pitch you out the door?"

"What's going on, anyway?" Lola called from the sofa, sitting up. She blinked dazedly at Michael. "Oh, my God, it's Flora's little boy friend! Now, Bobbie, take it easy!"

"Are you going to scram?" Bobbie demanded, swaying, and dropped his glass. It rolled unbroken on the rug.

"I'm going to leave in my own good time," Michael retorted scornfully. "I don't recognize your right to evict me!"

"Why, you little bastard, I'll show you — !" Bobbie stumbled toward him, swinging, and Michael, standing on the lowest step which made him higher than his opponent, drove his fist with full strength into the latter's eye. It was a soul-satisfying blow. Bobbie reeled back, stunned, and seemed about to charge again when he sat down suddenly instead on the chest by the stairway and covered his eye with both hands. Lola with a scream ran over to him.

"My poor sweet," she cried, "has he hurt you?" She turned angrily back to Michael. "Can't you see he's drunk? You might have killed him!"

"It was purely in self-defense," Michael said coldly.

"Send your little hell cat home, will you, Flora?" Lola demanded in a sharper tone, and Michael, turning, saw Flora above him on the stairway, clutching a dressing gown about her. She was staring down at the three of them with an air of stupefied surprise, but suddenly her expression cleared. She actually laughed.

"You'd better go home, Michael," she said. "I think Bobbie's got enough people to look after him. Only next time don't hit him quite so hard."

Michael went home and spent a fretful balance of the night trying to imagine the consequences of what had happened. Whatever they were, however, he was wonderfully certain of one thing: that he would never regret what he had done. When he stood by his window in the hot clear early morning and watched the thin long line of billows curving like a lemon peel under a bartender's knife, he felt the tears of happiness full in his eyes. At breakfast he hardly spoke to his mother or sisters despite their suspicious looks. Afterwards he telephoned Flora, but when Bobbie's voice answered, he quietly hung up, grateful, at any rate, that his opponent was still alive. He decided that he could not face the group at the beach club, and took an early train back to New York on the excuse of having work at the bank. The next morning he called Flora, knowing that Bobbie would have gone back to town. She sounded just a bit tense. Bobbie, despite an ugly black eye, had made no reference to the night's events. But he had told her she could go to the Cape, after all, for the Labor Day weekend, and she was to leave in a few days with Ginny. When Michael stammered that he loved her, she laughed in a rather funny way and said that it might be as well if they did not meet for a bit.

The next weekend, when he came down to Bradley Bay, he knew from his mother's severe glance at the station that the story was out. Lola Shea, of course, would not have kept such a tidbit from her friends. Gertrude said nothing in the car, but at home she came to his room while he was unpacking and, closing the door ominously behind her, sat down on the edge of the bed.

"Everyone seems to know about last weekend," she began. "Though I don't suppose *I*'d have heard it at all if Gwen hadn't told me. I hope you'll give it a chance to blow over before going to the beach club again."

He stared into his bag, a shirt in one hand. "If you think best," he agreed.

"I don't know what's come over you," she continued excitedly. "To strike a man in his own house and under *those* circumstances — well, it's really beyond anything, Michael!"

"You *know* such things happen, Mother. You know everything that goes on in Bradley Bay. I should think you might be almost relieved to find your son is not exempt."

"Are you implying that I should be *glad* about this?"

"In a way, maybe."

"Michael Farish! Where did you get your values from? Or don't you have any?"

"I got my values from the best of schools!" he exclaimed with sudden heat, turning now to face her. "Selected by you!"

He was immediately sorry when he saw the quick concern in her eyes and how her lip trembled. She was so helpless whenever her small list of tenets was challenged. Gertrude, however abrupt and practical, had an unwavering faith in "style," in the keeping up of appearances, that sometimes seemed her only creed. It was in this respect that Michael had offended her most deeply. He had exposed an emotion and exposed it crudely. She herself had never even hugged her children when they were little. She had converted the impulse into the fixing of their clothes, the adjusting of their collars, followed occasionally by a brief peck on the cheek that conveyed more affection than it was intended to. The world to her, particularly since the death of the husband whom she had so adored, had seemed a totally illogical place that only made a small amount of sense if one adhered to the standards of conduct laid down by the richer members of the preceding generation. The rules accepted, there was plenty of latitude for humor, even for cynicism, occasionally for belly laughs. But the rules were rules.

"I'm sorry, Mum," he said, sitting down beside her. "Try not to worry. People will forget all about it in a couple of weeks."

"I'm afraid you're optimistic, my boy," she retorted. "I

hear that Bobbie Dexter is planning to divorce Flora. Right here in Bradley Bay. And name *you* as corespondent!"

"What!" Michael's mind reeled. That *he* should be named in a lawsuit! That *he* should be the hero of a scandal! "That's obviously nonsense. He has no grounds. Everyone knows about him and Mrs. Shea."

"Yes, but Flora condoned it. She's condoned it for years. And he has *not* condoned you!"

"They're going to the Cape together!"

"That's what *you* think. You'd better catch up with your Bradley Bay gossip. Bobbie Dexter moved out two days ago. He's gone to his club in town." She paused as she took in his frozen expression. "Oh, my poor boy, don't you *see?* It's his chance to be free to marry Lola Shea without paying Flora a cent of alimony. He's been waiting for it for years!"

"Let him get his divorce then! What does Flora care about his wretched alimony?"

Gertrude's eyes flashed with sudden panic. "As long as you have no idea of marrying her! Oh, Michael, you couldn't be thinking of *that?*"

He recoiled from her. He jumped up and turned away. "And if I am?"

"Oh, Michael, you can't!" she cried. "That dreadful indolent creature! Married already and years older than you! Darling, you have no obligation to a woman like that! Don't you *see?*"

"Who's talking about an obligation?" he retorted, turning back on her. "I'd be the luckiest guy in the world if she'd consent to have me!"

"Consent!" His mother was on her feet now, her eyes blazing. "Are you crazy?" She shook her fist in the air. "There ought to be a place where parents could lock children up until sense was pounded into their heads! It isn't fair! It isn't *fair* that a lazy, loose creature like that should snap you up because she was able to drag you home *one* night!"

"Mother!" he cried, appalled.

"Well, it isn't!" she went on recklessly. "That she should be entitled for *one* night to my twenty-three years' work! That a fine, promising young man should be allowed to throw himself away, on *that!* Oh, if your father was only alive, this would *never* have happened!"

"I see no point in going on with this," Michael retorted coldly and left the room.

But he soon discovered that Gertrude in her desperation had carried her case to a higher court. Mr. Minturn himself, as it turned out, was staying with one of his daughters at East Hampton to officiate at the wedding of an Averhill graduate, and Gertrude had gone over to confer with him. He telephoned Michael on Sunday and asked him to call that afternoon. "Asked" was the word, but Michael quite understood that it was a summons. Mr. Minturn knew of no limits, geographical or chronological, to the jurisdiction of a headmaster. Being an "Averhill boy" was a life proposition, and nothing, Michael knew as he sat before the great man a few hours later, neither the silly small conservatory with its rather withered palms where they met, nor Michael's age, nor the wonderful events of the preceding weekend could alter the fact. Mr. Minturn with a single cough, a single grave shake of his head, transformed their location to his old study at Averhill.

"Your mother has been to see me, Michael," he said in a tone that was somber but not unfriendly. "She has told me of her concern about you. Which, of course, I share. You need not blame her for coming, for it so happens that I had already heard the sorry tale. I'm afraid you have not brought credit on yourself. Or on the school. I am the more surprised, for I had thought you a steadier man."

"It is a mess, I admit, sir." Michael answered more boldly than he would have thought possible during his nervous moments on the road. "But there was some coincidence in it. Some bad luck."

Mr. Minturn raised his grey, inquiring eyes to Michael's and held them there unblinking. "There's no bad luck about adultery, Michael."

The word hung there, the scarlet letter, strangely real in the fantasy of the little conservatory with the irregular plopping of the fountain in their ears. Michael was in the chapel again at Averhill, and Mr. Minturn again in his pulpit, warning, as he raised his arms slowly up and down, of the wickednesses, the temptations that would beset his boys in manhood, temptations that must have had their counterparts in the minds and hearts of most of them even then. But if it was sin to yield, if it was virtue to overcome, what was it not even to be tempted? And Michael felt again, even under the hard prick of Mr. Minturn's gaze, the throb of excitement that he had risen at last to the plane which the headmaster had opened to him as the ultimate reality, that he had become, thank God, an adulterer! Was it not even possible, he wondered irrationally, that there might be a hidden note of congratulation, at least of sympathy, behind the sternness of that glance? But no. There was no such note. Michael looked down at the flagstones.

"Well, Michael?"

"I don't know how to tell you this, sir. My feelings for Mrs. Dexter are entirely honorable. She has been grossly deceived by her husband. It is one of those situations where the ordinary rules don't apply."

"But it is precisely the situation for which the rules were made!" Mr. Minturn's eyes were wide with surprise now as well as indignation. "Do you mean to sit there, Michael, and tell me that one adultery justifies another?"

"In a way, sir, yes."

"Michael Farish!" The grey eyes were luminous now with concern. "You can't have so misconceived the teaching of our Lord!"

"Our Lord has nothing to do with it!" Michael exclaimed recklessly. "Why should He want a beautiful woman whose husband deceives her to live without love? I'm sorry, sir, but I love Mrs. Dexter. I love her more than anyone or anything! If you knew her, you might understand. But I know it's hopeless to explain." He stood up suddenly. "I've waited my whole life for something like this to happen to me. Something real and true. And now that it's happened, I won't give it up, sir! Not for you or anyone. It would be a betrayal of myself!"

Mr. Minturn looked through the glass at the lawn, shaking his head slowly. "You say you've waited your whole life, Michael. May I remind you that it hasn't been a very long one?"

"It's seemed long enough to me!" Michael cried passionately. "It's seemed an eternity of waiting. Of nothingness. Now I'm alive. And I'm going to stay alive!"

"You had better go home now." Mr. Minturn, too, was standing. "We had better talk no more of this now. You're too excited. When you're in a calmer mood, we'll meet. Or I shall write you. In the meanwhile I must ask you not to visit the school."

It was the famous interdict to erring graduates. Not to visit the school. It had been known, on the back of a post-card of the school chapel, to chill the hearts of middle-aged men in foreign parts, men who had not visited the school or thought of visiting it for twenty years. But to Michael speeding homeward, the early fall wind in his ears and hair, his heart full of a new goddess, it seemed that he held his Averhill diploma at long last in his hand.

10

MICHAEL, LEAVING THE Hone Club after his revelation to Ambrose, headed for Third Avenue to make a tour of its friendly bars. In the second that he visited he told a complete stranger all about Flora's infidelity, but the stranger, although sympathetic, immediately embarked on a diatribe against women which included a bill of particulars on his own wife, compared to whom Flora was evidently as chaste as an angel. Michael, formerly the perfect listener, found suddenly that he could no longer bear it. Why had he ears when he wished only to talk? He stumbled from the bar in the midst of the stranger's story and wandered uncertainly up the Avenue in the hot night. Leaning against the window of an antique store he stared at the hideous bronzes and pictures and wondered dully at the flat, fatuous elegance which Victorian painters attributed to the eighteenth century. Could he go to his mother? And have her sadly shake her head as he confirmed the very suspicions that had once so maddened him? Or to his sisters and be told, again and again, to "buck up"? No, there was only one person in the world who would be glad to see him, who would really sympathize, but she would be dining out or entertaining, or at the very best home with a husband who would not want to see him. Yet the idea, once fixed, became obsessive and after two drinks in the fourth bar, he found himself, without conscious premeditation, in a telephone booth, dialing Alida Parr's number. He slumped into the seat, overcome with relief, when she answered herself.

"It's Michael," he murmured. "What are you doing?"

"What am I doing?" Her voice was startled, almost irritated. "Why, I'm reading to the children. What should I be doing?"

He pictured her, sitting on the big white sofa with Ambrose II and Julia, beautiful, grave, blond children, listening intently on either side. He pictured the big, clean, handsome, dull room and the Leger, the Utrillo, the Vuillard, conscientiously purchased. A modern Cornelia in black velvet, Roman in her calmness, her firmness, her stalwart figure. It was all painfully inviting to his distracted soul. "Is Jimmie there?"

"No, he's dining with Ambrose at the Hone Club. What's got into you?"

"I want to see you!"

"Michael, what's wrong? Has something happened?"

"Everything."

"You sound as if you'd been drinking."

"I *have*. Please, Alida, let me come and talk to you. I'm desperate!"

"Oh." Her voice relented. "Very well. In half an hour. That'll give me time to send the children to bed. And, Michael!" Her voice was sharp again. "Don't you dare have another drink. Get out of that bar or wherever you are and drink a big cup of black coffee."

"Yes, ma'am."

"Michael! Do you promise?"

"I promise."

He did exactly what she said, and when he arrived at the

lobby of her apartment house he felt more sober. But when she opened the front door herself, and he saw the expression of concern in her searching, worried eyes, he burst into tears. For it was suddenly the Alida of Baymeath again, the lonely and sympathetic Wave ensign, as vulnerable as she was large, who had not yet learned the assurance that bordered on arrogance from a ten years' schooling in money and unhappiness.

"My poor dear," she said quickly, "come in, come in. Tell me at once: has anyone died? Is anyone sick?"

"No, no," he gasped. "It's not that at all."

"Then it can wait. Have you eaten?"

When he shook his head, she led him to the big living room and the white sofa where he sat, shaking with diminishing sobs, while she went to the kitchen and returned with cold chicken and salad and more coffee.

"Now," she said. "Tell me all."

She sat still, her eyes intently on him, while he told her the whole thing. Even the humiliating details of how he had peered through the transom. Somehow, the formality of the room, its very coldness, made it easier.

"So," she said finally. "You've found out at last."

"You mean, you *knew?*"

"What a bitch Flora was? Of course I knew."

"Alida! How can you talk that way?"

"How can *you?*" She glared at him indignantly. But her violence was not the self-assertiveness that she had shown in recent years. It had a note of her old clear schoolgirl resentment. "Who but a bitch would behave that way?"

"You mean you knew about Jones?"

"Not about Jones, no." She shrugged impatiently. "Simply that there were Joneses."

"How many?"

"I haven't tried to count them. What's the point? How should I know how many taxi-drivers, how many Fuller Brush men, how many —"

"*Alida!*"

"I tell you, I know her type!" Her voice rose sharply, and they stared at each other as opponents. But Michael was silenced by the genuine anger of her reddened cheeks. "I tell you she's an African bush girl! She wants one type of man, the type who'll kick her around! How could anyone of your sensitivity and taste ever hope to please a woman like that? Ever in a million years! And why in God's name should you want to?" She sniffed disdainfully. "She's common as dirt. Everyone knows she had the luck of her life to catch you. Except it was cradle-robbing. There ought to be a law against it."

"No! I went after *her!* She was beautiful, Alida. You didn't know her then!"

"I know more than you think." She sniffed again. "Everyone agrees she took you in."

"But look at her now!" It was ludicrous, he knew. He was arguing like a heated boy, but he couldn't stop. "She can still pick up young men!"

"*One* young man," she corrected him. "And probably he was looking for a mother. I wouldn't boast about it. You think you see yourself, Michael. You don't. It's possible to be a good father to a poor son. And a good husband to a poor wife. It doesn't *have* to be your fault. Seymour's not your fault, any more than Flora is."

"Seymour's not a poor son!"

"Either we face facts," she said firmly, "or we stop pretending to face them. Seymour is a singularly unlovable child. That's something *else* everyone's always known but you."

There was a pause in which she outstared him, unblinking. The Wave ensign had faded, and she was again the daughter-in-law of Ambrose Parr.

"I know it, Alida," he said with a little moan. "I know it." He buried his head in his hands, thinking that he was going to cry again, but he didn't. "What do you leave me to live for?"

"Try having nothing to live for," she retorted bitterly. "Try it for a while! You'll find you can do it. God knows, I have. For ten years!"

He was about to protest, but the words died on his lips. For there in the doorway was the frog-shaped face of Jimmie Parr, his small black eyes fixed on Alida with a peculiar glitter. When she turned and saw him, however, she didn't even start.

"Why do you have nothing to live for, Alida?" Jimmie came slowly toward them, into the room. His tone was ominously gentle. "Would you mind telling me why?"

But Alida made not the slightest effort to answer him. She simply looked away, across the room, with the glazed expression of one accosted by a drunk.

"If you have nothing to live for," Jimmie continued, "don't you think you ought to tell your husband? Even if *he's* not worth living for?" As she continued to be silent, he turned to Michael. "What about it, Michael? *You* must know the answer. You've been sitting here listening. In your best trust company manner, no doubt." The sneer cut the cords of Michael's paralysis.

"I guess I'd better go," he said, getting unsteadily to his feet.

"No!" Alida had jumped up. "No, stay, Michael!"

"I think Mr. Farish is being tactful, my dear. This can hardly be an agreeable scene for him to witness."

"Get out!" Alida turned on her husband in sudden fury, and he stepped back, astonished.

"Get out? Whose apartment do you think this is?"

"Mine!" Alida retorted. "It's in my name! Get out!"

"Why don't you call a policeman, dearie?" Jimmie smiled nastily. "We'll see which he is most anxious to evict. Your husband or your gentleman caller."

"I don't need a policeman!" It seemed to be true. As she advanced on him, Jimmie began to retreat. "I'll throw you out myself!" she cried. "Go on now and get back to your club and your drinking pals!"

"And leave you here with *him?*"

"What's it to you? Michael isn't feeling well. I'm putting him up in the spare room."

"A likely story!"

They were glaring at each other across a table now.

"You can believe anything you want," she retorted, "as long as you get out. *Now!*" There was another pause, and then, with a quick movement of her right arm, she swept a Tanagra figurine to the floor. "Get out!"

Jimmie stared at the pieces with the puckered face of a child about to cry. "Alida! That was *mine!*"

"Will you get out then?" She turned menacingly toward the Utrillo.

"Alida, no! Alida, please! I'm going!"

"All right, then." She watched him contemptuously as he ran to the hall.

"But I'll be back!" he screamed from the door, his face contorted. "I'll be back tomorrow, and you'll be sorry, you bloody bitch!"

They heard the front door boom behind him, and both stood for a moment in silence.

"I don't suppose you should have done that, Alida."

"I suppose I shouldn't." She sat down, seeming suddenly exhausted.

"He can do things to you. Spiteful things."

"I know he can. But I'll be ready for him. Tomorrow, however. Not tonight. Tomorrow I'll gather my wits together and think of something. But not now. Let him have Round One. For all the good it may do him."

She settled back on the sofa for the evening and drank whiskey after whiskey without showing, by so much as a slurred syllable or a flicker of the eyelids, the smallest effect of it. By tacit agreement it was her turn for revelations, and she talked of her life with Jimmie, grimly and dispassionately. It was almost enough to turn Michael's mind from his own problems, this somber inventory of the details of a life that had crushed out her old spontaneity and enthusiasm.

"Jimmie's very existence is money," she concluded. "It would take a Balzac to do justice to it. He can't abide the fact that his mother left more money to Ambrose than to him. That's the clue to everything. He has to make more money to compensate for his small stature and his father's domination. When he and I were first married I could actually tell the state of the stock market by the vigor with which he made love."

"How did you ever marry him?"

"I thought he had changed." She shrugged, as if to express the hopelessness of anyone's doing that. "I thought he had changed from the small, cocky boy I remembered at subscription dances at the Plaza. You didn't know him then, but you can imagine. With those popping black eyes and that frog-shaped face. The kind of boy who would pinch your fanny at the very moment he was bowing unctuously to your grandmother."

"What could have changed *that?*"

"The war. At least, I thought so, then. As if the war changed anyone. Except for the worse." She handed him her empty glass and paused while he refilled it. "I was at San Anton in the winter of 1946. I was still trying to forget you. I was very keen on skiing. Attempting, I suppose, to recapture my innocence in the snow of a hundred mountains. I was good, too. Which Jimmie wasn't. But he had been in the Navy. His ship had been sunk, and he had been a prisoner of war. Some of the dignity of those events had attached to him. At least in my mind. I began to admire the plucky little figure who picked himself up so doggedly after his spills. I spent my evenings at the bar while he told me of his plans for the future."

"Were they romantic?"

"Oh, no." Alida shook her head emphatically. "I'll give the devil his due. Jimmie never tried to misrepresent what he wanted out of life. He wanted to get home as soon as possible and look after his money. Or, rather, look after his father looking after his mother's money. *I* was the romantic. *I* was the one who insisted that the *real* Jimmie was a brave, little man of generous instincts who had suffered from a domineering father. Oh, poor Michael, you were a realist compared to me!"

"And then?"

"And then? 'And then' is the story of my marriage. Jimmie was a favorite with my family and all my friends. Why not? On the surface his worldliness seemed like theirs. And maybe it *is* like theirs." She sighed. "Maybe that's what I really resent. Not that he's taken away my old world. But that he's proved that it was always his."

"That, I agree, would be unforgivable."

"So there you are, my friend." Putting her drink down, she clasped her hands behind her neck and continued in a contemplative tone. "There you are. As I told you the other day, I haven't a thing to live for. Except my children. And they're so good, poor darlings, they hardly need a mother."

"You see it bleakly."

"I see it clear." She roused herself. "And I see something else. I see it's time for you to go to bed."

He followed her obediently while she turned down the neat pink coverlet in the neat pink guest room. He swallowed without a murmur the pill that she gave him and the fizzy water that followed it and lowered his forehead for her good-night kiss. When she had left, he took off his suit and climbed into the cool sheets in his underwear. In the darkness he began slowly to imagine himself in a hospital and to feel the relief and surrender of one who has borne too long a mysterious inward pain and gone at last to a surgeon and has now no cares beyond the spotlessness of the walls and sheets, no duties beyond stretching back and accepting the silent ministrations of his nurses and waiting, in euphoric dullness, for the knife.

II

SITTING IN HIS office late the following morning with the door closed, Michael idly turned the pages of a bulletin of recent court decisions affecting banks. The early hours, since leaving Alida's apartment, had been wadded like cotton between the sharp-angled events of the night before and their inevitable consequence. The telephone rang, and, of course, it was Flora.

"Michael! Where have you been? Why didn't you come home last night?"

He moistened his lips. "Because I didn't want to."

"What do you mean, you didn't want to?"

"I suggest, my dear, that you take a peek into your own conscience for the answer to that one."

"*My* conscience!"

"That's what I said."

There was a short pause, and then she hurried on: "I'm in town. I called you earlier from the country, but I couldn't reach you. I was so worried, I drove right in."

"I'll tell Danny Jones. Do you want him to meet you? It seems a pity we're to get *no* work out of him at the bank." He listened to her heavy breathing in the pause that followed this.

"Michael, will you have lunch with me?" she asked abruptly.

"I'm afraid I'm rather busy today. I can't get uptown."

"Suppose I come down?"

"If you'll just wait till Amelia checks my calendar — "

"Please, Michael!"

"All right. Come on down now. I'll meet you at Raider's."

He sat back and wondered how many years had passed since Flora had been downtown to lunch with him. But even as he was wondering, he heard his door open and saw Charlie Meredith himself on the threshold. Now things *were* happening. Old Charlie blinked at him in a grave, embarrassed way and then, without a word, came in and closed the door behind him. He walked over and sat down in a chair by the desk, elaborately hitching up his carefully pressed trousers.

"I have to talk to you, Michael," he said, looking down at the floor. "Frankly, I don't know how to begin."

"Mrs. Winters again?"

"Dear me, no. This is quite personal. Uncomfortably personal, in fact."

"Oh?"

"I've just been talking to my son-in-law, Jimmie, on the telephone." Meredith was staring now at his knees. "He told me something rather distressing. He told me that you spent last night in his apartment."

"Why should I not have? Your daughter asked me to."

"Quite so, quite so." Meredith pursed his lips and touched the tips of his fingers together. "But apparently Jimmie did not. He seems to think that you and Alida may be — well, may be — a bit too partial to one another."

"Alida and I are friends! We always have been."

"Well, I know that, of course, my dear boy." Here Meredith looked up at him for the first time, and a sudden dignity took the place of his embarrassment. "But Jimmie told me something else. Something I had *not* known. And something that I was very sorry to learn. He told me that you and Alida had been — shall we say, intimate? In England, during the war."

Michael was appalled that even Jimmie could have been so cruel as to tell the old man this. For there was no world outside the bank for Charlie but his wife and daughter. Michael had watched the gradual dignification of home affairs to the rank of "work," the consecration of his superior's time to the family insurance situation or the unraveling of Mrs. Meredith's income taxes, as if a bustle of manila folders and typed memoranda around personal matters could convince him that he was again engaged as a competent bank president on work that he understood. But there was no manila folder for what had happened in Baymeath, no list of figures, checked by tax experts, that could cope with adultery. Charlie Meredith was at bay, but he raised his fine white head with the dignity of an old stag at the surrounding jackals. "What have you to say to that, Michael?"

"Jimmie has no business bothering you with his jealous suspicions! He ought to take them to a psychiatrist!"

"They were more than suspicions, I'm afraid." Meredith paused to look gravely again at his knees. "He said that Alida made no secret of it." There was another heavy silence. "That she even boasted of it," he added softly.

"That was long ago, Mr. Meredith!"

"I know that, Michael. And I have no reproaches, believe me. All I ask, and I don't think it's too much for a worried father to ask, is that you reassure me that the past still *is* the past. At least that it was last night."

Damn him, Michael thought. Why did he always, with

his innate decency, that innate gentlemanly decency that all his fatuity and fussing could never quite obliterate, have to have the last word? He beat at the rising tide of pity around him with fretful strokes. "Well, what should a father want for his daughter?" he cried. "To have her forever loyal to a man she despises? What sort of a life is that?"

"The life she chose."

"But don't you see that means nothing to Alida? Or to me?" He throbbed with the difficulty of saying all he meant. How was it possible to convey to this old friend the impossibility of telling him the one thing he wanted to know: that nothing *had* happened the night before? "Don't you see that Alida and I can't understand why *we* should always be the ones to give things up?"

When Meredith finally answered, his tone was sad and dignified. "There's always been something I never quite understood about you, Michael. A kind of lurking sullenness. Well concealed, I grant. Oh, very well concealed. But there. Always there. A kind of resentment. As if you were never quite on the team. One had to know you well to sense it. But then I have known you well. Better than you think. Perhaps I've even had a glimpse into your secret."

"What secret?"

Meredith rose and walked slowly to the door. He turned before going out. "That you believe in nothing," he said with a sudden sharpness. "In nothing at all."

Happily for Michael there was little time to contemplate this scene, for he had to meet Flora. In the dark corner of the seafood restaurant, only fifteen minutes later, she took a sip of her martini and looked him straight in the eye. "This business about Danny Jones," she said with determination. "There's nothing in it, you know."

"But I know all about it."

"Because you found a rumpled bed in the house! Is it illegal for me to take a nap when I come to town?"

"Look, Flora. *You* know you've been having an affair with Danny Jones. *I* know it, too. The only thing you don't know is *how* I know it. I'm afraid you'll have to accept it, that's all."

She stared. "Have you been talking to Danny?"

"No."

"Have you hired a detective or something?"

"I'm not going to tell you."

"Oh, all right." She gave it up now and raised her chin defiantly. "What do you propose to do about it?"

"What do *I* propose? I'm not the one who's having the affair."

"No, but you're the one who's making the fuss about it. What do you expect me to do? Give him up?"

"Would that be so unreasonable?"

"Look, Michael." There was a sudden tense note of exasperation in her tone. "You say that you and I both know about Danny. Very well. But don't you and I both know something else? Don't you and I both know that you're not interested in me any more the way Danny is?"

Michael rubbed his lips that had suddenly become dry. "I thought it was mutual."

"All right, it's mutual," she agreed roughly. "But is that anyone's fault? Have I ever flung it in *your* face?"

"No." He paused. "No, you haven't."

"I've carried out my other functions as Mrs. Farish, and we've been friends. At least I thought we were." Flora, evidently sensing that she was gaining her point, paused for a moment and then changed her tone. "But we have different natures," she continued with a shrug. "You're quite happy with your bank and friends and the kind of social life you lead. But I have to have something else. From time to time. Maybe it's my Spanish blood. I don't know. But as long as I'm discreet, and nobody finds out — "

"*I* found out."

"Yes, but God only knows how. I don't think other people have. The point is, this thing with Danny isn't doing you any harm. There's no law that says you *have* to behave like an outraged husband!"

"Suppose I were to give myself the same liberty of action that you — "

"Go ahead!" she interrupted. "Go ahead! You have my entire blessing!"

Michael retreated uncomfortably from this position. "You propose, then, to continue meeting Danny in the middle of the day? In *my* house?"

"Or elsewhere." Flora's eyes were fixed and sullen now. But then, unexpectedly, she seemed to jump at him. "Have you no imagination, man?" she cried. "Can't you see what it means to a woman my age to have a young man like that?"

"Well, what do *I* do about it? Sit by admiringly and clap my hands?"

"But it won't be for long!" Flora's tone had changed suddenly to one of passionate pleading. "I can promise you that. How much longer do you think he's going to care about me?" She shrugged again, impatiently, bitterly. "A few weeks perhaps. Months at the most. And then he'll drop me flat. Don't worry. You'll have all the revenge you want. And what the hell? Why fuss? It's probably my swan song, anyway."

Michael, listening, knew that the whole pattern of his

life pointed that way. It was the ancient feeling that he had failed and was consequently without rights. To play the role of the complacent husband and to play it gracefully was a destiny that seemed to have been his since the earliest summers under the gay umbrellas, amid the sand piles of Bradley Bay. His heart was full of panic that he was going to give in, that his little romp in the park was over and that he was headed back to school. But then he felt the sudden spurt of his revived resolution.

"You say we're different," he exclaimed, "and that you can't help being what you are! But if I must face the fact that you have a lover, you can face the fact that I resent it. And that I can't help resenting it! And that I'm going to go right on resenting it!"

Flora stirred the olive in her drink. "Very well," she said, looking up at him calmly. "I'll face your resentment. What shape is it likely to take? Am I to be smothered, like Desdemona, with a pillow?"

Their eyes met, and he could read the incipient laughter in hers. He felt a sudden terrible impulse to laugh with her and knew that he was lost forever if he did. "No," he cried, jumping up to go, "you won't sneer me out of this one, Flora! I don't know what I'll do. You'll find out when I've decided. But I'm not coming home again while you're Danny Jones's mistress!"

Back in his office again he contemplated, stunned, the wild possibility of a new life. Might he not actually have developed the courage to snatch at it? Did everything *have* to be over? If the forces of his old world now rallied to repossess him, if from behind the waxy figure of an irate Flora, toppled over like a bowling pin, there sprang up an anxious Meredith, desperately appealing, was it not that they sensed instinctively the full range of his defection and moved in unison to save him? But he was beginning now to make out, beyond the frenzied clamor of their appeal, a small flickering hope in himself that he might not be overcome, that he did not *have* to be overcome, that Danny Jones, instead of a nemesis, might prove his deliverer, swinging a clear silver blade to sever the multitudinous umbilical cords that lashed him to his earlier role.

Even Amelia Brown opposed him. He could tell by her set expression as she came in with his letters that she had guessed about him and Flora.

"Tell me, Miss Brown," he asked her suddenly, "do you ever feel that life ought to be continuously exciting? That it's our own fault if it's not?"

Amelia did not seem in the least surprised. "I don't think life's meant to be exciting," she said flatly. "And I doubt if it's healthy to think so. People who think that way are apt to go smash."

"You think I'm going to go smash?" He looked at her with a small fixed smile.

"You will if you take off," she said with a shrug. "But I'm sure you have too much sense for that."

"And what's my alternative? To spend the rest of my life on the ground? Sitting in an airport, watching the planes? Doesn't that strike you as rather depressing?"

"Why an airport? Why planes?"

"Well, I suppose people who go smash have to go up in something?"

"In balloons maybe. Full of their own hot air."

"Oh, damn the metaphor!" he exclaimed. "Are you worried about me, Amelia?"

Her eyes hardly flickered, though he had never used her

first name before. "I'm worried now," she came back at him. "*Mr.* Farish."

"You think I'm going to make a fool of myself?"

"I think you're a bit young to do that."

"But the sooner I come to my senses, the better?"

Her lip quivered suddenly as she turned away, and he was ashamed, as he had been with Charlie Meredith. "I simply don't want to see you get hurt," she said classically and turned to leave as Danny Jones's head appeared in the doorway.

"Am I bothering you, sir? I have the probate petition in the Maltby estate. It's ready for your signature."

"Oh, fine. Come in, Danny." He took the papers and glanced over them rapidly before reaching for his pen. But his eyes took in nothing, and his heart was beating fast. "Did you get to the Willoughby box opening?" he asked without looking up.

"Oh, yes."

"Everything in order?"

"Quite in order, sir."

"Good." Michael glanced up suddenly, straight into the other's eyes, but Danny seemed unabashed.

"By the way, sir," Danny said easily, "if you're not too busy, could I have another word with you about the question of the Winters commissions?"

Michael stared at him coldly. "I wasn't aware there was a question."

"Well, that's the point, isn't it?" Danny sank into the chair beside the desk and started scratching his black hair. The sudden informality of his demeanor seemed to suggest the democracy of a shared intellectual problem; it conveyed annoyingly the attitude that however superior Michael might be, a construction question was still superior to both of them. "I've been talking to a lawyer friend of mine."

"That hardly seems discreet."

"Well, naturally, I didn't name any names. I just showed him the clauses in the will and in the letter. He thought the word 'total' definitely covered all commissions of any kind, and he gave me a couple of cases which I thought might interest you. The first is 'Arden's estate,' and I've got a quote from it here." Danny, without waiting for assent, pulled a piece of paper from his pocket. "There the will limited commissions to two per cent of principal, but the testator had written this letter — "

Michael's cold fury gradually turned into fascination as the irrepressible Jones read on. Had the stern god of Averhill, the god of the gargoyles on the chapel tower, sent this fury expressly to destroy him? Because of his *hubris* in dreaming that he, too, might one day become a man? From the murky cold of a New England winter, from the stale sweat of a thousand gymnasiums, from the jeering faces of a host of small boys, had this terrible god created the avenging demon of a Danny Jones to sleep with his wife in his own bed and to tear down the whole structure of his banking career? It was almost in a spirit of cooperation that he prepared to challenge the demon to do its worst.

"Before you go any further, Danny," he interrupted in a tone of mild sarcasm, "I think you ought to know that I'm not in the least interested."

"Oh?"

"I don't care what your cases are. I've already made up my mind. And I think it highly indiscreet of you to have talked about it outside the office. Even if you didn't mention names. A clever lawyer can put two and two together."

"But suppose I could *prove* to you, sir, that the word 'total' included our real estate commissions?"

"Why should you want to do that? So the bank can have

the privilege of paying back three hundred thousand dollars to Mrs. Winters?"

Danny stared at him with sullen eyes in which suspicion was beginning to take the place of perplexity. "But if the bank *should* pay it back?"

"Where's your loyalty, Jones?" Michael snapped at him. In the silence that followed he looked away, but he could hear Danny's heavy breathing. When Danny spoke, the last pretenses were dropped.

"Where's your integrity, Mr. Farish?"

"Don't be a child!" Michael swung around and slapped the desk in sudden fury. "Ever since you first came here, you've been absurdly naïve. I begin to wonder if you'll ever get over it. But get this through your head, Jones, once and for all. I do *not* propose to have my old decisions raked up by idle subordinates who have nothing better to do than get their boss in trouble. As far as I'm concerned, the question of the Winters commissions is a closed one. If I ever discuss it again, you may rest assured it will *not* be with you. That'll be all now, thank you." He looked down at his desk, but Danny did not move. "I said, that's all, Jones!"

"Not quite all, Mr. Farish, if you please."

"What now?" He looked up to meet Danny's sullenly staring eyes.

"I'm wondering if there's very much point in my continuing to work for a trust officer who finds me 'absurdly naïve.' "

"That's a question you'll have to decide for yourself."

"Would I get an even break?"

"I've said all I'm going to say."

"In that case it's obvious I quit." Danny's voice was ominously soft. "Only tell me one thing, will you, Mr. Farish?"

"What?"

"Are you quite *sure* that your attitude toward me has nothing personal in it?"

Michael looked up boldly and outstared him.

"Why should it have?"

"No reason, I guess." Danny shrugged. "I just thought I'd ask, that's all. It can't hurt, can it?" And he actually grinned as he shrugged again and turned to amble out of the room.

Michael, alone, tried to bring calm into the tumult of his emotions by thinking of Alida. Over his shoulder was the glare of a whole horizon ringed with the flames of his burning ships. But his feet, at least, were on the shore; there was no alternative now but to head resolutely inland. Alida, happily, would know her way. He seemed to sense her firm stride ahead in a darkness that had no terrors for her; he seemed to hear the crackling of branches as she blazed the trail. He would not lose sight of her a second time.

12

THE AMERICAN NAVAL BASE at Baymeath, England, in the summer of 1944, was the focus of that little port's activity. In peacetime it had been a seaside resort, but never a very fashionable one; quiet, elderly couples had come for quiet summers in the big, plain boardinghouses on the cliff that overlooked the Channel and had nodded little nods to each other in dining rooms whose drowsy silence was broken only by the clink of passing china. Abandoned now, the houses looked bleakly down at the busy comings and goings of the small amphibious vessels and submarine chasers as if to protest sullenly, in conceding their own current uselessness, that *they*, at any rate, had had no part in the moral disintegration that had preceded this unseemly armageddon.

The commanding officer of the base, Sam Stookey, must have seemed to the inhabitants of Baymeath the incarnation of the Yankee invasion. When they heard the wail of the siren of his black official car with the stars and stripes fluttering on the hood and saw his round, red angry face glaring out the window, they must have wondered if he did not consider himself a kind of colonial governor. Nor would they have been far wrong. Sam, although only a commander and a reserve officer at that, felt possessed of an unbounded authority over the environment of his little base. He loved the war; he loved small puddles, and, certainly, he was a most impressive frog. His voice was loud and gravelly, his tread heavy, his blue uniform unwrinkled. He would have been almost handsome, or what is called, at any rate, "a fine figure of a man," had he been forty pounds lighter. As it was, everything about him, the thick cheeks, the swelling neck, the widening girth seemed just a bit comically bulbous. But Sam, fortunately for the maintenance of his authority, had a temper, the kind of roaring temper that promotes obedience by itself without the aid of other qualities of leadership. It was quite adequate for his purposes.

Yet he was not, as most reserve officers were apt to expect, the kind of shore-based commander who found in a small authority a needed compensation for some failure in civilian life. Before the war he had been a senior partner of an old family real estate firm in Manhattan, and Michael, who had often had to deal with him, knew that in Stookey's field ignorance and bluster were by no means inconsistent with success. Sam at a New York title closing was always overpoweringly friendly. He would take for granted, blandly and prematurely, that all were in agreement; he would scoff at any difference of opinion as something "to be worked out by the lawyers"; his arm would be around everyone's shoulder or waving for celebrating drinks, until suddenly, at a harmless objection, at the first threat that he might miss his four-fifteen train and his daily golf, his face would redden and he would start shouting, quite willing to jeopardize even the most profitable deal for the indulgence of his own bad temper. Michael, in each case, with patience and impassivity, had managed to save the deal. Was it just luck on Sam's part? Or did he know, expertly or instinctively, when there would be a Michael to save the day and when not? That he was fully aware, at any rate, of Michael's diplomatic talents was evident on their first wartime meeting in London. "I've got the perfect job for you, Mike," he had cried, gripping his shoulder. "I want you to be my executive officer at Baymeath." And he had laughed loudly in his own humorless way. "In case you had any ideas about not being worthy of the honor, I took the precaution of getting your orders signed in advance."

The position was considered a good one. Stookey was even able to get his new assistant a spot promotion to lieutenant commander. But Michael was soon to discover that in carrying out the administrative policy of his superior officer he needed all the tact and subtlety of a Talleyrand dealing with a Napoleon and at least some portion of the former's disloyalty. For Stookey's ambition was as appalling as it was simple: he wanted his base to *look* the best and smartest base in England. Michael at times even wondered if Stookey did not seriously believe that to look the best base and to be the best base were synonymous, that Stookey the martinet would be identical with Stookey the naval hero. And there were those who seemed to agree with him. All the scrubbing and cleaning and painting that went on may have been a source of amazement and ridicule to the crews of visiting craft, but the gleaming results were unquestionably gratifying to inspecting officers from London. Stookey delegated the office management to Michael and spent his own few work hours striding about the base, accompanied by his first lieutenant and three petty officers, pausing here and there, as an artist might before an almost completed picture, to add an improving touch. But unlike the artist he had no technical competence, not even an ordinary seaman's acquaintance with the *Blue-Jacket's Manual*. He would simply point to the things that he found unsatisfactory and shout until they were made to meet his rather murky criteria. If one conceded his premise that the primary function of a naval base, like a pyramid, was to glorify its master, Stookey was a successful commanding officer. On his inspection tours the Quonset huts and machinery shops rang with shouts of "Attention on deck," and the general effect of drilling and stamping feet, of sudden staccato orders and presented arms, was more that of a military institute than a workaday dockyard. At night, in the big brick house on the hill that had been purchased by the U.S. Navy for officers' quarters and requisitioned by Stookey for himself, he held forth with the splendor of a Napoleonic marshal at dinners for the local gentry and the favored of his staff, while stewards' mates in dress white uniforms passed wines and champagnes smuggled from recently invaded France. For every skipper whose ship ever came into Baymeath found it politic, if not indispensable, to contribute to the base commander's cellar.

Michael's job, under the circumstances, was easy enough to define: it was simply to run the base. Stookey being entirely absorbed in the mystique surrounding his command, it was up to the executive officer to see that the amphibious craft which plied their weekly journey between Baymeath and the Normandy coast received adequate provisioning and repairs. This was possible only by freely conceding to Stookey the number of men that he needed for painting and scrubbing and making do as best he could with the rest. Michael, having a natural disposition to accept the nonvariables in any given situation, even managed to derive a small satisfaction from what he was still able to accomplish. What he did not like was his second task, which was to keep Stookey "legal." For the commanding officer had no deeper knowledge of means than he did of ends and had scant patience with the limitations of naval law. If he caught any sailor, either from his own command or from a visiting ship, with his cap not properly "squared," he would have him taken to the base barber to have his hair shaved off. He would hold a crew responsible for the behavior of each of its men and restrict the liberty of a whole ship for any infraction of his uniform regulations or a failure, however late at night, to salute an officer in the streets of Baymeath. Solitary confinement on bread and water was the penalty for the least untidiness in the barracks. Promotion, on the other hand, was meted out by standards equally bizarre. If a coxswain was suddenly made chief because of the spic and span condition of the commanding officer's car, it was up to Michael to see that the records showed elevation in the proper degree. It was up to Michael, in short, to fix, arrange, ameliorate, placate; he had to act as a buffer zone between what Stookey liked to describe as his own raw but efficient practicality and the unworkable world of paper requirements in distant Washington. Yet it worked, the whole thing; it *just* worked. The body of men who made up the base pulled together with Michael in a silent conspiracy to insulate the commanding officer and to satisfy his requirements at the smallest cost. It was as if their work had to be spasmodically interrupted for the production of Stookey's musical comedy concept of a war. The men trusted Michael to keep to a minimum the number of rehearsals. The real war, after all, was bound to be won if there were only the Germans and Commander Stookey to beat.

The outward relations between Michael and his boss were good. Stookey was a snob and rather truculently conscious of the difference between the Wall Street Farishes and his own family to whose name clung much of the trickiness and greed of three quarters of a century of real estate deals. To have a Farish at once his subordinate and friend was gratifying to his pride, and Michael knew how to get through the volume of work that Stookey expected of him without having the bad taste to appear more industrious than his commanding officer. He always turned up at Stookey's dinners and joked conscientiously with his little court. He even acted as host to bid the other guests good night after Stookey, thick of speech and unsteady, had staggered upstairs with the British Wren of his choice. But it was at such moments that Michael most doubted the becomingness of his wartime role.

"You know I'm worried about you, Mike," Stookey told him one night while they were drinking brandy. "Unless it's the best kept secret of the base, you haven't had a girl since you came to Baymeath. What do you do? Save it up for those weekends in London?"

"Oh, I thought you knew. I'm the Unknown Soldier. A happily married man."

"Aw, can it, will you? We're all happily married." Stookey had been happily married three times. "That doesn't mean you have to be a vestal virgin all the time you're in this God-forsaken island, does it?"

"There are different ways of looking at these things."

"Yeah? And how do you look at them? Down your long Farish nose?" Stookey's face was beginning to flush, but Michael did not blink an eye.

"You know I don't do that, Sam."

"Don't 'Sam' me, you prude."

"Excuse me, Commander. We can't all have your hot blood."

Sam, mollified, relaxed his expression. "It's not good for you, Mike. Take it from me. After all, you're my exec. I don't want anyone on my staff having a nervous crackup from overwork. Relaxation can be a duty, damn it. A patriotic duty. You ought to have a girl, Mike."

"Is that an order, sir?"

"Yes, damn it!"

Michael smiled sardonically as he walked home to his quarters that night. It was not that he felt that he had to carry out Sam's over-brandied instructions. But it was curious how persistently he seemed to find himself on the side of a despised and reprehensible virtue. If as a boy he had been ashamed of his innocence, did he now as a husband have to be ashamed of his fidelity? The very absence of such concerns had, up till now, been one of his reasons for regarding the war as a kind of holiday. True, he had the duties of his base, but these had none of the reality of his duties in Wall Street which no armistice would put an end to. The war, in its simplest terms, was something for which Michael Farish had not been responsible and which he could therefore look upon as a period of suspended animation, an interlude, a thing, in short, almost to be enjoyed. Away from Flora, away from his mother, away from Hudson River Trust, overseas and buoyed up by the constant reassurance of a rank and uniform that seemed to take the place, with only a moderate effort on his part, of a façade that in the past he had always had to erect out of the raw materials of his personality, he was discovering the pleasures of a comfortable, unimaginative masculine world in which one knew, more or less, all that was expected of one. And if one knew that, what was there really left to complain about except boredom, and how bored could one be with the constant reassurance of drinks at the officers' club every night at six, a movie in Stookey's parlor and a night of uninterrupted sleep? What complaint, indeed, as long as Stookey wasn't *too* much of a bore?

But it almost seemed as if he was going to be. When word came of the impending arrival of four Wave ensigns to work in Michael's office, Stookey made him the butt of his heaviest humor. Michael, he would point out to the respectfully laughing juniors at the officers' club bar, was a wily hypocrite. Scorning the native product that was still good enough for the rest of them, he had been pulling wires in London to arrange for the delivery of a veritable harem of his own compatriots.

"But don't count on having them all to yourself, smarty," he would warn Michael with a roll of his eyes. "I get first pick, you know. You may find me becoming a swivel-chair sailor, after all." For Stookey liked to consider his own inspection trips of the base as practically sea duty in contrast to Michael's desk job.

When the Waves arrived they reported to Michael's office, and he lectured them informally on the nature of their duties. They were attractive, disciplined young women and seemed serious about their work. One of them seemed particularly serious; she stared at Michael while he was talking with rather brooding brown eyes. She was a tall, square-shouldered girl, in her late twenties, with a pale, reflective countenance. She had a classic, almost a Minervan build, with just a hint of the bovine. It bothered Michael that he seemed to know her. Later, when she was seated at her desk outside his office, studying the file of base orders, he paused in passing to ask how things were going.

"Fine, thank you. But you don't remember me, do you, Commander?" And, then, of course, he did.

"Alida Meredith!" he exclaimed, suddenly remembering the name on her orders: Meredith, A., Ens. USNR. "My gosh, of course, I know you!"

She smiled. "I thought you'd forgotten."

"One forgets a lot of things in wartime, but not the boss's daughter!" His mind leaped back to the long slow dinners with the Charlie Merediths in that dark, Elizabethan house in White Plains. And to the near impossibility of getting Flora to go. He smiled as he remembered the big, shy only daughter who wouldn't talk. "You've changed."

"I suppose that's a compliment."

"How's the boss?"

"Daddy? Oh, fine. Rather in a snit about my going overseas, though. He'll be glad to hear I'm in such good hands."

"Hudson River Trust looks after its own."

"Thank you, Commander."

Michael went on to lunch with rather mixed feelings. The prospect of an observer from his old world was not altogether unpleasant; he liked to think that Charlie Meredith should hear of his importance as executive officer in Baymeath. Yet at the same time it cut into his concept of the war as a holiday; eyes from home were legendarily critical. He could not be sure that Miss Meredith's wouldn't be. She had seemed terribly pleased that he remembered her name, but he could not flatter himself, in the days that followed, that she showed a corresponding desire to capitalize on their prior acquaintance. She said good morning as she might have said it to any superior officer, and when she consulted him about her work there was nothing in her demeanor to suggest the least connection in their pasts. Michael even began to be disappointed. If he shunned female company of the kind sought by Stookey, it did not mean that he had no need of women at all. Before a week was out he found himself almost resenting the impersonality of Miss Meredith's attitude and her unquestionable efficiency in the office. He was disgusted to find himself playing the role of the old salt to the bright-eyed midshipman, if for no other reason than that those bright eyes saw so much. He decided that it was time he asked her to dinner and to a movie. It was certainly the least he could do for old Charlie's daughter.

"Oh, I'm so sorry!" she exclaimed. "I told Sylvia I'd go to the movies with her."

This took him aback. Sylvia, he remembered, was another Wave ensign. "Can't you do that another night?"

"Oh, but I'd hate to disappoint her."

"Tell her it's business. It's not every night one gets a chance to go out with the exec."

She smiled nervously. "That wouldn't be quite fair to her, would it?"

He had to be content to be postponed to the following evening. Miss Meredith was not one of those who felt entitled to ditch her own sex for the other. A commitment was a commitment. When Stookey asked him to dinner the following night Michael was taken by surprise and actually blushed. He stammered that he had another engagement. Stookey looked at him shrewdly.

"An engagement or a date?"

"Well, it turns out that the father of one of our new Wave ensigns is an old friend of mine, and I asked her — "

"Don't give me that father business. Which one?"

"Meredith. Alida Meredith."

"Oh, the big one."

"She's not all that big."

"Bit of a cow." Stookey shrugged. "But if you like 'em that way, what the hell? Bring her around. We need some new talent."

"If you don't mind, I think I won't. Not tomorrow anyway. We have a lot of things to discuss."

"I'll bet." Stookey winked suggestively. "You and she can talk about Daddy all night. That's okay, Mike. I'm delighted. I was beginning to worry about you." His big jaw fell as a thought suddenly struck him. "Say, you don't mean she's Charlie Meredith's daughter, do you?"

Michael felt a small prick of disappointment at being deprived so quickly of his new role of seducer. "That's what I was trying to tell you."

"Well, I'll be damned! Isn't he trust officer of Hudson River?"

"And probably the next president."

Stookey whistled. "I guess you *do* have to take her out. And buy her champagne, too. You'd better pick up a bottle at my house. You won't find any in town, that's for sure. And next time bring her around. I know Charlie Meredith myself."

But Michael's next discovery about Alida was that it was not going to be so easy to comply with Stookey's request. In the small pub to which he took her for dinner she seemed, despite her rather girlish and exclamatory enthusiasm for everything that smacked of local color, of a decidedly independent frame of mind. When he mentioned the fact, thinking that it might impress her, that they could have dined with the base commander, she wrinkled her nose in distaste.

"Well, thank heaven we were spared that!"

"You'd have had a much better dinner."

"But I like this one. Anyway, I can't abide Commander Stookey. You should have seen what Daddy wrote me about him."

"What?"

"He called him a cheap blow-hard. Can you imagine Daddy using a term like that? He must feel terribly strongly."

Michael, at the risk of seeming stuffy, decided that he had to say something to re-establish the shattered authority of the Baymeath command. "After all, he is the skipper," he reproved her. "We have to show some loyalty."

"But not off duty! Not when we're alone in a pub." She seemed to dismiss the naval hierarchy as a kind of game that only had to be played in school hours. "The man ought to be court-martialed."

"Miss Meredith!"

"Please call me Alida. You used to."

"*Did* I?"

"Certainly. And I called you Michael. But I won't if you'd rather not."

"Oh, no — no. It's all right, I guess."

"Only after office hours, of course."

Michael nodded uncertainly. "Why are you so down on Stookey?"

"Because I've talked to the boys on the boats. Ships, I mean. I bet you have no idea how they hate him."

"They probably feel the same way about all the base officers."

"Oh, no!" She seemed very intense about it. "They don't at all. It's only him. How would you feel if you'd been out on the Channel attacked by E-boats and came in to find your liberty cut because the gangway watch wasn't in dress blues when Commander Stookey called?"

"I know, I know." He glanced uneasily at the other tables as she raised her voice. "I do what I can about those things. There are way and means."

"I know there are. But how does that excuse *him?*"

"My dear Alida, this is war. We have to make do with what we've got."

She looked at him searchingly. "I guess Daddy's right," she

said. "You *are* a diplomat. He always said you were marvelous with the old lady depositors."

"So that's what you think of me?" he asked with a small dry smile. "Old ladies in peacetime and Stookey in war?"

"Oh, you're quite wrong!" she exclaimed quickly. "I admire you very much. I always have."

"Always?"

She paused. "Well, Daddy had such a high opinion of you."

"Of a lowly assistant trust officer?"

"Funny, I never thought of it that way." She reflected for a moment. "It always seemed to me that you were the young heir and that Daddy was a kind of caretaker."

Michael laughed in sheer surprise. "What on earth gave you that idea?"

"Well, aren't you a Farish? Wasn't your grandfather president of the bank?"

"Yes, but what does that mean?"

"Oh, everything! Mummy was always in a dither when you and Mrs. Farish came to dinner. She's so attractive, your wife. I don't suppose it was very amusing for her at the family's."

"On the contrary, she loved it."

"Oh, Michael, you liar!"

He found himself suddenly laughing. There seemed no point, far away in Baymeath, in keeping up these little appearances. "Anyway, *I* liked it. I'm very fond of your father."

"You were always nice to him, anyway. And to me. I won't forget that in a hurry. Shy girls don't."

"You seem to have conquered your shyness."

"I've learned to wear a mask. Haven't you?"

"Have I?"

"Isn't that what being a diplomat is?" She looked suddenly troubled when he frowned. "I know all you have to do to get around Stookey," she went on hastily. "I know you really run the base. Everyone admires you for it, too."

"*You* don't," he retorted abruptly. "You'd defy Stookey if you were in my shoes, wouldn't you? You'd stand right up to him!"

Their eyes met. He felt that she wanted to compromise, but that her nature prohibited it. "I might."

"And what would happen then? You'd get the sack, and Stookey would find himself a real stooge. Would that help the war effort?"

"I suppose I'd let the war effort take care of itself."

"You're not very practical."

"I admit it." Her eyes pleaded with him not to spoil their evening. "Look, I'm being absolutely bloody, as they say over here," she apologized. "What do I care about Stookey? Let's forget him, shall we?"

"He wants to meet you," Michael persisted. "Will you let me take you there sometime?"

"I'd rather not."

"After all, he does know your father."

"And we know what Daddy thinks of him."

"Won't you really? Just once?"

She sighed as if she really minded. "The boys at sea will think I'm a traitor."

"You can tell them it was an order."

After this they dropped the subject. He wanted to know more about her life, and she told him, dryly enough, its simple outline. As the only child of elderly, nervous parents she had been fussed over, fretted over, made to dress up in too many ribbons and sashes. She had always felt conspicuous, somehow perspiring, as out of step with her own contemporaries as she had felt her parents to be out of step with theirs. Yet they insisted on offering to a heart yearning for the immolation of recognized defeat the ludicrous fantasy of a happy hearth for which she should be articulately grateful. She had finally achieved, after years of a rather truculent noncompliance, a grudgingly yielded independence, a summer on a ranch, one in Newfoundland and the chance to develop a degree of competence in handball and skiing. It intrigued Michael that she should remember — as he did not — his own intervention with her mother on the question of a progressive college.

"But I can never forget it!" she exclaimed. "I owe you everything. Mummy had this idea that you were *the* authority on where girls could go. Nice girls, that is. She regarded you as a social arbiter. When she said you would never approve of Bennington, I was prepared to hate you. And then, when you came for dinner, and said you'd like to send your own stepdaughter there, Mummy didn't have a leg to stand on!"

"By gosh, I do remember!" he exclaimed in sudden astonishment. "I said something about people having to do the things they really wanted, didn't I?"

"That's it! And Mummy was shocked. She said if we did the things we really wanted, we'd be like monkeys in a zoo."

"Which shows what *she* really wanted!"

This time, when they had stopped laughing, he knew they were friends. They finished up the evening more agreeably and went out again together twice that week. Everyone on the base immediately assumed that their relationship was something it wasn't. Michael hardly cared. It was even rather warming to have such a thing assumed, to catch a sense, conveyed in the friendly "good morning" of the chief yeoman, in the knowing smiles of the mess hall, in Stookey's lewder wink, of sharing in the human conspiracy to achieve in wartime at least this pleasure. He could easily enough shrug his shoulders, smile and tell the officers of Stookey's circle that they were leaping to wild conclusions.

But were they? What exactly was his relationship with this girl? There was an immediate sympathy between them that made the most ordinary topics interesting. She was inclined to criticize him for his habit of compromise, his tendency to regard the ideal as being wholly dependent on the practical, but he felt in the hasty way in which she backed down whenever he was really irritated that her very criticism might have sprung from an earlier admiration of himself and a corresponding disappointment not to find him all that she had pictured. He was reminded that she had remembered him vividly — far more vividly indeed than he had remembered her. But now it was her image that was growing in his fantasies to the point of obliterating other things: Stookey, Baymeath, even Flora and home. He would shake his head, and the image would dissolve. But he knew it would come back, and he found it odd that this should not give him even the smallest sense of guilt.

The next time that Stookey asked him to bring his "girl" for dinner, he felt that he had to. To his relief Alida accepted.

"Well, I suppose if we must, we must," she said with a sigh.

The dinner was like every dinner at Stookey's, but Michael, seeing its full shoddiness in Alida's unsmiling eyes and straight lips, kept waiting apprehensively for something terrible to happen. Alida was seated on Stookey's right, and on her other side was Lieutenant Doyle, his "aide." Whenever Michael considered himself too much a sycophant, it was his consolation to contemplate Doyle. A grinning, balding, be-spectacled Detroit lawyer, younger than he seemed, his culti-vation of Stookey was comically obvious. Michael, whose position he coveted, knew that tyrants in the end preferred the grosser flatterers. But what of it? It was only a matter of time, in any event, before Stookey would want another exec.

They were ten at dinner in the dark wood-paneled dining room of Stookey's Victorian villa, waited on by five silent, well-trained stewards' mates. Their host addressed himself to Alida in the loud, suspicious tone that he adopted with any naval guest whose obsequiousness was not yet assured. Every-one else was silent.

"I had a letter this morning from Jimmie Parr," he was saying. "I thought I might read it aloud. Jimmie's an ensign who used to be stationed at Baymeath. Did you ever know him, Miss Meredith?"

Alida looked in surprise at the rather glazed hostility in his eyes. "I think I did, as a matter of fact. If he's the same one. But why? Should I know him?"

"He just happens to be the son of Ambrose Parr, that's all."

"And who, pray, is Ambrose Parr?" Alida's voice had a thin edge of defiance.

Stookey glared down the table. "I guess Michael can tell you that," he retorted. "Would you say the biggest depositor in Hudson River Trust, Michael? Or only the second?"

"One of the biggest, surely."

"Oh, *Mr.* Parr," Alida said with a faint flush. "Yes, I do know his son. But I've never met *him.* Daddy keeps his home life and his business quite separate."

"Unlike his daughter, eh?" Stookey retorted with a guffaw, winking at Michael. This remark was received in silence except for Doyle's dutiful snicker. Stookey cleared his throat and took a letter from his pocket. "I thought it might interest you all to hear what a smart, observant kid like Jimmie Parr thinks of our little effort at Baymeath." He proceeded to read aloud several paragraphs of fulsome praise of himself, interspersed with such comments as "It may not be the province of a junior officer to compliment his superior" and "Trusting that I do not seem impertinent." Michael decided the most nauseating thing about the letter was its evident sincerity. When Stookey had finished everyone followed Doyle's lead of murmured congratulation. Everyone, that is, except Alida.

"You didn't like the letter, Miss Meredith?" Stookey demanded.

"I haven't been in Baymeath long enough to judge for myself, Commander," she said coolly. "And I'd rather form my own opinion than take Jimmie Parr's."

"Well, that's right," Stookey said ominously. "Be cautious. A girl should always be cautious. Particularly in a war. And *particularly* on a naval base."

The situation was momentarily saved by the chief steward who presented a bottle of wine for Stookey's inspection.

"Oh, yes," he said, examining the label. "I think you will all like this. A Montrachet that the skipper of the LSM 621 brought me back from Le Havre. That was the ship that had the dirty laundry on deck, wasn't it, Mike?" He winked again at Michael. "Well, now we have a case of Montrachet. Live and learn, I always say. Live and learn."

As the chief steward leaned down to serve Alida, she turned her glass abruptly over. Stookey flushed very red, and there was a silence around the table. As the meal drew on, Stookey, who had already had many cocktails, drank glass after glass of the constantly poured Montrachet and became more and more flushed and sullen. At length he began to grumble about women in the service, addressing himself to nobody in particular. Women in uniform, apparently, were activated by every possible motive but that of patriotism. They wanted to ape men and usurp their position; they were bored at home or bored at their jobs; they were abnormal sexually, or if normal they were lacking in sex appeal, or if normal and not so lacking they were nymphomaniacs. It was not entirely clear in which category Alida fitted, but it was manifest that in Stookey's opinion she had put on her uniform only for the opportunity to take it off.

"And what about men?" she asked finally. "Why do *they* join the service?"

"Because they want to fight!" he snapped. Dinner was over now, and he stood up. All stood up after him.

"From where I'm looking I don't see so many fighters," Alida retorted. Stookey turned scarlet.

"You'd better remember where you are, Miss Meredith!" he shouted. "You'd better remember you're only an ensign. And that I'm your commanding officer!"

Michael had to admire the coolness of Alida's high, clear tone. "I'll remember that you're supposed to be an officer, Commander," she said, "when you remember that you're supposed to be a gentleman."

Michael came forward and took her by the arm. "Let's call this the 'Montrachet evening,' Commander," he said in his most diplomatic tone. "It seems to promote dispute. I think I'd better take Miss Meredith back before she's hanged to the yardarm, don't you? How could I ever explain it to her father?" It was the best he could do, but obviously nothing could save the situation. He considered himself lucky that Stookey simply turned away without bidding them good night.

In the jeep driving back to the base Alida was very quiet. He waited for an apology that didn't come.

"It's all right, you know," he said.

"No, Michael, it's not."

He glanced at the rigid profile in the dark beside him. "I don't really give a hoot," he tried to assure her.

"Perhaps not. But *I* do."

"We've agreed a dozen times the man's a lout. What's new about that?"

"It wasn't Stookey," she said firmly, turning now to glare at him. "It was you."

"Me!"

"Yes." She nodded. "The way you sat there. With that nervous half-smile."

"But I wasn't smiling!"

"Oh, but you were, Michael! And you *heard* what he said about the Waves!"

"Of course I heard it. And very offensive it was, too. But also quite unimportant. You should have ignored it."

"Ignored it! When he insulted us that way?"

"Certainly," he retorted. "You ought to expect it from a man like that."

"What about the position it puts me in?"

"What about the position you put *me* in?" he exclaimed.

"What position?"

"The position of having to stand by while he was rude to you. It was most humiliating."

Alida's mouth fell open. "I'm so sorry!" she cried sarcastically.

"You should be," he said calmly. "An executive officer

can't get into a fight with his skipper. Particularly in front of English guests."

"Oh, I *see!*" she exclaimed in the same tone. "I'm lucky, I suppose, to have got off so cheaply. He might have ordered his stewards' mates to shave my head while you watched! Fancy your humiliation then!"

"I see no reason for dramatics." Michael held his arms out straight to the steering wheel, staring fixedly ahead down the road. "Obviously there are limits to what I have to take from Stookey. In my opinion they had not been exceeded tonight."

"How fortunate!"

He pulled up abruptly before her quarters, and she got out of the jeep and strode quickly down the flagstones to the door. He had meant to drive off without a word, but it suddenly struck him as impossibly disagreeable.

"Alida!" he cried and hurried after her. When she turned he saw in the light from the opened door how exhausted she was. It was a despairing, crumpling exhaustion, and he had a sickening intuition that it had been there all the time, that now, under this terrible pressure and because she had thought him gone, her guards were down, and it had swept devastingly over her features. Pity hammered inside him. "Alida, my poor dearest," he said and took her in his arms.

Her reaction surprised him. Everything in her seemed suddenly to go tense, and she clung to him passionately, her hands gripping his shoulders, her lips pressing hard against his, forcing them open. "Oh, my darling," she gasped, "you have no idea how I've wanted this. And how long! Forgive me. Flora can have you forever and ever when the war's over, but it's my turn now. Oh, yes, it's my turn now!" Gently he disengaged himself and led her back to his jeep. She clung to his arm silently as they drove to his quarters where he never even turned on the lights. In the unbelievable darkness their relationship became all that Commander Stookey had from the beginning assumed.

From this point on, Michael's life in Baymeath became a very different thing. Almost overnight he stopped living, as he had been living hitherto, in the minor pleasure around the corner: the evening drink, the movie, the weekend trip into London, small events that glittered like shiny silver cups in the immediate future, children's trophies at a lawn party. Now it was enough to know that every evening after work Alida would come to his quarters, and they would have a drink and cook dinner and make love. With incredible speed, they had settled into a solid domesticity which excluded the base and everyone on it. He was not at all sure that he was in love with Alida; it seemed enough that she should be so obviously in love with him. For the first time in his life he had the experience of being listened to and admired by someone totally, almost alarmingly acquiescent to him. All Alida's defenses, her disapprovals, her criticisms of him had collapsed in a single night; the former valkyrie gazed at him now with the tousled hair and limpid eyes of a beached Rhine maiden. It was gratifying to his vanity; it was exciting, but it was also worrying. He could never quite get out of his mind what a fool he would look if people knew that he, Michael Farish, were considered by anyone, even by this lonely and undiscriminating girl, the perfect lover. It had always been his misfortune to believe that a desire for himself might be a mark of inferiority. He could be grateful for such a mark in a woman, genuinely and humbly grateful, without necessarily wishing to advertise it.

What bothered him even more was Alida's complete loss of interest in the maladministration of Commander Stookey.

She seemed to be adopting Michael's attitude of tolerance just as he himself was beginning to shed it.

"Oh, to hell with Stookey," she said brusquely when he started once, rather handsomely, to re-examine his behavior at the famous dinner party. "He's not worth an argument. And besides, darling, you were quite right. I behaved outrageously. Just like a petulant ten-year-old. After all, as you said, we *are* in the Navy."

"But there are limits," he protested, dissatisfied with so easy a victory. "I've been thinking it over. Surely an officer is not expected to sit by while the service is vilified. I should have taken you out the moment he started."

"And run the risk of being bounced out of here? No, sweetheart. I've suddenly discovered that I *am* a practical woman. After all."

"Who taught you that?"

"Who do you think?" She leaned over to kiss him. "I'm not going to let anyone as small as Stookey take you away from me, darling. It's not worth it. We have too little time." She put her head on his shoulder. "I don't like to talk about it, because it's too painful, but I'll say it just once. We're not going to have forever, sweetheart. I'm not the kind of girl who breaks up a home. This is strictly a wartime affair. And I'm going to keep it that way. No matter *what* it costs me."

Michael was too much a gentleman not to despise the relief that he nonetheless felt at hearing the limits of his commitment. Gravely he asked her: "Do you think it won't cost me as much?"

"Oh, less, darling, much less," she said with an unresenting smile. "But never mind that. I've never had anything like this before. And it's going to take more than Sam Stookey to get it away from me now."

Stookey was very surly with Michael for several days after the dinner party, and Lieutenant Doyle must have had his hopes that the fall of the executive officer was at last on hand. But the reports that he spirited to his master of Michael's increased infatuation with the insolent Wave had an effect just the opposite of what he intended. Stookey was invariably sympathetic with sexual involvement. He decided it would be more fun to be paternal with Michael than to break with him, and he summoned him for a drink at the officers' club.

"I've been hearing a lot of things about you, old man," he said in his friendly tone. "Baymeath is a small place. You'd better watch your step if you want to find that cozy job waiting for you when you get back to Wall Street."

Michael saw immediately the role Stookey wanted to play and refused to join in the game. "I'm not sure I want to go back to Wall Street."

"Oh, come now," Stookey remonstrated with something like concern in his voice. "You've got a golden future there. You can't take the chance of having it blow up in your face. And that's just what'll happen if Charlie Meredith hears about you and that snotty daughter of his. It's not worth it, Mike." He put his hand on Michael's shoulder and added, in one of his rare moments of realism: "Keep your eye on that future, boy. All this navy business is so much crap. One day after the armistice all the braid in London will look like small boys sailing boats in a bathtub. You've got the real thing back home. And don't you forget it."

"I'm afraid that will have to be my decision, Sam."

Stookey looked at him in surprise. "Let's not be like that, Mike," he said with an ominous softness. "After all, I know how it is. I've been married three times myself."

"It's not the same thing."

"Oh, it's not, isn't it?" Stookey retorted, flushing. "What you're getting is different? Is she so special, this big Wave of yours? She's not made like the rest of them? Maybe she's not, at that!"

Michael made no answer to this, but turned and left the bar. His shoulders trembled with anger as the loud, sneering laugh broke out behind his back. But he knew that he had hurt Stookey, and he was glad.

"He's just too cheap to be borne," he told Alida that night. "It's high time I did something about him."

"Oh, but, darling, what?"

"There are plenty of ways I could cross him up. After all, I run his base for him."

"Yes, but wouldn't it be dangerous?"

"Perhaps it's time I did something dangerous."

"Oh, sweetheart, the war's going to be over soon," she protested anxiously. "Maybe in a few months. And then Sam Stookey can go back to selling brownstones. Who cares?"

"*I* care."

"Darling, don't do anything rash!"

Yet it was her very protest that most incited him to action. His failure to stand up for her at Stookey's dinner party was beginning to be something of an obsession. He had always tended to look upon life as a moving belt bearing dummies in different costumes and attitudes, from the study of which, as it slowly passed, one could figure out in advance the costumes and attitudes expected of oneself. But there had never been any idea of stopping the belt or altering its direction, far less of changing the costumes or even knocking off the wax figures. All the big events of his life had been planned according to a schedule: school and the trust company and marriage and even doing his duty as an officer in wartime. But Alida had not been planned; Alida had simply happened. And the idea that other things might simply happen, or even be made to happen, was intoxicating. He found himself at his desk feverishly devising different methods of asserting an independence from Stookey. He would publicly remit all the illegal penalties and advise the men at quarters of their rights. He would have Stookey's wine cellar destroyed and dare him to protest. He would get himself transferred to London and harry his former boss with carping demands from headquarters. But these were only fantasies, after all. The days went by, and he did nothing.

The opportunity, as it turned out, like most opportunities, did not have to be sought after; it fell into his lap. Stookey could never abide an official inspection; he would contrive any sort of excuse to be away, either on a sudden visit to another base or on a trip to London to report to the very officer who had just journeyed down to see him. His transparent excuses were usually accepted, partly because of Michael's smooth handling of the inspecting officer and partly because of the latter's satisfaction with the gleaming aspect of the Baymeath base. It was no surprise to Michael, therefore, to learn one morning at his office that Captain Fowler Kean was expected from London in two hours' time and that Commander Stookey had just departed in an army plane for Glasgow.

"He wants to interview a chaplain up there," the chief yeoman explained soberly. "He thinks he might have him transferred here."

Michael nodded, also without expression. Their understanding was complete. His heart, however, was beating a bit faster, for Fowler Kean was an old acquaintance of his.

A New Yorker bought up in England, a famous yachtsman with a handsome boy's face and white hair at fifty, Kean was one of those modern rich whose life had been a constant and graceful apology for his fortune. Because he lived in fear of seeming superior he was almost fatuously enthusiastic about the commonplace. He adored the Navy and the opportunity which it offered him to live in a hierarchy of distinct classes unseparated by money. His own high reserve rank he regarded, with some justification, as the peak of all his accomplishments. Michael knew that he would lean over backwards to avoid discovering the kind of man Stookey was and that he would tolerate no disloyalty in his executive officer. On the other hand — Michael looked at his watch. Yes, he decided with a deep breath, he still had time. He summoned Mr. Doyle and gave him his orders abruptly and coolly. The thing that surprised him most about the new excitement tingling in his veins was that he actually seemed to be enjoying it.

Two hours later he met Captain Kean at the main gate of the base and took him to the officers' club for lunch. He was careful to address him as "Captain," though at home they had used first names. "I think everything points to a drink and a very good lunch before our tour," he said blandly as they entered the bar.

"You serve drinks in the morning?" Kean asked with a little frown. "On a working day?"

Doyle, who was hovering behind them, edged forward. "Only in honor of your visit, sir."

Michael eyed him coldly. "Nonsense, Mr. Doyle. You know as well as I do that Commander Stookey has this bar open every day at noon." He allowed himself the boldness of a small wink. "The commander's a man of the world,

Captain. Like yourself. He believes if a man can't do his job after a couple of dry martinis, he probably can't do it at all." He took a glass from the bar that the chief steward had just poured and handed it to Kean. "Here you are, Captain. A Stookey special. And I'll bet you won't find a dryer, crisper martini even at the Savoy. But then I'll bet you don't get the gin that we get."

"What gin?"

"Ask me no questions, Captain, and I'll tell you no lies."

Kean drank half his martini in silence while Michael smiled benignly and ordered a second for himself. "I think we'll have a bottle of the Montrachet with lunch, Fred," he said to the chief steward. "In the Captain's honor."

"Not for me, thank you," Kean said dryly.

"Open it up anyway, Fred," Michael continued airily. "Maybe the Captain will change his mind. We get the best from France, sir. It's one of Commander Stookey's little prerogatives." Holding his cocktail glass he guided Kean toward the officers' mess. "Some of our amphibious skippers are apt to bring him back little presents. It's very nice."

"It must be."

During lunch Michael purported to amuse his superior with little stories about the night life of Baymeath. He even managed to introduce the subject of segregation and spoke with pride of the color line that Stookey had established for American sailors in English pubs. "Well," he breathed, with a satisfied sigh when the meal was over. "You will admit that's not bad chow, Captain? Perhaps a bit more than you expected from an amphibious base?"

"Just a bit." Kean's laugh was more like a grunt. "What are you trying to do, Mike? Bribe me to give up the inspection?"

"On the contrary!" Michael rose from his seat. "We want you to inspect the base from top to toe!" As Kean rose also Michael shook a finger at him. "I know what you're thinking, Captain. You're thinking we live a bit too well, aren't you? You're wondering if the work gets done. Well, you'll see! I think it's generally conceded we're the smartest base in England!"

"I'll be the judge of that."

Michael watched the Captain out of the corner of his eye as they walked down the road past the machine shops. As he had expected, Kean seemed agreeably surprised at the trim appearance of the row of grey Quonset huts.

"Neat?"

"It is, rather," Kean conceded. "It really is."

"I'll bet you're wondering where we get all our paint? *And* the men to do the painting?"

"Where do you?"

Michael smiled a bit roguishly. "I told you, Captain, ask me no questions!"

"Oh, come off it, Farish," Kean retorted brusquely. "Where do you get the men?"

"The LST crews are *very* anxious to go on liberty," Michael answered mysteriously, dropping his voice. "And a base commander, as you know, can withhold liberty." He shrugged his shoulders. "Q.E.D."

"Q.E.D.?"

Michael reverted suddenly to his normal tone, as if fatigued by the necessity of spelling out the obvious. "The LST skipper is only too happy to provide a working party to contribute to the beauty of the base."

"Do you mean to tell me, Farish — ?"

"Oh, Captain," Michael interrupted softly, "I mean to tell you nothing."

The Captain became very grave indeed at this, and Michael decided that he was ready for the coup. Preceding Kean into the largest machine shop he shouted: "Attention on deck!" When Kean entered he saw twenty sailors standing rigidly to attention. Suddenly he started.

"Why are their heads shaved?" he exclaimed. "What does this mean, Farish?"

Doyle was staring at Michael with narrowed eyes. He understood at last. The executive officer had told him earlier that morning to assemble all the men with shaved heads in a single hut which he would undertake to keep off the Captain's itinerary. Michael simply gave him a defiant wink and turned to Kean. "It's a most effective little punishment if I do say so, sir," he explained. "Devised by Commander Stookey himself. To teach the men to keep their hats squared."

"Damn it all, Farish, it's not legal!"

"Damn it all, Captain, it's practical!"

After this he had Kean where he wanted; the point of no return had been passed. The Captain, silent and grimly frowning, followed him about the base while Michael suavely uncovered all the shoddy makeshift behind the outward gleam. Everyone in the inspecting party now understood the executive officer's little project; intrigued, half hypnotized, they watched with alert eyes his graceful maneuvers. When the inspection was over Kean went alone with Michael to his office and sat down, looking tired.

"What's your game, Mike?"

"I thought you ought to know."

"And what the hell do you expect *me* to do about it?"

Michael shrugged. "Tell it in Gath. Publish it in Askelon."

"But the Admiral *likes* him!" Kean protested unhappily. "Upsetting Stookey's applecart is more of a job than you think. It could get me in one peck of trouble."

"The war won't last forever."

Kean shook his head gloomily. He did not like the idea that as a rich man and a reserve the blast of naval retribution might be only a zephyr to him. If others feared it, then he, too, must fear it. To admit otherwise would be to concede his unique distinction, and to concede this would be to upset the thought habits of a lifetime. "Whatever happens," he said with a sigh, "you're washed up with Stookey. That man Doyle will tell him."

"Don't worry about me."

"I'm afraid I'll have to." He rose, sighing. "Why did I ever come down here, anyway?"

"In answer to a silent prayer."

That night at the officers' mess, when Kean had gone, Michael felt himself the subject of an awed and fearful staring. No one wanted to be associated with the vengeance that Stookey was bound to wreak on his return, yet all recognized that a miracle had occurred and that the executive officer was no longer in the ranks of ordinary mortals. Michael continued to feel rather dizzily elated, but his mood sank afterwards when he told Alida. She burst into tears.

"It's all my fault," she kept repeating. "I mocked you into it. I did. I've brought this on you."

"I brought it on myself," he said firmly. "I did it for my own good. Everything's going to be all right."

When Stookey returned from Glasgow two days later he did not send for Michael immediately. Doyle had met him at the airport and motored him to the base. It was not until late that afternoon that he summoned his executive officer and silently handed a dispatch to him across the desk. Michael read it, but did not register on its contents for several seconds. Then he realized that it was his orders from London and that he was being transferred to Captain Kean's command.

"Well, that's fine, isn't it?" he said, looking down at Stookey's expressionless face. "It saves you the trouble of getting rid of me."

To his surprise, the commander's voice was not unfriendly. His eyes evaded Michael's as if he and not Michael were the one at fault. "If you wanted a soft berth in London, you didn't have to go sucking around Kean, Mike," he protested. "You didn't have to square yourself with him by running me down. I'd have arranged your transfer if you'd asked me."

"I don't expect you to believe this, sir, but I had nothing to do with these orders."

"No? Well, watch out for those buzz bombs. I'm glad I'm not in London. How about a party before you go?"

So there it was. Incredible as it seemed, Stookey wanted to remain friends. If Michael was to be at headquarters, Michael was to be placated. It was as simple as that. That a subordinate should doublecross one to improve his own position was only to be resented if the subordinate failed. It was all in the simple law of nature. Michael felt deflated that this *deus ex machina* should have so robbed him of all the glory of being martyred. He returned to his own office and sent for Alida. Her eyes were deep with concern as he told her.

"Why do you think Kean did it?" she asked.

"Because he found he was helpless to do anything about Stookey. Or unwilling. And he's too much of a gentleman to leave me in the lion's den."

"So it's all come to nothing? Your great gesture?"

"Like all my gestures."

"Oh, poor sweet," she said sadly. "How like you to see it that way. But *I* think you were terrific. You were very brave. That's what counts."

"Is it?" He laughed bitterly. "The lights have gone on in

the school theater, and the mothers and nurses are clapping. And I find I'm just another little boy who has finished reciting 'Horatius at the Bridge.' "

"I *like* 'Horatius at the Bridge.' "

He leaned forward to squeeze the hand that rested on his desk. "Luckily for me. But don't worry. You can come to London on weekends. Stookey will allow it, never fear. And after a bit I'll get you transferred there. We'll have fun."

"No, Michael."

"No what?"

"I'm not coming to London." Alida was very grave now, and her eyes were fixed on the floor. "I want you to get me a transfer if possible, but not there. To France. Or even to Germany."

"What's this?" he cried. "Must we all be heroes?"

"I want to have something to distract me," she said firmly. "When I'm no longer seeing you." She paused, but still did not look up. "I think I'm going to want a good deal of distraction."

"But why must you stop seeing me?"

"Because this is the time. The indicated time. I told you I'd know when to pull out, Michael. Well, I do."

Michael would not have believed that it was possible to be so torn by conflicting impulses. On the one hand there was the sudden vivid picture of the return to his wartime freedom, to be once again a Michael whose every action was so comfortably predictable to himself. On the other was poor Alida whose resolution, he was quite sure, was not nearly so firm as she made out, who only needed one note of conviction in his voice to throw all her plans and resolutions to the winds. He felt something tearing in his heart as he watched her drooping shoulders, and then it seemed to him as if only in and through her could he ever find life and hope.

"Alida!" he cried. "Alida, darling, you're mad. Don't you know? I want to marry you!" It seemed incredible that words that expressed such sincerity should ring so false. "I want to marry you!" he repeated violently. "Flora will give me a divorce. She doesn't really care. She never has. It's only a question of alimony."

"Oh, dearest," she said, taking both his hands in hers. "I know you mean it when you say it. Even if you'd die if I took you up on it. And I love you for meaning it. We can't help what we feel. After all, I was the intruder."

"Darling, we need each other!"

"I think we do. But even so." She shook her head and sighed. "Even so."

"Don't decide it now."

"I've got to. Now is the time. I've got my strength up now."

"Will you come and see me in London?"

"No."

"Alida! Please!"

"I'll write you first, then. Before I come."

Which she did, three weeks later. She wrote that she was coming up to London on a weekend pass and wondered if they could meet for dinner. That was all. There was no emotion expressed in the letter, not even a suggestion that anything of the sort be renewed. Holding it in his hand, Michael looked out of his office window at Grosvenor Square. Three weeks had been long enough to make Stookey and his little court seem like people of a different planet. London, even drab, war-weary London, was a veritable riot of friends and color and warmth and talk. It was as if the great grey curtain of his Baymeath existence had been suddenly slit down the middle and his whole past were tumbling through the gap. He dined now with men who had seen Flora only a few days before, who had held Seymour on their knees, who had telephoned to his mother and sisters. He attended cocktail parties and went to theaters. He even accompanied his new boss to a reception at the Palace. When he looked back to his quixotic little mutiny at Baymeath and the big, lonely girl who had inspired it, it was with something like incredulity. Captain Kean had suggested that he send an officer over to Paris for a few days to unravel some particularly snarled red tape, and he decided to go himself.

She did not suggest coming to London again. Or if she came, she did not look him up. Later he saw her name on a list of Wave officers being transferred to France. Obviously, she had been successful in obtaining her change of duty. The same day's dispatches contained a list of commanders promoted to captain. Stookey's name headed the list. Michael remained in London, consoled for the lack of heroics in his job by the sputter of the buzz bombs, and wondered bemusedly from time to time to what extent the episode of Baymeath had been a chapter without relation to the rest of his life.

13

ALIDA PARR KEPT MICHAEL explicitly informed of each step in her deteriorating relations with her husband. Jimmie first demanded that she give him her word of honor not to see Michael alone again, which was contemptuously refused. He then threatened to divorce her in a New York court, naming Michael as corespondent, and she defied him to prove his case. Thereafter he moved back into their apartment, but refused to speak to her. It was Jimmie, however, who first found the silence unbearable and took to dining at his club. Alida immediately sent him a typed memorandum informing him that as long as he preferred the company of his own sex to hers, she intended to dine out with her old friend and counselor, Michael Farish. She carried off her new role of estranged wife with considerable style, and Michael even suspected her of enjoying it.

"It was a mistake, my letting you spend that night in the apartment," she explained judiciously. "But, anyway, I called Jimmie's bluff. He didn't have a detective and couldn't take advantage of it. But from this point on we've got to be careful. You can be sure as blazes he has one now!"

Their life took on a definite pattern. Michael had moved to the Hone Club, and they dined together every night. There was never the slightest deviation from the rigid rules of their talks and meetings; on the telephone they were brief and matter-of-fact, and in restaurants they met at the table, and she always left first. Incredibly enough, they never discussed what their relationship would be when Jimmie had been disposed of. It seemed to be tacitly assumed that they would pick up where they had left off in Baymeath.

If Alida was calm, however, Michael lived in a daze. At the bank he kept his door closed and tried to immerse himself in routine work that should have been left to subordinates. Charlie Meredith rarely called him in now; when he and Michael met, their colloquies were dry and embarrassed. Amelia Brown, hurt by his detachment, was studiously formal; Danny Jones, to everyone else's surprise, had resigned. At the bar of the Hone Club where Michael repaired every evening before meeting Alida he was brief and clipped with friends who ventured to show solicitude about his rift with Flora. He hurt their feelings and derived a perverse satisfaction from it. He wanted to cut out everything in his life but his formal, oddly satisfactory dinners with Alida, filled with the well-told news of her day, and the peaceful solitude of his neat, plain room at the club. But there were parts of his old life that could not be entirely eliminated. One was Seymour who had returned, after the close of school, from a visit with Rex's family to find his mother on Long Island and his father in town. Armed with Flora's version of Michael's irrational jealousy he called one evening to extend a rather prickly olive branch.

"I'm sorry," Michael answered him. "I know it's hard on you, for all your independence. But you will remember how often you've rejected *my* advice. You must allow me to reject yours. This is something your mother and I have to work out for ourselves."

"But what can Mummy do?" Seymour raised his voice shrilly in their dark corner of the club bar. "She says you've made up the whole thing about her and Mr. Jones because you want an excuse to see Mrs. Parr!"

"That's *her* story," Michael replied softly, closing his lips in anger.

"You mean it's not true? You mean there *is* something between Mummy and Mr. Jones?"

Michael watched the dismay that broke through the superiority of Seymour's expression. Pity, pity, it would be the end of him. But he knew how dangerous it would be to injure Seymour's faith in Flora.

"I'm not saying that," he insisted. "But people who've been married as long as we have sometimes run into these difficulties. There's nothing anyone else can do to help."

"You mean you've reached the 'dangerous age'? I know about that. But which of you has reached it? You or Mummy?"

"Maybe we both have."

"Then it's *true* about Mummy and Mr. Jones?"

"No, I don't say that."

"What *do* you say?"

"Look, Seymour," Michael said wearily. "Why do you want to hang around Long Island this summer? Why don't you and Rex take a trip? Out west to a ranch? Or maybe Canada? I'll blow you to it. I'll be glad to."

"You must think I'm easily bribed," Seymour sneered, "if I'd fall for that one. I'll tell Mummy, of course. And I will assume that this crude offer of cash is proof that her 'story,' as you call it, is entirely true. You have made up an atrocious lie to justify your own debauchery!"

"Seymour, Seymour," Michael protested, shaking his head. "Don't say things that you're going to regret. Remember, I *am* your father."

"Well, you aren't behaving like it!" The boy rose proudly.

"I know where *my* place is this summer. Right with Mummy. And if you don't mind, I'd like to pay for my ginger ale!"

Michael was left alone, staring at the quarter which the irate boy had flung on the table, until he was summoned to the telephone to talk to his own mother. Gertrude sounded high and hurt and sharp; she had come in from Bradley Bay particularly to see him. He protested his dinner engagement.

"I know all about your dinner engagements," she snapped. "And they're not going to take precedence over explaining to your own mother why you're making such a stupid mess of your life. You can call Alida Parr right now and tell her that you'll be a few minutes late. If you don't, I'll call her myself!"

Michael knew only too well that she would do this and, sighing, he made his way uptown to the small, bright apartment to which she had moved years before after deeding her house, over family protest, to him and Flora. It always made him a bit sad to see the large inherited things confined to those two little rooms: the big Georgian silver which Gertrude polished herself, the tapestry after Fragonard, the nineteenth century paintings of Arabs and of Venetian canals. It was difficult not to think of his mother as caring more for her possessions than she did. He had offended her once, after accidentally breaking a china bird, by exclaiming: "But it's so dear and ugly, and you love it so!" It had not been pleasing to Gertrude, this glimpse of herself as brave and disciplined and rather pathetically caring about a few old relics, as keeping up, at any cost, a sad, proud little glitter. But there was nothing sad or in the least pathetic that evening about her frown or snapping blue eyes.

"I should think, Mother," he pointed out when she finally gave him a chance, "that you, of all people, would appreciate the delicacy of my position. You were always sympathetic to Flora's first husband."

Gertrude paused, taken aback. "You mean Flora really *has* been misconducting herself? You *know* that?"

"I know it."

"Oh." But Gertrude, torn with conflicting feelings, found refuge in irritation. "Well, I always warned you about her! I did from the beginning!"

"You're quite right. You did."

She puffed nervously at her cigarette for a few moments and then angrily crushed it out. "Well, she must have been very discreet," she concluded. "*I* haven't heard a word about it. Even from your aunts."

"Oh, she's been discreet. I grant her that."

"Then why can't *you* be?" Gertrude scrambled hastily out of these doubtful waters to the welcome sands of a scolding. "Why can't you behave in a civilized fashion? What do you think you're doing to Seymour? And to yourself? Holing up in your club and making a fool of yourself over Alida Parr?"

"Please, Mother!"

"Don't 'please' me! Do you want to ruin yourself with Ambrose and the bank just to spite Flora?"

"You condone Flora's conduct?"

"Don't be a perfect idiot." Gertrude jumped up to get another cigarette. "I condone nothing at all. I simply don't see why, as a man of the world, you have to upset the whole applecart because Flora's being Flora. A marriage is a marriage, after all. Think of all the European husbands who find it occasionally advisable to look the other way."

"But I'm not a European," Michael retorted. "And I'm not a Catholic, and my son's almost grown up, and I can see no reason why I should continue to pay lip service to a marriage vow that Flora no longer considers binding on herself."

"No *longer!*"

"Oh, I know!" Michael cried, suddenly exploding with anger. "You think she's been cheating for years! You can't imagine why a poor creature like myself should start objecting now. Well, I *do* object! And much as you may laugh and sneer, I've found someone who understands my objecting. Someone who understands *me.* Someone who thinks there may be something more for me in life than being Flora's lap dog!"

"And that's Alida?"

"Yes! That's Alida!"

Gertrude's expression changed from the irritation with which he could always cope to a solicitude that undermined him. "My dear boy," she said in her gentlest tone, and he shivered with resentment, "have you really persuaded yourself that you're in love with her? Don't you know that every man whose wife has done what Flora's done has to prove himself with someone else?"

"Stop!" he shouted. "Will you stop?" He stared at her, his eyes wide with fear. For as always, she would expose him, tear away with mocking affection the tattered cloak of his aspirations, dissuading him from the impossible, urging him to avoid the laughter of the crowd and remain safely the poor thing he was. And if he doubted her, if he persisted, could she not always carry her point by rising and disrobing and proving to him once and for all that he dared not look? "I refuse to discuss Alida!" he exclaimed. "She's a part of my life you could never understand!"

It struck him as he left her and hurried away to Alida's restaurant that he was turning into a repertory ham, that he was constantly running in and out of wings to clap on a helmet, to seize a spear, to declaim. And yet everything, he knew, was only a rehearsal for the big moment, the culminating crisis that Danny Jones could not indefinitely postpone. What in God's name could Danny still be waiting for? Had he not done *enough* to him?

"Don't worry about your mother," Alida said when he told her where he had been. "She's just being maternal. You should have heard *mine*. If things ever work out in this mess, you and I are going to be handing each other the damndest set of in-laws!"

When he arrived at his office the following morning he found a message on his desk to report immediately to Mr. Meredith. The president's door was closed, and as he pushed it open he sensed the sudden silence. Meredith, his face yellow and drawn, looked up from his desk.

"Of course, you know Mrs. Winters, Michael," he began in a tired voice. "I don't know if you've met Mr. Lincoln."

Michael felt something like exhilaration. He bowed almost gallantly. "Good morning, Mrs. Winters!"

"I hope you will *still* think it's a good morning, Mr. Farish," she said grimly. "After you've heard what Mr. Lincoln has to say. I hope you will!"

She sat before him, her large, bulbous face a solid of still tenseness, all the tenser for the shiny blackness of her unfashionable hat with its just quivering plume. Her voice had a high, dreary, not-to-be-interrupted tone, but he felt that at any moment it might jar into the screech of a parrot heard through a damp jungle and that her plump, moving hands, the only parts of her that did move, would suddenly snatch at him.

Mr. Lincoln was one of those lawyers who liked to play Clarence Darrow to a world of juries. He squeezed his long, worn cheeks; he ran a hand constantly through grey hair that should have been shaggy; he crossed and recrossed his legs and stared up at the ceiling for minutes on end with pursed lips. Without even turning now to face Michael he pointed a bony finger at a paper on Meredith's desk.

"Ever seen that, Mr. Farish?"

Michael walked over and picked up the paper. It was a typed copy of his letter to Mr. Winters. He did not even pretend to read it, but dropped it back on Meredith's desk. "Certainly. I remember it well."

"Was it ever sent to Mr. Winters?"

"No."

"Care to tell us why not?"

"It wasn't possible." Michael seated himself in the chair opposite Meredith's desk. He appeared to address himself to the latter, but Meredith only stared down at his blotter. "The letter was dictated by Mr. Winters and signed by me. In his presence. It constituted what I believe you lawyers call a 'delivery.' Later, Mr. Winters gave it back to me to have it retyped on the trust company's stationery."

"And that was done?"

"It was."

"But it's not your custom to mail out letters that have been typed and signed?"

"It's not our custom to maintain correspondence with the hereafter. Mr. Winters died before the letter could be mailed."

"I see. Very amusing, Mr. Farish. You didn't think Mr. Winters's family might have been interested in his final adjustment of your commissions?"

"It was all spelled out in the will."

"I suggest there's a difference."

"You refer to the word 'total' in the letter? I can't agree with you."

"But you *see* the point!" Mr. Lincoln's voice rose like sudden thunder. "You merely glance at a letter that you wrote sixteen years ago and grasp immediately that it contains a word that is missing from the will! A *vital* word, Mr. Farish. I suggest that this matter has been on your conscience for some time!"

"You forget that I have had reason to consider the question only a little while ago," Michael retorted coolly. "It was pointed out to me by the same eager young man who undoubtedly brought it to your attention. I refer to Mr. Daniel Jones who recently severed his connection with this institution."

"I am not stating who brought the matter to Mrs. Winters's attention. I will state, however, that in my opinion it was a person who had her welfare more at heart than you have had."

"In *your* opinion, yes."

"Well, how can you justify yourself?" Mr. Lincoln exploded altogether now. "In placing your own construction on a letter of which you had the only copy? Was it not your obvious duty to show it to Mrs. Winters? Or at the very least to submit it to a court?"

"I didn't think so."

"Well, you may find yourself thinking so when this business is aired in the Surrogate's Court! You'll be very lucky, in my opinion, if it's not held to be fraudulent concealment!"

"If I had wanted to conceal the letter," Michael said with a shrug, "I could have destroyed it."

"Well, you did the next best thing!"

"This is becoming acrimonious and hardly pleasant." Michael made a little bow of apology to Mrs. Winters. "Obviously, you will take the matter to court. Let us wait and see what the surrogate has to say. At least it should be interesting."

Mr. Lincoln's expression indicated that Darrow himself might have been confounded by such impudence. "Well!" he exclaimed as he rose to his feet. "Well, I guess that's that! Shall we be taking our leave, Mrs. Winters?"

"Just a moment, Mr. Lincoln." Mrs. Winters raised a judicial hand. "To you this is only a legal matter. To me it is something more. Mr. Farish was originally recommended to my husband by his own grandfather, Dr. Lear. The old gentleman spoke in the highest terms of his integrity and trustworthiness. Mr. Winters and I relied on his word." She turned now, magnificently, on Michael. "I want to ask you, Michael Farish, how you think your grandfather would feel if he were alive today and knew that you had robbed me of three hundred thousand dollars!"

"I haven't robbed you of a penny."

"Do you deny that my husband's trust is the poorer by the amount of your improper commissions?"

"Certainly, I deny it. If we had not been able to take our rental commissions, we would have turned the real estate over to a collecting agent who would have charged the trust the same amount. Probably more. The question that Mr. Lincoln is raising is simply whether the money should have gone to an agent or gone to us. In either case the trust would have paid."

Mrs. Winters looked puzzled, and puzzlement did not suit her majestic mien. She turned to Mr. Lincoln. "Is that true?"

"I should say it's hardly relevant."

"But tell her it's true!" Michael cried out suddenly. "At least do that much!"

"I'm not interested in doing anything for you, Mr. Farish."

"But he doesn't deny it, Mrs. Winters!" Michael exclaimed. "He doesn't deny it!"

"I cannot see that it affects the question of your fraudulent concealment," Mr. Lincoln said testily. "A fiduciary is held to the strictest accounting in such matters. The law requires — "

"I know what the law requires!" Michael jumped up now and started pacing the room in sudden excitement. "Can't we have a little honesty? Just for a few minutes before we go to court? All right, I made a decision on my own. I was young and scared, and I made it in favor of the bank. Suppose it was wrong? It cost the trust nothing. But let's look at you, Mr. Lincoln. What did *you* do? You saw a chance to make the bank cough up three hundred thousand dollars, and you grabbed it. Why not? It's pure gravy. You don't have to pay it over to a real estate agent *now*. The Winters trust will have had sixteen years of real estate management free and for nothing! And you will have earned a big fat fee! Fine!" He clapped his hands together a bit wildly. "But don't come in here mouthing about fiduciaries and what the law requires! I'm not impressed!"

Mrs. Winters rose now, too, and turned to the door. "Good day, Mr. Meredith," she said in her stateliest manner. "I'm sure this scene has been as distressing to you as it has to me. It is unhappy that our long relationship should end in a law suit."

"Unhappy!" Michael cried after her. "It's the luckiest break you ever had! You're getting something for nothing, aren't you? That should be the Winters motto!"

"Mr. Lincoln! *Come!*"

As the door closed behind Mrs. Winters and her lawyer Michael turned to his shattered superior. Meredith still would not look at him; he continued to stare down at the white blankness of his unspotted blotter, shaking his head again and again.

"Michael, Michael," he murmured. "Have you gone mad?"

"Don't worry, sir. If there's a surcharge I'll pay it. It may wipe me out, but I'll pay it."

Meredith seemed not to have heard him. "But to antagonize her so wantonly!" he moaned. "If there ever was a chance of settling with her, it's gone now. And Jones. What about Jones? Did you know that *he* knew?" Michael nodded. "And you let him go? No, worse! I remember, he told me! You *antagonized* him!"

"But he was so cocky and impudent."

"*Michael!*" Meredith looked up at him with eyes that quivered with panic. "Michael, do you realize this may ruin us!"

"Not *us*, sir. I'll take the blame. Why shouldn't I? It's all mine, anyway. And I resign. I resign as of now!"

"Oh, Michael!"

"Do you hear me, sir. I'm resigning!"

"What good does that do? *Now?*"

"Well, for whatever good it may do you, there it is. I'll write it out and send it up to you."

Fifteen minutes later it was done, and Michael, ignoring his telephone, Amelia, even the doorman with the urgent message, hurried out of the building and across Wall Street to turn and face it. His eyes rose slowly from row to row of the massive Romanesque arches; he took in the rugged whole of its beetling façade, its great craggy, disapproving face and laughed aloud.

"Goodbye, old pyramid," he whispered. "You can be Grandpa Farish's pyramid. He wanted that. Even poor Daddy's, though he didn't. But not mine. Not now. Not *mine!*"

14

WHEN MICHAEL AT LAST succeeded in convinc-
ing Alida that his rupture with the bank was final, that there
was nothing further to be gained by appeasement or delay
from either her father or Jimmie, she came forth suddenly
with a bold plan that she had been working out with her
lawyer. It was simply this: after Jimmie had departed for a
fishing trip in Canada with his friend Stark Terry, an
annual expedition that he would on no account put off, she
would quietly take the two children and their nurse to Idlewild and board a plane for Mexico City. A useful widowed
aunt, a sister of her mother's, Mrs. Fenester, had agreed to
fly down in advance to see to the accommodations and to
chaperon her niece during the visit. The house of a Mexican
friend of Alida's who was now in Europe had been loaned
to her, complete with staff. She showed Michael a colored
photograph, and he had to agree that it was beautiful: low,
white and modern, a series of connected rectangles in the
brilliant Pedregal gardens with a living room cantilevered out
over a sapphire pool. Once there she would file suit for
divorce, instructing Jimmie that she would not return to
New York until he consented to the terms of her decree.
Michael was to follow her in three weeks, but in Mexico he
was to stay in a hotel while he sued for his own divorce. The
faithful aunt was to chaperon them scrupulously on sight-

seeing trips and in restaurants. If all worked out they could be married in Mexico City and back in New York for the opening of the children's schools.

"Suppose Jimmie finds out?" he protested. "Suppose the police are at Idlewild?"

"Suppose they are?" Alida shrugged. "What have I lost? We come home, that's all."

"But the children! What a humiliation!"

"I'll have to take that chance. If it *is* a chance."

And, of course, she was right. The execution of the plan was as smooth as its conception. If Jimmie was having her shadowed, his agency had not been efficient, for he learned nothing of Alida's departure until his own return from Canada. Then he called up Michael in a high, tense, almost screaming tone.

"I'll have you prosecuted for this, you son of a bitch!"

"Call Alida's lawyer, Jimmie," Michael said as prearranged. "That's all I can tell you. Call Alida's lawyer."

He was not bothered again by Jimmie, for he departed himself for Mexico shortly afterwards. He mailed letters to his mother and Flora from the airport and drank whiskey intermittently during the seven-hour flight, enjoying as fully as he could what he was quite aware would be only the fleeting satisfaction of turning his back on ancient obligations. When he saw Alida and her aunt in the waiting room to greet him, both in gay Mexican skirts, he was quickly reminded of new ones.

"Did you get your securities out of New York?" Alida asked as she gave him a quick peck on the cheek. He nodded. "Good boy."

The matter, however, had been a rather sore one. Alida's lawyer had advised him that it would be folly to leave any property in New York that Flora might attach. He had suggested that his stocks and bonds, for example, be shipped across the river to New Jersey. Michael had objected.

"But of course, they must!" Alida had exclaimed. "Flora may try anything when she finds you've gone."

"It seems so shifty."

"Shifty? It's elementary. Do you know what *I'm* doing?"

"I'd rather not know, Alida."

But he had acted as they suggested. He had carried his securities to New Jersey himself, and he had felt like a thief in doing so. It seemed a pity that Alida should have reminded him of this straight off, just as he was trying to feel a new man in the thin, Mexican air. But he had little time to think of it. Mrs. Fenester had just placed a bottle of pills firmly in his hand and was advising him in graphic detail of the health problems of Mexico.

It had not been difficult for Alida to persuade her aunt to come to Mexico. Mrs. Fenester had married young and so had her two children; alone, rich and a widow at sixty, she was a fair example of an American type that has for decades amused, confused and outraged the males of other continents. Loquacious, self-possessed, dogmatic, healthy, with uninteresting good looks and uninteresting good clothes, she had been four times around the world, carrying the same stories and the same judgments, as unaffected by her travels as the great planes that bore her through the ether. Mrs. Fenester had seen riots in Hong Kong and starvation in India; she had been in typhoons and tiger hunts; she had even met, though without shaking hands, head-hunters and the chiefs of communist states. She had observed it all carefully and described it all accurately. But it was simply impossible to listen to her; she was like an album of postcards without a single snapshot.

Her attitude toward Michael could be described as tolerant. Michael might be charming, but Mrs. Fenester did not
recognize charm. Michael might be amusing, but she did not
discriminate between people who amused her and bores. But
if Alida wanted him, it was enough for her faithful aunt. The
good lady professed to set great store by morals and the
sanctity of the home, yet she saw no necessary connection
between the principles that she loved to enunciate and the
behavior of the female members of her own family. And, of
course, it was convenient to have a man to order meals and
tip and to act as a fresh audience to thrice-told tales.

"I know, Alida, you've heard my story about that strange
little man with the blue fez I met on the plane to Ankara,"
she would say. "But, if you don't mind, I think it might
amuse Michael."

"Certainly, Auntie."

"Oh, yes, Mrs. Fenester, do tell me."

Their tripartite life fell into a regular tourist's pattern of
churches and restaurants. There was no legal business to
attend to in view of Jimmie's ominous silence. In fact,
Michael's only communication from home had been a brief,
tart note from his mother to tell him he was a damn fool. He
thought more than once of this through the long evenings in
the night clubs on Mrs. Fenester's comprehensive list. The
latter found it twice as much fun to go to two night clubs
as one, three times as much to go to three. For her there
seemed to be no diminishing returns.

Eventually he brought himself to ask Alida about her
money arrangements. He had to satisfy himself that she
wasn't spending her last penny on the elaborate scale of
living that she had established in Mexico. He need not have
worried. She had moved three hundred thousand dollars in

securities out of a joint account in her and Jimmie's names to her own account in a New Jersey bank which she would not identify even to Michael. It seemed incredible that Jimmie should not have forestalled her in this, but as Alida pointed out, people who thought all the time about money were just the ones to miss the most obvious tricks. She had done the same thing with the stocks that Ambrose had given her as custodian for the children. And, in addition, she had her own income and a supplementary allowance that she had extracted from her father. Not to speak of Jimmie's mother's jewelry, a mere loan from Ambrose, which had nonetheless been removed to Mexico in a small, tightly clutched black bag. It seemed to Michael that possession might be even more than nine tenths of the law.

"Now don't fuss," she warned him. "There's nothing that can't be returned. It's simply a question of maneuvering for the best bargaining position. I think you'll agree that Jimmie has lost Round One."

Michael was beginning to wonder if Jimmie Parr had been the only loser. He had a curious feeling which he tried to attribute to the altitude, but which persisted long after he should have become adapted to it, that he, like Jimmie, had been left behind in New York. He found it difficult to identify himself with the bright colors of Mexico, either with the faded pink and yellow grandeurs of its Spanish past or with the blues and whites of its rectangular modern; he was like a dark brooding protestant crow in an aviary of squawking macaws. This feeling was intensified by the contrasting enthusiasm of Alida and her aunt: they shopped happily with large wicker baskets; they clapped their hands at night clubs to Mexican dancers; they read sad, sentimental books on Maximilian and Carlotta and discussed their unhappy fate as they paced the memory-haunted terrace of the castle at Chapultepec. If they remained, for all their Mexican sympathies, as unmistakably Yankee as himself, there was a piercing note of the Latin in their resounding appreciations.

On their day excursions Michael would stand apart from his companions and their loquacious guide; he cared nothing for dates and statistics and wanted to contemplate in silence the engrossing monuments that they visited. But however fascinated he might be with the cathedral at Puebla, the shrines of Cholula, the Aztec pyramids, the gaudy Rivera murals, it was a depressed fascination. In the incense-laden interior of the churches, with their glittering Churrigueresque altars and their great, grotesque dolls of bleeding Christs, he felt in the presence of a strange, hostile god.

"As far as I can make out," Mrs. Fenester observed as she closed her guidebook, "the history of this country has been one long revolution. It makes it easy to remember, anyway."

"Violence," said Alida. "Violence in everything. Even in their churches."

"Oh, especially in the churches!" Michael exclaimed, but when the other two looked at him in surprise, he quickly buried his nose in a map.

At Teotihuacán he left Alida and her aunt in a market of souvenirs and climbed alone to the top of the great pyramid of the sun. It was cool and windy, and the sweeping view of the green plain and the ring of surrounding mountains made him feel giddy in his exalted isolation. It was as if by the hard climb he had finally forced himself on the attention of the angry god of this country, and here, too, on the very spot where the sacrificial obsidian knife had cut out so many thousands of human hearts. The great panorama spread out before him had been a last view for these victims; drugged, bedecked in flowers, they had made their grotesque rhythmic ascent to the presence of this terrible god to find peace from the high wind and the roaring in their ears. What god would permit it? *Any* god! Michael closed his eyes and breathed in the reassurance that there was always the answer of death. It was the only answer to Mexico, the only relief from the glare of colors. That was her message: violence and death, the same for the Aztecs, the same for Spain. In Rivera the sacrifice on the pyramid was always balanced with the Catholic auto-da-fé. The obsidian knife was quicker than the flames, the sacrificial flowers less humiliating than the heretic's peaked cap; there was nothing else to choose between Montezuma and Rome. If the fury of religious struggle ended in the stake, the agony of social strife ended in the robot life of the blocky, marching workers of the communist murals. Both were death, but death was the only answer to violence. If Mexico seemed a reproach to himself, even a sneer, was it not because violence was what he had been avoiding all his life, violence that was man's estate, violence that was the shunned heritage of his father? And without violence was it possible to achieve the release of death? Would the god accept the sacrifice of his heart even now, on the top of his sacrificial pyramid, or did he read his sentence in the chill, rejecting wind to go down the steps and take up again his disembodied career until he had found a heart that the priest's knife could reach? He rose to go back, pausing for one more look across the plain. How absurdly simple, he thought. One had to live before one could die.

"Did you really go to the top?" Alida asked.

"All the way."

"So it *was* you. You seemed so alone, way up there." She looked worried. "So tiny."

"I *felt* tiny."

"You shouldn't do it, you know," Mrs. Fenester reproved him. "Until you're used to this altitude. You may be younger than I am, but you're still getting to the age when men have to watch their hearts. My husband wasn't much older than you — "

"But I *am* used to the altitude," Michael interrupted firmly. "That's the difference."

Only two days later he had a rather similar experience. He was walking alone on the Paseo de la Reforma one afternoon when it began to rain, and he took refuge in a movie house. An American short subject was being shown, a nature film dealing with insect and animal life in a simple rural pond. The narrator's tone was familiar and condescending, and his point of view was the conventionally anthropomorphic one: animals were interesting only when their actions seemed a ludicrous imitation of humans. But what kept Michael's attention fastened to the screen after the first few minutes — not at all as he had wanted, for he had expected to sleep — was the contrast between what the animals were doing and what the narrator was saying. They seemed all unconscious of his benign chuckles and of his vulgar chatter about "Junior" and "Grandpa" and the inevitable mother-in-law; they seemed, ever tense and jerky, with big, beady, concentrated eyes, wholly absorbed in the task of eating each other. The fly into the beetle into the snake into the frog into the heron, it reminded him of the Chinese wooden figures he had been given as a child which he kept taking apart to find smaller ones within. And it seemed so unending; there was never any respite for the poor creatures in the business of eating and being eaten, only tense, trembling moments while black eyes, unblinking, watched for their prey, while still, crouched bodies waited to strike or be stricken. It seemed to Michael, tensely watching now, that the process was ultimately the same whether one ate or was eaten; if life could only live on life, the very act of being was cannibal. Sex, relegated to brief seasons, in snatched moments, seemed almost inconsequential in the terrible battle of the jaws. Nor was there any difference in this between the sexes; males and females, of equal strength, tore at each other with equal ferocity. When he came out of the theater the clouds had gone, and he blinked in the unexpected sunlight. On a raft adrift in mid-ocean, would he, with other humans, eat the weakest? Or would he simply want to? Or would he be himself eaten? Ah, that was it; that was the saving grace. One did not *have* to do such things; that was the beautiful simplicity of being weak. One could always die. He stopped at a bar for several drinks.

That night, when he arrived at the dining room of the Hotel del Prado, his head felt distinctly wooden. Alida and Mrs. Fenester were there before him and in festive mood.

"I think frogs' legs," Mrs. Fenester was saying. "Or what about the *cervelles?*"

"No, I feel like kidneys tonight."

Michael shuddered and closed the menu. He would have an omelet. Or, better yet, a salad. Looking up, as the ladies chattered with the waiter, at the great Rivera mural of the artist's dream in Alameda Park, at all the shiny faces and beady eyes, like the creatures in the nature film, surrounding the central figures of the skeleton in lady's finery and the small boy, he was startled at the confirmation of his afternoon's feeling. That was the thing about Mexicans: they could face what man was! When he looked at Alida, he saw that she was watching him narrowly.

"Is something wrong, dear?" she asked.

"Nothing at all. I was just thinking how gay you both seemed tonight."

"No reason for that, is there, Auntie?" Alida and Mrs. Fenester exchanged smiles. "We just had a wire from New York. Jimmie has filed suit for a separation. On the grounds of desertion."

"Desertion?" Michael blinked at both of them. "Well, that's not so bad, is it?"

"As long as he sticks to desertion," Mrs. Fenester answered firmly. "Don't think he hasn't got someone down here watching you and Alida! And don't think at the very first indiscretion he won't add a juicy little something to that petition!"

"Michael knows all that, Auntie."

"I know, my dear, but one can't be too careful."

"We *are* being careful. That's why you're here."

In the silence that followed this Michael felt that something was expected of him. "Will you defend it?"

"Of course I'll defend it!" Alida retorted. "I'll defend it with everything I've got!"

"You mean, you're going to keep the jewelry and the securities?"

"But those things are yours, anyway, my dear!" Mrs. Fenester turned on Michael as indignantly as if he had been Jimmie Parr. "What are you talking about? Do you expect *Jimmie* to wear the jewelry?"

"No. But he might want them for his daughter."

"Alida will take care of that. After all, Julia is *her* daughter, too."

"Or his wife might want them. If he marries again."

"And have them go out of the family?" Mrs. Fenester looked as if her gloomiest doubts about Michael had at last been justified. "Is that what you want? Alida's lovely things on some tramp?"

"Auntie, you don't get the point," Alida said impatiently. "Neither of you do. There are two issues. One is the property. That's only a matter of trading. That's a question of *things*. But the big issue is the divorce. That's harder. That's a question of words."

"Words?"

"Words, petitions, answers, law." Alida took a crumpled telegram out of her evening bag and tossed it on the table before him. "Jimmie has started the word game. 'Desertion.' 'Cruel and inhuman treatment.' And he's just itching to add 'adultery.'" She shrugged. "Well, he may have started the game. But that doesn't mean he's going to finish it."

"What words will *you* use?" Michael asked.

Alida looked from him to her aunt who seemed, he thought, suddenly embarrassed. "Shall I tell him, Auntie?"

"Oh, that's your affair, my dear. All yours."

"Very well." She regarded Michael with a searching gaze in which he could read more than a touch of defiance. "My lawyer has already drawn the answer. In it I accuse Jimmie of misconduct justifying my removal with the children to Mexico." She paused, with a fixed little smile. "I accuse him of having 'unnatural relations' with Stark Terry."

Michael stared at her, moistening his lips. "And *has* he?"

"Who is to say?" Alida shrugged again elaborately. "In my opinion his relations with all that group have been highly unnatural. I keep a diary, and I can show all the fishing trips, the club evenings, the drinking. I can show a lot more, too."

"But can you show *that*?"

"That's for the court to decide. I can't cross every 't' and dot every 'i,' no."

"Then it's not fair!" he cried. "Even if Jimmie wins, that's the kind of mud that's going to stick!"

"The answer will be submitted to him before it's filed," Alida retorted. "It's entirely up to Jimmie whether it ever gets in the papers."

"Then it's blackmail!"

"All right, it's blackmail! But who drove me to it?"

Michael caught sight again of the skeleton in the center of the mural and shuddered. Mrs. Fenester, embarrassed, tried to keep her dignity and composure by taking little sips of water and gazing distantly across the room.

"Alida," he argued in a more reasonable tone, "you don't see what you're doing. Jimmie's just the kind of man who will suffer most from such a charge. It'll kill him."

"Well, let it!" she cried angrily. "He's always accusing other men of that kind of thing! Let him feel what it's like! When you deal with a man who makes a career of tossing labels, you have to toss them, too. It may be a silly game, but by God I can play it as well as he. 'Cruel and inhuman treatment'!" She snorted contemptuously. "Maybe he'll learn what those words mean!"

"I don't like it, Alida." He turned suddenly on her aunt. "Do you like it, Mrs. Fenester?"

"Oh, don't ask *me!*" Startled, she threw her hands in the air. "Mr. Fenester always said I was no good at these intellectual games. 'Follow your heart, Sylvane,' he used to say. 'You can't go wrong, then!'"

"And what does your heart tell you now?"

"Auntie's entirely on my side," Alida said brusquely. "She knew all about it from the beginning. But before you start condemning me, you might as well know the full story. I'm not relying solely on my answer to drive Jimmie to the wall.

Oh, no. My lawyer is going to make it very plain to him that we're also retaining a public relations counsel to see that my charges get the widest possible publicity!"

"He can't be a very reputable lawyer!"

"He's not! It's too tough a fight for a reputable lawyer!"

"Alida." He leaned over and stared down at the table, closing his eyes. "Alida, I'm serious. I beg you not to do this thing."

"And who are you to beg me not to do it?" she demanded furiously. Mrs. Fenester now hid her face entirely behind the menu. "Who was it who lost his job in the bank? Who upset the applecart while I was waiting to bring Daddy and Ambrose around to our side? And for whose sake do you think I risked losing my children and my reputation to come down here? And *you* have the nerve to sit there and 'beg me not to do this'!"

There was nothing that Michael could say to this and nothing that he did say. He lay awake most of the night afterwards and decided that she was incontestably right. He was not only in her hands; he had placed himself there. It was some consolation, anyway, to know the worst.

The following day there was a bullfight, and he lunched early at his hotel before meeting Alida and her aunt at the arena. He had two letters from New York, one from Flora and one from the trust company, and each required its fortifying cocktail. Flora's note was short and bitter. Danny Jones, it appeared, had left her. She congratulated Michael, in wry terms, on his own better luck and signified her consent to a divorce. Her lawyer, she wrote, would get in touch with his. When he opened the second envelope from Hudson River Trust and took out the letter, a newspaper clipping fell to the table. Picking it up he recognized the small print of the *New York Law Journal*. "Matter of Winters": it was the surrogate's decision on the commissions question. Breathless, he read through the long statement of facts and paused, incredulous, before this paragraph:

> The claim of the widow is denied. The record abundantly reveals that her husband was a man closely acquainted with banking practice. He certainly must have known that the collection of rentals was above and beyond the regular services performed by a corporate fiduciary and that special compensation had been allowed by the legislature. There is no question that the limitation in his will applied only to ordinary commissions, and to hold that he meant to deny his fiduciary all extra compensation for managing real estate would be to give too great a significance to the word "total" in the letter dictated just prior to his death. It might have been better practice for Farish to have submitted the letter to the widow, but under the circumstances his failure to do so cannot be deemed a breech of fiduciary duty.

He turned, dazed, to Charlie Meredith's letter:

> Congratulations, my dear boy! You were right from the beginning! And kept your head "when all around you were losing theirs and blaming it on you." Mrs. Winters may not even appeal. She's furious at the bill Ted Lincoln sent her and is telling everyone he trumped up the case to earn a fee. We all want you to come back to Hudson and forget the whole thing. Ambrose Parr says not to worry about him. He says Jimmie's and Alida's marriage was on the rocks, even without you. And here's what I'm getting at, my dear fellow. Alida's mother and I have decided that we feel the same way. We have talked it all over, and we

feel that you and Alida have to work out your own lives without interference from the old folks. We happen to feel strongly about divorce, but we also realize that we belong to a generation that is rapidly passing. Our mores cannot necessarily be yours. And we are both deeply gratified to hear from Sylvane Fenester that your conduct in Mexico has been beyond reproach in its tact and discretion. God bless you, my boy.

Staring out the window down the Avenida Juárez, Michael was able at last to identify the particular discouragement that invaded him. In the spring of his second form year at Averhill he had been sent home, after a series of colds, for a check-up and diagnosis. The family doctor had looked grave and finally pronounced that he was suffering from a virulent sinus infection for which the only cure was Arizona. The dear old man had even advised against a school there as too tiring, recommending instead life on a ranch with a tutor, possibly for several years. To Michael the prospect of hot air, solitude, rest and reading, no boys, no marks, no jangled sounds, no hate, had been nirvana, and the fact that he was at the same time overwhelmed with family sympathy was the final piece of pink icing on his great cake of relief. But, of course, it did not last. A specialist had been called in who had scoffed at the diagnosis; the family doctor, he had whispered to Michael's mother, was notoriously past his prime. It was no secret in the profession that the old man had an obsession for recommending the places and cures that he longed for himself. As for Michael, he could jolly well spend a week in bed and then go back to school. He was right as rain.

He met Alida and her aunt outside the arena. They arrived, once again, in wide Mexican skirts with jangling silver bracelets and a Mexican gentleman of smooth middle age called Mr. Silva who represented Hudson River Trust in the capital. He was very gay and full of knowledge of the arena and even managed to imply that Mrs. Fenester, with her faded but loquacious memories of Madrid, of Manolete, of greater days, was a welcome mentor in the Mexican bull ring. At any rate they all seemed to be in unison; they applauded frantically the parade of the matadors; they shouted together and waved programs and scarfs when the first snorting bull bounded onto the sand and looked suspiciously about for his human antagonists. Michael tried to find consolation in anonymity, but as the afternoon wore on he felt that something extra-ordinary was happening inside him. It was not exactly that he was turning into a bull; he had not the arrogance to imag-ine that with muscle and black weight and two great horns he could send young men with ripped capes scattering on agile feet behind the nearest shelters. But it was unquestion-ably the bull with which he identified himself, the bewildered bull in what was turning now into one of the worst of fights, the bull whom seven clumsy saber thrusts had only tortured, the panting, desperate bull, with its own wide cape of scarlet blood clinging to its raven flanks, pawing the earth, stum-bling, with the derisive shouts of several thousand angry spec-tators in its ears. As the crowd roared with anger and frustra-tion, as they hissed matador after matador and screamed at them to leave the ring, Michael felt with a detached numbness that he was one with each bloody, staggering beast, and his own kind, his own chattering, screeching Latin brothers were so many monkeys, so many saber-toothed, carnivorous monkeys, whose souls could only have jointly deserved a black infinity of extinction.

"But see how many Americans are here today," Mr. Silva

protested. "Will they go home and call this a bullfight? Oh, shame. Shame for Mexico!"

"Look at that man! He's afraid of the bull!" Mrs. Fenester turned to explain the action to Michael. "You see how he keeps stepping away from it. That isn't the way at all. He should remain in one spot. Watch his feet, that's how you tell a bullfighter. The feet should be still. Only the arms should move on a pass." And she moved her arms back and forth, jostling Michael, passing a bull as she had learned from Manolete. "Do you see it, Michael? And when it's well done — ah, then you know it immediately. Then it's art. Then it's ballet!"

"It ought to be time for the warning," Alida observed, looking at her watch. "This boob has had his five minutes."

And just then the aviso sounded, the first warning that the matador must make his kill or give up. It was the eighth bull, the last; the air was already dark, and the crowd was tired and angry with disappointment. People were starting to leave, edging their way slowly down the aisles, laughing, dropping beer bottles. Pillows, like black meteors, whizzed through the air over their heads and landed in the ring below. Some landed in the crowd, and one struck Michael on the side of the head, a shocking, hard blow that dazed him and brought sudden tears to his eyes.

"Oh, my dear sir, I'm so sorry, I am *so* sorry," Mr. Silva cried.

Michael stared at him blankly. "But you didn't do it, did you?"

"No, of course not, good heavens! I'm apologizing for those that did."

"There's Mexican manners for you!" Alida exclaimed, laughing, but seeing that Michael was upset, her expression changed. "Oh, I'm sorry, darling," she murmured, "did it really hurt you? Come on, let's go home. It's a rotten fight anyhow."

"I'm ready," her aunt agreed, looking up at the dirty, darkening sky. "Besides, I think it's going to rain."

"No!" Michael cried suddenly. "I want to stay! I want to see it!"

The other three looked at each other in surprise.

"It's all right, Auntie," Alida said, smiling. "It's only another minute."

Michael turned away now and ignored them. He could only see the bull which had less than a minute to wait. The animal stood there, panting, too tired to move, and the matador pointed his sword again, rising to his tiptoes, as tense and formal, as stylized and beautiful as if he were trying to kill for the first time, as if the arena, not laughing and leaving, were silent and poised, ready to award him an ear, to make him walk around once, twice, to an inundation of flowers and hats. The blade flashed in the murky air and glanced off the bull's back, and the stunned animal hardly moved. For just a moment the departing crowd paused; for just a moment there was silence as they took in the glittering blade on the sand, and then the air was torn with the exasperation of final jeers. Michael saw Alida and her aunt and Mr. Silva rise; he jumped up himself, but only to see better. The gates opened, and he saw three oxen trot slowly out onto the sand to lead the bull away.

"Oh, for God's sake, Michael, let's go," he heard Alida's voice in his ear. "It's over, darling. Can't you see it's over?"

"No!"

And as he exclaimed this, he saw that he was right; he saw the arena darken with a sea of humanity. Young men, boys, from everywhere, swarmed over the wall and descended into the ring. The matador and his bull were surrounded by a mocking crowd; the former turned away in disgust and was forgotten. But not so the bull. One youth grabbed its tail; another tried to mount it; a third threw sawdust in its eyes. Michael, standing, closed his eyes and prayed passionately. "Dear God," he whispered, "*dear* God, make that animal charge and kill!" When he opened his eyes, his heart leaped to see the bull make one last, desperate charge, right into the thickest of the crowd. They fled as he approached, but not fast enough; two boys went down, and Michael in ecstasy felt that there was, after all, a God. But in another moment the boys had picked themselves up unhurt, and the bull was docilely following the oxen through the gates.

"Mr. Silva!" he cried. "He's made it, hasn't he?"

"Who?"

"The bull, of course."

"Oh, yes. It's a great disgrace."

"What will they do with him now?"

"They'll kill him, of course."

"But *why?*"

"Why? What else can they do? He's badly hurt. And, obviously, he can't fight again."

"Why not?"

"My dear Mr. Farish, he knows too much. Next time he might go for the man and not the cape."

Michael stared at him for a moment and then closed his eyes and fainted.

He had vague memories much later of being carried down a flight of stairs, one arm around Mr. Silva and the other around a stranger. There was also the recollection of sitting in the back seat of a car with his eyes closed and Mrs. Fenester's voice sounding very far away. Then he must have blacked out again, for he remembered nothing more until he regained consciousness on a sofa. Alida and a strange man were staring at him. She handed him a glass, and he drank some whiskey.

"It's all right, darling," Alida was saying in a soothing tone. "You're going to be fine. The doctor says it's just a touch of fever from the altitude and overdoing it. A day in bed, and you'll be right as rain."

He stared past her out the huge window and saw the lighted pool. "But this is your house!" he protested, almost in panic. "I'm not meant to be here! Alida, please, I must go!"

She smiled at him and then at the surprised doctor. "It's all right," she said again. She placed a cool hand on his brow. "I didn't tell you at the bullfight, but I had a telegram from my lawyer this morning. Jimmie's given in. He's dropped his suit and agreed to a Mexican divorce. On *my* terms. So you see, darling. It's all going to be all right!"

Michael turned away to the wall because he felt his eyes suddenly filling with tears. He could not explain to them that he had suddenly remembered the bull and how it was to be killed even though it had survived the fight and the dozens of hateful boys. But then he had learned on the pyramids to expect no mercy. Only, how could he explain it to them? How could he explain it to anybody?

15

IN JUNE OF THE following spring an item appeared in the social column of a New York evening paper that provoked considerable comment in Bradley Bay, especially in Gertrude Farish's circle. It read:

> We have just learned that Mr. and Mrs. Michael Farish are planning to spend the season in "Port of Call," Mrs. Farish's villa in Bradley Bay. "Port of Call," the friends will remember, was part of that very handsome settlement which Jimmie Parr signed without a murmur (Ahem!) when he and Alida parted company last fall. If Alida and her Michael care to stroll up the dunes a few hundred yards they can call on Alida's former father-in-law, Ambrose Parr, who has rented "Bonniecrest" again this season. If, on the other hand, they take a jaunt to the south they may chance on Michael's "ex," Flora Cameron Farish, who has kept her little cottage on Smith's Point. A happy summer should be had by all!

Michael sympathized with his mother, but he still thought her agitation was unreasonable. He could not entirely bow to her sense of dynastic priorities in the summer colony, nor allow that Flora, as a Cameron, had a first claim on Bradley Bay over Alida. It was so like his mother to espouse the cause of Flora for the first time just when the latter had ceased to be her daughter-in-law, but it was not like her to carry her peppery independence to the point of being barely civil to Alida. Michael in the past, despite his mother's sharpness, had always been able to rely on the basic throb of that umbilical cord, but now that throb seemed to have ceased. Her bitterness could no longer be overcome with a kiss, and they viewed each other with surprise across the sudden chasm that had opened between them. When he saw her in the morning, walking down the terrace at the beach club, her thin arms so brown and wrinkled against the spotless white of her dress, her pace so brisk, her smile for others so immediate and warm, he could hardly believe that they were not going to sit down together and gossip as they had in the past. They sat down together, yes, but they did not gossip. Alida was always between them, and the new barrenness of their relationship made all the more exasperating Alida's unjustified jealousy. For Alida could not seem to get rid of the idea that her mother-in-law was her one serious rival; it was an odd exception to her attitude of otherwise consistent realism. She resented even the picture of Gertrude on Michael's dresser and refused to listen to any rebuttal of her favorite thesis that every serious flaw in his character came from his mother's early possessiveness.

"Your mother goes on as if she *owned* Bradley Bay," she complained. "Why shouldn't we spend the summer here if we want? I'm sure Flora doesn't care. As a matter of fact, I saw her at the clubhouse the other day, and she was positively genial. Your mother might at least recognize that I have a right to spend the summer in my own house!"

Michael deferred to her opinion. He had discovered in the eight months of their marriage that life was a good deal easier when he did. Immediately after their wedding in

Mexico they had returned to New York to settle Alida's children in school. There Michael had developed a cold and more of the fever that he had had in Mexico; it had persisted stubbornly, and Alida had finally taken him off to Nassau for six weeks where a life on the sand and in the sun had baked it out of him. By the end of his convalescence he had become more used to his new role. It was not too difficult, after all, if one accepted the rules. It was Alida's pleasure to take care of the mechanics of their joint living, and she did so with her usual ease and efficiency. So long as he took care to satisfy her regular but not inordinate physical demands and to see the people she wanted to see, things went well. When they returned again to New York and moved into her apartment, she decided that he was to go back to the trust company. He had dreaded this, but under her firm encouragement his reinstatement was achieved.

Everyone at the bank seemed glad to have him back. Charlie Meredith, now that the bitterness of the divorce was over, was happy enough to enjoy the double comfort of Michael, his first assistant, and Michael, his son-in-law. It did not, after all, take too much wishful thinking to reconcile even his conservative soul to the pleasure of having his daughter married to a man who was not only the probable next president of Hudson River but the grandson of his revered old patron, Maury Farish. Public opinion made matters still easier, for Michael's and Alida's stock was rising steadily. The very sympathy that Flora had engendered as an abandoned spouse had invested her with a faint dowdiness, and there were rumors extant about Alida's reasons for leaving Jimmie which appeared to be countenanced by old Ambrose himself. Divorce, in any event, was far too common to be held against anyone for long, particularly a couple upon whom fortune appeared to smile as happily as it did upon the Farishes.

Yet Michael at the trust company found himself unable to resuscitate his old interest in the work. He got by with delegating most of his matters to juniors. He was perfectly aware of the dangers of this; he had seen too many bank officers ruin themselves by becoming figureheads before their importance justified it. But he was not going to allow it to become a habit; that was the point. He was simply going to get over this difficult period as best he could, and then he would resume his old standards. It was like the step-up in his drinking; that, too, was only temporary. But two cocktails before lunch, five before dinner and several drinks afterwards helped to keep in the background the image of the old Michael Farish who was gazing so steadily, so sadly, so even rather quizzically at the new. Alida, oddly enough, did not mind his drinking; she drank a great deal herself, in a rather thirsty way, and never showed the least effect from it. He felt closer to her, indeed, when they were drinking; at least then they were sharing a weakness, however little it appeared one in her. The rest of their life together had too much the gaudy appearance of success. Success, in fact, which had always in the past seemed to him the most elusive, the most precarious, the most evanescent thing in life, now appeared to have taken on the attributes of a soiled stiff shirt after a long and tiring evening. It was almost impossible to get off.

The last friendship that he would have expected to be strengthened by his marriage to Alida was that with Jimmie's father. Yet such was the case. Ambrose, it appeared, had no intention of losing the competent services of his daughter-in-law, who had for years acted as his hostess, or the sympathetic ear of his favorite trust officer, merely because his son had proved himself unable to hang on to a wife. If Alida, then, was to be promoted from the position of in-law to that of daughter, Michael had to move up in turn to take her vacated place. All this had been made clear to him one night at the Hone Club bar by Ambrose himself.

"Your Alida's a good girl!" he exclaimed. "Don't think *I* don't know it. No screams, no moods, no female skittishness. She's straight as an arrow and holds her drinks like a man. I like that girl. Always have. As for Jimmie, you can imagine how an old guy feels when he finds his only son is nothing but a goddamn pansy!"

"Oh, Ambrose, no! I'm sure —"

"I know what I know, Michael!"

And Michael had been silent. After all, he had gone so far already with silences that it had not been much further to go. Besides, it was not quite as if he had faced a mortified old warrior, turning his stricken eyes from the sight of a smoking battlefield and a fleeing son. The angry snort of Ambrose's interruption had signified an actual reluctance to be consoled. Homosexuals were favorite butts of the jokes and stories at the Hone Club bar; the old men warmed their hands against the conversational fire with which they burnt them. Whatever we are, whatever we have been, to *this* we have not fallen. There was some savage satisfaction for Ambrose in damning Jimmie with the damned.

"I hope you and Alida will come to Bradley Bay this summer," he had continued gruffly. "It would mean a lot to this old man to have you there. It would help make up."

But Ambrose had changed during the winter; he had suffered a stroke, and it aged him badly. All his violent characteristics became more violent: his laugh, his roar, his crudeness. He was almost incapable now of listening; he had to talk constantly, repeating over and over the same stories and the same arch-Republican sentiments. He was more and more restless, harder and harder to amuse. Basically Ambrose needed only two types of acquaintance: the casual friends at the bar with whom he exchanged loud banter with a habitual, static violence, and the smaller but scarcely more intimate group of semi-dependent house guests who spent the summer with him. It was to the latter group, into which Michael and Alida found themselves incorporated, that the job of amusing the old man primarily fell. They constituted a permanent little court of adulation: the fair fat male secretary who shook with such basely genuine laughter at Ambrose's jokes and his frumpy, pink-haired wife, the middle-aging nephew with the perennial sun tan who taught Ambrose golf, the small, dark old maid cousin who said so little but hated to be left out of anything. Ambrose wanted only to be surrounded by people; he had no ambition at Bradley Bay beyond being king of the club bar. Anyone, fundamentally, would do, anyone, that is, who didn't interrupt him, or if they did, like the pink-haired secretary's wife, if they didn't expect to be answered. He couldn't be left alone, that was the only thing, for then he would slump, as he sometimes did even in crowds, at gay parties, his mouth half open, his colored shirt wilting, his beady eyes staring in front of him. At home, with his court, he was like a monarch in a cartoon with an ermine robe and a crown awry, roaming through the great rented rooms that his decorator had only half finished before he had fired her, never so much as glancing at the fake Gainsboroughs and Lawrences that he had bought for even less than *they* were worth, bellowing for a servant, a drink, a jester, deciding after dinner to take his party on to the gambling at Montauk, the dancing somewhere else, or just "on." And off they would go in the big car, laughing and screaming, as if there were nothing funnier in the whole of Bradley Bay than themselves, a ghost party of Scott Fitzgerald characters awakened after twenty years and still fighting despair.

Michael made the mistake of introducing Ambrose to his mother one Sunday morning at the beach club. Their mutual dislike was instant. It was a hot, clear day, and the three of them sat at a table on the terrace with a view down over the sand and the yellow umbrellas and the small, spoiled, angry children.

"I hope you like Bonniecrest, Mr. Parr," Gertrude said gravely. "My parents built it, you know. We always found it a very pleasant house to live in."

"I've had to make changes," he grumbled. "Those old shingle barns aren't adapted for modern living."

"Those 'old shingle barns,' as you call them, have lasted pretty well. Bonniecrest is almost as old as I am. There have been a lot of storms and hurricanes since then." She paused significantly. "But Bonniecrest manages to survive most anything."

"Even me, Mrs. Farish?"

"Even you, Mr. Parr." She allowed him a thin smile. "You wouldn't believe how Bradley Bay has changed since I was a girl."

"All for the worse, no doubt."

"Oh, I don't say that. *Autre temps, autres moeurs*, that's all."

"I don't speak French."

"No, I suppose not."

Just then, spotting a golf crony passing behind Gertrude on his way to the bar, Ambrose shouted at the top of his lungs, directly at her and without averting his eyes: "What about it, fat-gut? Did you *win?*" And when the crony, failing to hear or at least, in Ambrose's own style, appearing not to notice, hurried on, he jumped up and went after him.

Gertrude's eyes flickered with unbelief, and she clutched Michael's arm. "What did he call me?" She shuddered. "Fat what? Oh, Michael!"

Michael, embarrassed, but smiling in spite of himself, put his hand on her clutching one. "No, no, dear. Not *you*. He was speaking to that man. It's his way, that's all."

"His *way!*" Gertrude withdrew her hand and sat up even straighter. "Well, I may not be modern, or whatever you call it, but I'll never understand *that*. I'm afraid your Mr. Parr and I will never really understand each other."

"You're not very sympathetic." He was irritated that she would not even try, for her own son's sake, to get on with Ambrose. "Ambrose is an important man. To me particularly. He has great responsibilities. When he relaxes, and he *needs* to relax, he does it differently from the way you or I do."

"I'm sure he's an important man," Gertrude answered icily. "You forget that I've known a great many important men in my time. But the ones I've liked have always been gentlemen."

"It's a great luxury to be able to afford such old-fashioned standards."

"It's not a luxury, Michael. It's a necessity."

"It seems hard that you should take that tone with me. After all, I learned about the world from you."

"No, you didn't! You learned about *your* world from Mr. Parr and Alida!"

"Really, Mother, you can't bracket Alida and Ambrose!"

"Can't I?" Gertrude's blue eyes were ablaze with indignation. "I'd like to know why not! They're both after what they can get, and they don't care how they get it!"

"And Flora, of course, was never at all that way!"

"Flora had a heart! Which is more than I can say for Alida. More, I'm afraid, Michael, than I can say for *you!*"

"Please, Ma." He closed his eyes, suddenly flinching. "Must we hurt each other so?" When he looked up at her, he saw her sudden tears, but she turned away.

"I'm sorry, dear," she said, in a sad, rather puzzled tone. "Something in me just seems to have snapped. I would never have thought that my disapproving of Alida would affect my feelings for you. But there you are. It has." She stood up, looking suddenly frail and old, and pity struggled with bitterness in his heart. But he said nothing.

"Yes, dear?" he heard his mother say, and looking up, he saw that she was speaking to Flora's daughter. Ginny Dexter was glancing past her with a vivid, covert curiosity at her former stepfather. Her big round, intense eyes seemed even poppier, and her hair was bleached.

"Mummy says she'd love to lunch with you on Sunday," she was saying to Gertrude. She paused. "And if you don't mind, Mrs. Farish, would it be too much to ask — well, could I come, too?"

"Of course, you could come, my dear." Gertrude looked with renewed defiance at her son as she turned to leave. "You will be *most* welcome."

Michael and Ginny were left to face each other with the same self-consciousness.

"Are you still working?" he asked.

"Oh, yes."

"What sort of a job?"

"Come, Michael, you don't have to be the good stepfather any more. You don't have to pretend to care."

Michael regarded her with interest. She had no claim on him now, so he knew that she would be at a loss how to act. If he had no reason to be nice to her, how could she think he would be? Why should anyone? She stood there hesitantly, sullen, guarded, confused. Through his torpor of a year's standing something stirred.

"You think I was only pretending?" he asked. "All those years?"

"Why not? I was an awful brat."

"You always thought I was faking, didn't you? But that's been your trouble, of course. You always thought everyone was faking. If you could ever relax, you'd discover what a really attractive girl you are."

Ginny stared at him in astonishment. Suddenly her brow puckered, and he was afraid she was going to cry.

"You don't have to say that, Michael."

"I know I don't."

"I'm sure you've forgotten all about Mummy and me." She turned away and sniffed into her handkerchief. "Why not? You're much better off without us, really."

"I haven't forgotten in the least. In fact, I've been thinking a good deal about you recently. You shouldn't go on living with Flora, you know. It's not the right thing for either of you." When he saw how immediately she responded to this treatment, he was suddenly aware that what he was saying was true. When she looked at him attentively, the way she was looking now, she *was* an attractive girl. She tried too hard, that was all. "I worry about you both," he continued, trying to satisfy the interest that he had aroused. "You're going to get terribly on each other's nerves. Flora won't be able to help her bitterness about the divorce, and she's bound to take some of it out on you."

"Well, thanks for the advice!" Ginny unexpectedly exploded with resentment. "And whose fault is it that Mummy's 'bound' to take it out on me?"

"Mine, of course."

"And where does that leave *me?*"

"Oh, you'll be all right, Ginny," he continued in the new tone that he was already becoming used to. "You've got a hell of a lot more on the ball than you think you have. Plenty of people would be very pleased if you stopped hoarding it. Believe me."

She turned at this and walked off, her high heels tapping angrily against the terrace tiles. But Michael only laughed. After twenty years of appeasement it was rather exciting to meet Ginny Dexter as an equal.

That night he and Alida went to a party at Ambrose's. It was the kind of great shapeless crush that he always gave that summer: dozens of people of all ages asked in after dinner to drink and dance. As anyone could bring any number of guests, the party soon took on the quality of a roadhouse evening. Which was exactly what the host wanted.

"Come on now, God damn it!" Ambrose was shouting at the man at the piano. "I want the 'St. Louis Blues.' What do you think I *pay* you for, you big baboon!"

Standing alone by the fireplace, his back resting against the white marble, a tilted drink in hand, Michael looked across the room at the copied Lawrence with its white young faces of eighteenth century children in billowing dresses and sailor suits, under dark, leafy trees, captive, transplanted, appealing to him. His mood, Chekovian after five scotches, was as nostalgic as his mother's. He thought of his grandmother and her sisters, on long rainy afternoons, pacing up and down that very room for their exercise, arm in arm, straight-backed. There had been no copy of a Lawrence then, only two great big pointless photographs of rocks and sea. A young couple from the beach club, whose names their host probably did not even know, danced slowly past, their bodies interlocked; he saw the granite envy in Ambrose's face, watching them, the ashes from his cigar falling to the floor. "I want the 'St. Louis Blues'! How many times do I have to tell you?"

"But this is the 'St. Louis Blues,' sir."

"Then play it so I can recognize it!"

Just then Michael spotted Ginny. She was dancing with a young man who looked as if he had been dancing with her quite as long as he wanted. Michael saw that she was watching him over the young man's shoulder; on a sudden impulse he smiled and winked at her. The impulse had caught him unawares; he was sure that he had never done such a thing before in his life. But oddly enough he had no desire to undo it. There was even a sharp little schoolboy pride at his own boldness. Ginny glanced away quickly, with the jaded expression of the debutante that she should have dropped years before, and continued to swing her hips to the music as if dancing were the most boring occupation in the world. He finished his drink and crossed the floor abruptly to cut in.

"What did you mean by that?" she demanded.

"I wanted to dance."

"No, I mean by winking at me."

"Oh, so you noticed?"

"Of course I noticed! I couldn't help it. What did you mean?"

"What does a man usually mean?"

"Well, really, Mr. Farish! And you old enough to be my father!"

"Not quite. Only your stepfather. Remember, my dear, I know your age."

"You ought to be ashamed of yourself!"

"What for?" The impulse that had made him wink came over him again, and he found that he was holding her close.

To prove to himself that it was *he*, Michael Farish, who was doing this, he suddenly held her even tighter. She tried to pull away, but when he refused to let go, she submitted with an affected shrug. "What for?" he repeated, and he sounded fierce, even to himself. "For thinking of you that way? Do you suppose it's all *my* fault?"

"Well, of all the nerve! You've been drinking, haven't you?"

"Don't be fresh, Ginny. You always were fresh with me." He had a sudden vista of males through the centuries talking this way. With an extraordinary relish he threw his last discretion to the winds and plucked the words from the recesses of his consciousness. "You may as well realize I've got your number. You can't snuggle those little breasts against me and wiggle that big fanny and pretend you're not as excited as I am."

She pushed herself away from him and stared in horror, her breath coming in little pants. "Oh! You beast!"

"Come on now, don't make a scene." Michael moved quickly forward and put his arm again around her waist, propelling her backward across the floor. "Keep dancing or someone will notice. It's bad style to be shocked. And you've always had bad style, Ginny. Too many frowns and too much fanny-wagging. I wish to hell I didn't find bad style so enticing."

"I hate you," she whispered tensely, but she was dancing with him again.

"Well, I wish I hated you." He saw the prospect of tears in her eyes and knew, miraculously, that he was all right. "Come on, kid, pull yourself together. It's not the end of the world because a man finds you attractive. If you'll only relax, you can face the fact that there's always been a bit of a thing between you and me."

"There has not!" She had regained her calm already. Girls apparently did. But, of course! They were *used* to this. This was simply the way *other* men behaved! "I never even dreamed," she continued coolly, "that you thought about such things."

"Thought I was too old, eh?"

"Well, no. Not exactly. I thought you were too — well, too pure."

"I'm as pure as you are." He held her off suddenly and stared in her eyes. "Would you care to tell me what you're thinking right now? No, don't make it up. Right *now!*"

"Well, really, I'm not thinking about anything."

"Not much you're not." He threw back his head and laughed recklessly. "Not *much!*"

"At the moment I happen to be thinking of your remarkably bad manners." She nodded primly as she pulled away from him. "Good *night*, Mr. Farish."

Michael smiled as he watched her twitching hips across the room. How she *knew* he was still watching! Then he went back to the bar and drank with Ambrose until Alida came from the bridge table to get him.

"It looked to me as if you were having rather a fling with Ginevra Dexter," she said as she drove home. It had been tacitly agreed between them, as his drinking increased, that she would drive at night. "Does one have all that much to say to one's ex-stepdaughter?"

He became cautious again, and when he spoke to her, it was with what seemed like a lifetime of new experience. "Do you know something, Alida? That girl's the only casualty of my break-up with Flora. It may sound conceited of me, but I was really a father to her."

"You didn't look so damn paternal tonight."

"We were having a little tiff. Naturally, she resents me

and takes her mother's side. But she's a lost creature at Flora's, darling. She'll always be in the shadow there. I hate to ask it of you, but I think we've got to be nice to that girl. Have her for dinner and that sort of thing."

"Flora's going to like *that*."

"Who cares what Flora likes? Ginny's twenty-seven. She can go where she pleases."

There was a pause while Alida considered this. When he glanced at her profile, however, he saw that she did not seem unduly concerned. "Oh, all right," she said with a shrug, "I don't mind. So long as you keep your interest in her strictly fatherly."

"Oh, darling, you don't mean you could be jealous of Ginny? Poor Ginny?"

"Couldn't I?" She glanced at him bleakly and then back at the road. "Couldn't I just?"

Michael said nothing for the rest of the drive. But while he lay awake that night long after Alida had gone to sleep and listened to the dull boom of the breakers down the beach, he thought wryly of his "fatherly" feelings for Ginny and what his own father might have thought of them. In the damp air, in the darkness, he was able to visualize the paternal countenance almost without pain, with little more, in fact, than a grim and half surly sense of shame. He saw the sympathetic, anxious smile fade from Maury's blue eyes and heard the resonant half-whine of his mild protest: "Ah, Mikey, what did you have to do that for? Why, boy?" And then the hopelessness of ever ceasing to disappoint this loving and all-forgiving parent once again invaded his being, and he tossed and turned through the night until it seemed to him that his childhood friend, Bertie Anheuser, must have at last succeeded in his early game of replacing Michael as Maury's son.

16

MICHAEL'S PICTURES of his father were all glowing ones. There was the young bank executive whose portrait, posthumously painted, hung in the directors' room with that square, detached look, a kind of nobility in a void, which fashionable artists used to attribute to those about to die, as if the subject, conscious of his doom, were trying to make his remaining span a bright example to his company. Then there was the paragon of husbandly virtues that Gertrude Farish always lauded to her children. And last was the athlete, the popular friend of men. "So you're Maury's son? Well, well. He was quite a guy, Maury. *Quite* a guy." This remark was usually followed by a regretful shake of the head and a little smile which seemed more than the superiority of the living toward the dead, which seemed to imply indeed that "good old Maury" was at the same time innocent old Maury, even possibly naïve old Maury. It struck Michael early in life that if people had obviously liked his father, they seemed to have very little to say about him. It was quite possible, he came to suppose, that his father, for all his worthiness, had been a limited man.

Yet when he put them all together, these concepts, and combined them with Gertrude's snapshots of the smiling, physically powerful Maury and added to these the sharper observations of his father's sharp but loving sisters, the total picture had more charm than any of its elements. And his own memory confirmed this. He remembered his father as a big, hearty, lazy man with sky-blue eyes, thick rumpled blond hair, a disposition that nothing could disturb, and boundless physical energy. He always thought of him as playing tennis or squash or raquets, closing in on a ball with the only hard look that his eyes ever wore and smacking it with a long clean stroke. Maury had been, obviously, a man's man, enormously popular with his own sex, almost revered, with a name to be found on shields in lockerrooms, on silver cups and punch bowls. He had certainly not been an intellectual, nor even, by all reports, particularly acute in his own line of banking, but whenever he would have ambled up to a group at a bar and smiled his broad smile, there would have been an immediate interruption of conversation and a seeking of his opinion on no matter what subject. Maury would only shrug and laugh and protest that he did not have one, as was expected and accepted; the question would have been put only as a matter of deference, a bow of recognition by the other males to an acknowledged superior in the line of maleness. Yet for all of this there was a protective impulse in the men who loved Maury; it was as if, recognizing that the world which they had created was dangerous to the natural strength and innocence which they inwardly admired, they had to protect him from its toils while at the same time letting him feel that he had overcome them. They had, so to speak, not only to send him the business but to help him handle it. Life, in fact, had been a bit of a conspiracy around Maury, woven by his own charm, to be as agreeable as he took it to be, and nowhere had this conspiracy been more intense than in his own home. Gertrude adored her husband and could never quite get over her amazement that he should have loved her — and loved her faithfully. Sometimes her incredulity would manifest itself in little outbursts of irritation at his slowness, his maddening tolerance, his general inertia, in small, shrill protests which would be effectively stifled by a wink, a pat on the arm and her name drawled protestingly: "Ah, now, Trudy, are things *that* bad?"

Maury loomed to Michael across the years of his childhood as a vast, too encouraging figure, constantly throwing balls that had somehow to be caught. It was not that his father was critical or unsympathetic; he was kindness itself. He never seemed to expect any more prowess on the part of his only son. But there was no end to it. Michael had flashes of pride on Bradley Bay Saturdays when his father would give up a game of men's doubles to give him a tennis lesson, but such flashes could never quite compensate for his own failure to bridge the hopeless gulf that separated his ball-striking capacities from those of this benign and overfriendly god. Gods were all very well; they had even their lovable side, but their place was not with mortals. Even after a Saturday night picnic on the beach when a sleepy Michael would be carried home in the arms of an easily striding, jovially singing father and could smell the comforting smell of his perspiring neck and shoulders, he would derive a guilty little comfort from the thought that the next day would take this magnificent parent back to the city, and normalcy, even a dull normalcy, would settle again over the old shingle house on the dunes.

The last year of Maury's life was his thirty-eighth and Michael's twelfth. It was always to be indelibly associated in the latter's mind with the ludicrous figure of Aribert Anheuser, the unwelcome clown whose lines almost ran away with the tragedy. Aribert was a classmate of Michael's at the Branford Day School for boys on Fifth Avenue; he was fat and soft, with long, sticky blond hair and beady, suspicious eyes.

"A goon," the other boys had classified him in disgust. "A real goon."

"Not a goon but a goof," Michael's father corrected him when he pointed out Aribert in the park. "There's nothing wrong with that kid that a summer in camp wouldn't cure."

But that was so like Maury. When one was on top of the world one could afford to be tolerant. A god could not be corrupted. But how was a contemporary expected to tolerate someone like Bertie Anheuser who enjoyed all the wrong things, and in an absolutely free and shameless manner? He wore tailor-made suits from Brooks Brothers with long pants though the rest of the boys had knickers. He lived in an apartment hotel called "the Delphinium" on Central Park West with an indulgent mother who sent him to school in a yellow Hispano-Suiza that made a tremendous rattling sound and had a dashboard that was the admiration of their class. Exempt, because of a murmuring heart of which he was duly boastful, from all exercise requirements, he would come to the park while the other boys played baseball to sit on the sidelines and chew gum and make waspish comments about the players in a high singsong voice that seemed never to pause.

"Would you like to be friends?" he asked Michael un-expectedly one afternoon on their way back from the Park.

"Oh, I might," Michael answered guardedly. "And then, of course, I might not."

"It might be a job to fit you in," Bertie retorted.

"Why?"

"Because I have so many."

"Friends? Who, for example?"

"Our whole class!"

Michael wondered if it was possible for Bertie so to misconstrue the enthusiasm of their classmates for the shiny metal trinkets that he had always available for trade. Surely he must see that this was as ephemeral as their interest in the dashboard of the Hispano-Suiza. Yet Michael, who could never be really rude, found himself accepting Bertie's company and even going to the Delphinium for lunch on Saturdays with Bertie and Mrs. Anheuser, a soft, dumpy, chalky woman, another version, in fact, of Bertie himself. Michael marveled at the Anheuser way of life which seemed the very reverse of his own family's. They had all their meals in the great gilded restaurant downstairs and ice in their water glasses and sherbet for dessert; they never had to go to the country ("If you see a tree, give it a kick for me," Bertie would say), and the rattling Hispano existed only to bear them to the movies. It did not surprise Michael that his own mother should disapprove of Mrs. Anheuser, but he wondered that she should be so unimpressed by the splendors at her command.

"Who *is* Mrs. Anheuser, anyhow?" his father asked one morning at breakfast when Michael announced that he was going there for supper.

"Oh, one of those rich widows nobody's ever heard of," his mother retorted. "If she *is* a widow. You know. Lives on the wrong side of the Park and goes to matinees. I don't know what Branford School's coming to."

Michael thought it rather arrogant of his mother to condescend to the Delphinium from the sober dullness of her own brownstone house. After all, she didn't even keep a car in town, much less a Hispano! But Gertrude's low opinion of Mrs. Anheuser was succeeded by active hostility when

Michael brought Bertie home to lunch. He could see how badly things were going by his mother's straightened jaw and averted eye, but Bertie, sure that he was making a hit, chatted happily away about Mrs. Anheuser's jewelry and how much she spent on her clothes and what a bore the old Hispano was.

"I think your mother's divine!" he whispered to Michael as he went out. "Absolutely divine!"

That evening, when Maury came home, Gertrude Farish blew up. In front of a mortified Michael she detailed the triviality of Bertie's conversation, his "girlish" appearance, his family's "vulgar yellow" car and seriously suggested that Michael be transferred to a school with higher standards of admission. Maury listened in his smiling, tolerant way and shook his head.

"Now, Trudy," he said in his low, resonant voice. "Now, Trudy, dearest, aren't we going just a bit far? How would you like it if Mikey told me what he thinks of some of *your* friends? They aren't all roses now, are they?"

"Maury, that has nothing to do with it! You should see this boy. Do you realize he actually told me that he wished men used lorgnettes? He said they were so much better to *stare* through!"

But her husband only laughed his rumbling laugh. It was like a low breaker along a pebbly beach; Gertrude's attitudes and worries were for the moment overwhelmed and scattered. "The poor kid's an only child, Trudy," he pointed out. "And brought up by a widow. I'm sure there's no harm in him. I'll tell you what, Mike." He turned and put an arm around his son's shoulder. "We'll have him down for a visit this summer in Bradley Bay. We'll get him on the tennis court and take him out fishing. I'll bet his mother won't even recognize him when she gets him back!"

Much to Michael's surprise Bertie accepted the invitation to Bradley Bay. The charms of summer life in the city, so much extolled, were readily sacrificed, and it was an even more irrepressible Bertie who clambered down the steps of the old Long Island train in a scarlet blazer, waving an obviously new racket and crying "Tennis, anyone?" in happy parody, as Gertrude later pointed out, of all the drawing room comedies that he should never have been allowed to see. He was bubbling over with curiosity; he wanted all the big houses on the dunes identified as Gertrude drove them home from the station and asked shrill questions about the name posts that they passed: "Dillon? Is that the Dillon girl who married the Haitian?" or "Morton? Is that the Doctor Morton who went to jail?" Gertrude paid no attention; she had something more important on her mind. Only the day before Maury had complained of feeling "fagged out" and had excused himself from the club tennis tournament.

In anyone else such a complaint might not have seemed serious; with him, it was alarming. The doctor did not appear unduly anxious, but he took a blood count and put Maury to bed for a day. After that he was allowed up, but not to exercise, pending laboratory tests. Gertrude preserved an outward demeanor of calm, but Michael knew that she was miserably anxious. Yet he couldn't help feeling a secret relief that she would now pay no further attention to the extravagances of his house guest. For Bertie "adored" Bradley Bay. He loved to go on walks with Michael down the dunes to explore the big shingle houses and to climb about the abandoned hulk of one at the end of a little point, a deserted castle of a summer cottage with a bell tower around which gulls squawked and from which they could see even the furthest fishing boats, little bobbing black spots on the heaving, glittering sea. Michael was surprised that Bertie should be so dominant in his own bailiwick. His friend's imagination seemed positively to explode with new source material, and he invented a game of peopling the various summer houses with imaginary families and endowing them with a rash of jealousies and intrigues. He made up five characters to Michael's one; he was never at a loss for passionate heiresses in love with chauffeurs, for tyrannical, splendid dowagers dimly suspected of murder, for embezzling bankers who blew their brains out with aplomb when the game was up. The evenings were as full as the days of heady, unaccustomed liberty; Gertrude, for the sake of peace and quiet, would give them each a dollar and send them to the movies in the village, and Bertie would assign faces of the silver screen to the characters he had made up in the daytime until his version of Bradley Bay fairly bristled with the personalities of Constance Talmadge and Pola Negri, of Erich von Stroheim and Valentino.

A minor liability on their expeditions was Susan, the younger of Michael's two sisters, whose enthusiasm for their enterprises was as boundless as her capacity to accept rebuff. She would tag along behind, even when they wouldn't talk to her, and she was with them on the fateful day when they discovered the abandoned playhouse on a large wooded property on an inlet from the sea. It was a neatly constructed log cabin with two rooms and a front porch, and the door was fastened, but Bertie found an unlocked window, and he and Michael, pushing hard, opened it suddenly with a bang. Startled, they both jumped back and then together stuck their heads cautiously in.

It had been a playhouse for the children, now grown up and moved away, of the old lady who lived in the big stone house at the end of the drive. Obviously it had not been used for many years, but it must have received a thorough cleaning every spring, for it was in perfect condition. Michael even seemed to remember his mother saying that Mrs. Lord, the old lady, kept it up that way because of one of her daughters who had died in childhood. Or had he imagined it? At any rate, there it was, with its lonely, rather ominous neatness, its brightly painted chairs and tables, its set of china with Mother Goose figures, its round blue rug and yellow curtains, all designed for little people. The intruders stood silently before the scene momentarily awed by its still dignity, like barbarians before a Roman villa. Then Bertie laughed.

"Well, isn't it sweet?" he said in his jeering tone. "Isn't it too, *too* sweet?"

It surprised Michael that he should feel the sudden tremor of a hostility that equaled his friend's. What was it? Why should the innocent aspect of an abandoned playhouse be so vexing? What had those dead or grown-up children ever done to him? In later years he was to ponder the question in more psychological terms. Did the playhouse represent in miniature his own home? Was it the mutual and excluding love of his parents that he saw in its bright imperturbability? And if this were so, what about Bertie? Was it the symbol of a home which he had never known that he could not bear to contemplate? In any event, their joint hostility had been aroused; glancing about, their fingers twitched with a sudden urge. They climbed in, followed by Susan, and proceeded to examine the drawers and closets like stealthy burglars. Susan went into the kitchen, and they had forgotten all about her when they suddenly heard her shriek. Hurrying in, they found her already abandoned to that flood of perfunctory tears that accompanies, in the lives of nicely brought up children, the breakage of expensive crockery. At her feet were the multitudinous remains of a green china soup tureen.

"Shut up, you little fool!" Bertie shouted at her. "Do you want to have the whole neighborhood in here?"

But Susan, who had a passion for ritual, would never listen to reason or reprimand until she had enjoyed to the full the exhausting emotionalism of her remorse. She stood there, utterly unmindful of their danger, her head thrown back, her whole body given over to the luxury of emitting those ear-piercing, methodically spaced yells. When Michael tried putting his hand over her mouth, it only made matters worse, for she was strong and broke away, and then her cries became really deafening. He was at wits' end when Bertie suddenly darted into the other room, and, seizing a serving dish, flung it to the floor with a crash. Susan's eyes widened, and her shrieks died away to incredulous gasps. A violent impulse made Michael follow this example, and, almost without thinking, he pushed a stack of plates after the tureen and the serving dish. Susan at last gave a delighted cry and rushed into the next room to break a lamp. Madness seized them all, and they broke every bit of china and glass in the little house.

Michael had never before committed such an act of van-dalism, and he was always to remember the fierce and heady pleasure of it. They worked with speed and thoroughness, in tacit recognition of the transiency of their mood and the limited time that they would have before the swift and in-evitable return of reality and retribution. He used to think of it years later during the war when he read descriptions of the sack of cities. Man, he had learned, could be made to do anything. There would always remain the picture of Bertie throwing finger bowls through the windowpanes, intense and concentrated, and of fat little Susan earnestly wasting her energy breaking into even smaller pieces parts of the crockery that she had already smashed.

When they had finished, and the little house stood windowless and unadorned, its floor littered with rubble, Bertie and Michael exchanged an awful look.

"Let's beat it," Bertie said in a low, tense voice, and they hurried off, dragging the protesting Susan from her pile of pieces. A sober silence was maintained most of the way home. Michael was pondering the blackness of a future mortgaged with such an intolerable load of bad conscience, and he assumed that his speechless friend, however sophisticated, was thinking the same thing. Only Susan seemed unconcerned, walking along in her demure, self-conscious smugness.

"Michael," she said as they approached the house. "Michael, we'll tell Mummy, won't we? We will?"

He stopped and looked at her, appalled. "I'll lick the pants off you if you do!"

"Mummy won't let you. And, anyway, I've got to tell. You know that."

They had all three stopped now, and Michael and Bertie were staring at her.

"We'll never take you with us again if you do," Michael threatened.

Susan only smiled at this. "Mummy'll make you," she said confidently.

"But, Susie," Michael implored, "you don't want to get me in trouble with Daddy, do you? I'll give you the new freight car from the electric train. Honest. The one you liked so."

For a moment she wavered. "With the little packages too?"

He nodded quickly. "With the little packages."

She shook her head. "I'd still have to tell."

"But why?" he cried.

" 'Cause I do."

Michael knew, from bitter experience, that she would be only too good to her word. There was a resolution in Susan, a stalwart determination that linked her in the history of fortitude with the Saint Cecilias and Teresas of more heroic times. What Susan said she would do she would surely do. To others was left the ugly and uninspiring field of consequences. And yet, as he and Bertie walked on ahead leaving the wretched girl to herself, refusing even to speak to her now, he was already beginning to feel an unexpected throb of relief that the heavy load of their shared crime was so soon to be lifted from his shoulders and the slate to be washed clean.

Susan had some difficulty in making her story believed, for her mother was too often assailed with her ready overflow of confession to give heed to every detail of her imagined crimes, and had it not been for the guilty silence which Michael maintained during supper, Susan's clamor for retribution might have gone unnoticed. As it was, his mother finally asked him what *had* happened in the playhouse, and he told her that they might have broken a dish or so.

"A dish or so!" she exclaimed reprovingly. "But, Michael, you know that it's not *our* playhouse. You had no right to go inside at all. How did you get in?"

"The door was open."

"It was? How careless of Mrs. Lord's superintendent. Still, a door being open gives you no right just to walk in, much less to break dishes. I'll ask your father to go over in the morning and offer to pay for it."

And with these ominous words the subject was allowed to drop. It was a long time before Michael got to sleep that night, but he was impressed by Bertie's sang-froid. "After all," he pointed out from the adjoining bed. "What can he do to us? He can't put us in jail, can he?"

Michael wasn't so sure, and neither, apparently, at ten o'clock the following morning was Maury Farish. He had gone over after breakfast to call on Mrs. Lord, and on the way he had stopped at the playhouse to collect what his wife had described to him as the pieces of some worthless kitchen china which they would have to replace. As he approached the paneless windows and stared at the scene of destruction within, his first reaction was that he had come to the wrong playhouse. His second was that the playhouse had been looted the night before, presumably after his children's visit. His third was a ghastly suspicion of the truth. He returned home and in a brief, grave interview with his son elicited the whole sorry story. He then opened the door and caught Bertie listening.

"Come with me," he said to them both. He silently preceded them down to the cellar and turned around, removing his belt. Michael felt his stomach turn over. His father had never so much as slapped him before.

"Now I tell you what I'm going to do," Maury said in an even, almost matter-of-fact tone. His expression was serious, but there was not a shade of anger on his face. "I want you both to take down your pants and accept a good licking. And not a squawk out of either of you. See if you can't take it like little men."

"You can't to do that!" Bertie shouted, white with fear. "It's against the law! You have no right!"

"That may be," Maury said equably. "But then you had no right to destroy Mrs. Lord's playhouse, did you?"

"Mummy'll pay for it!"

"She'll pay half," Maury corrected him. "I'll pay Mike's half. But that's not going to get you out of your licking."

"Let me call my mother in New York. I insist on calling my mother in New York!"

"You can do it afterwards."

"She'll sue you! I swear she'll sue you!"

"Very likely. But that's my affair, isn't it? Come on now, Bertie. Nothing's going to get you out of this, so you might as well behave. Show Mike here you're as brave as he is." The incredible thing was that he acted, with obvious sincerity, as if he were doing Bertie a favor. Maury's charm never left him, even at such a moment. "Come on, Bert," he continued, almost coaxingly. "Let's get it over with, shall we? You don't want me to take down your pants for you, do you?"

Bertie stared at him, dumb with terror. When Maury took a step toward him, he suddenly turned and ran whimpering into the corner. "Come on, Bert," Maury repeated and took another step. With a little sob Bertie suddenly took his pants down and leaned over to expose his great white trembling backside. Maury gave him four strokes with a belt, none sharp enough, however, to cause more than a faint red mark. Yet Bertie howled, Michael noted with astonishment. He actually howled. When his own turn came Michael did not utter a sound although he received five strokes, each one, as he well knew, more than twice as hard as those meted out to Bertie.

"There you are, boys," Maury said as he slipped his belt back on. "And that's all you're going to hear about it from me. As far as I'm concerned, the episode is closed." His tone was as serious and polite as if he had been talking to one of his own friends. "You, Bertie, of course, are free now to call your mother. Tell her if she wants you back in town I'll take you in on the morning train. But Mrs. Farish and I hope very much that you will finish your visit."

Which Bertie, to Michael's astonishment, elected to do. There was no further threat to call his mother: there was no further reference, in fact, to the episode of the licking. Bertie simply turned away and shook his head coldly when Michael later tried to apologize for his father. What struck him as even odder was that Bertie seemed to harbor no resentment against Maury. Instead of continuing his daily expeditions with Michael to the old houses on the dunes, he now evinced a sudden enthusiasm for sailing with Maury. The latter was still looking badly, but his doctor allowed him to sail, and he took the boys out each day for the rest of Bertie's visit. Bertie on board the sloop *Genie* was a different person. He scrambled around the deck, coiling rope, handling sails, doing everything that Maury told him. He did it all very clumsily, it was true, but he tried, and Maury watched him with a pleasant smile and occasionally patted him on the head and told him he would make a sailor yet. On picnics in the evening Bertie would sit beside Maury and listen intently as the latter sang songs in his deep baritone, joining in excitedly and off key in a shrill soprano as soon as he had picked up the words. He seemed to have transferred whatever interest he had in the Farish family to its head and to have forgotten Michael completely.

It was possible, Michael always thought later, that if Bertie's visit had been prolonged his father might have effected a permanent improvement in his character. But it was only a week after the episode at the playhouse that he returned to the city, and Michael did not see him again until the fall. By then the effect had quite worn off, and Bertie was, if possible, even more arrogantly self-sufficient than before. The intervening two months at the Delphinium and, no doubt, the resumption of his movies and matinees with Mrs. Anheuser had effectively closed out the sea air of Bradley Bay.

By the time school opened it was generally acknowledged that Maury Farish was seriously ill with a rare blood disease. He was in bed most of the time now, and as he wanted to stay in Bradley Bay where he could watch the autumn breakers from his window, Michael and the girls were moved into New York under the indulgent care of one of their aunts. It was all rather exciting for them. Not actually seeing their father, it was harder to imagine him ill, and the atmosphere of solicitude and sympathy with which they found themselves surrounded, together with the novel liberties of the aunt's regime, made them feel at once sophisticated adults and stricken orphans. Michael discovered that he was becoming adept, when older relatives called, at casting a manly dry eye at the floor and answering questions with "Well, we can only hope for the best, can't we?" or "Mummy's quite wonderful, thank you" or even, with a quick sigh: "At least, he's more comfortable."

At the beginning of the school term Bertie seemed distinctly bent on avoiding him. He never allowed himself to be alone with Michael and made sarcastic remarks about him in the presence of others. Only once did he give Michael a clue to his behavior, and that was after classes when he called to him from the window of the Hispano.

"Say, Mike!" The tone was guardedly friendly, and Michael went over to the car. "You never told anyone about your old man giving us that licking, did you?"

"Never."

"Cross your heart?"

The use of the childish expression and the tenseness of his wide moon face convinced Michael that he meant it.

"Cross my heart," he said solemnly.

"And you won't?" Bertie's expression still did not relax.

"Of course not."

"Oh." He nodded dubiously. "Oh, all right."

Michael was amused. To have it known at school that Michael Farish's father had given a licking to the prince of the Delphinium would have been more than Bertie's pride could have borne. Gone now in the cool air of autumn was any enthusiasm on Bertie's part for the memory of his own meek submission to Maury Farish, of his clinging, rather slobby devotion. That he, Aribert Anheuser, should have been first the victim and then the hypnotized admirer of so ordinary a mortal was not lightly to be forgiven the mortal's son.

Michael soon discovered that his diagnosis was correct. The very next day at recess Bertie actually made a crack about his father. "What else can you expect," he sneered to the others about a gaffe that Michael had made in current events class, "from the son of a semi-professional ball player?"

Michael did not have to say anything. Every boy there knew of his father's illness except Bertie. "Shut your fat face, Anheuser." "Lay off Mike's father, will you?" "Go on, fatso. Waddle home to Mummy."

Bertie was waiting for him at the door after school, his round face sober with apology. "Look, Mike, I'm sorry. I didn't know about your father. Honest. Tell me about it, will you?"

And Michael, with a dry, lofty pleasure, told him in detail, first the official version of his father's disease, as he had heard his aunt, parrotlike, repeat it so many times over the telephone at home, and then, in dropped tones, the gloomier, confidential version, still bravely hopeful, ending with the shake of the head, the sudden skeptical shrug and rhetorical: "But just how much do these doctors *know*, after all?"

Bertie might have been an undertaker, so solicitous was his immediate concern. As one who had already the distinction of losing a father, he took it upon himself to prepare Michael for his new and solemn role. The other boys in their class who enjoyed the superficial, the possibly even rather vulgar merit of two live and kicking parents, became the objects of a bemused and faintly scornful tolerance. Michael, according to his friend, was about to pass through the portals of maturity into a new world where even a twelve-year-old could own, if not wear, the paternal gold pocket watch and sit opposite his mother at the family board. Bertie went so far as to imply, in his "Now you can be told" voice that Michael would find himself in charge of all sorts of awe-inspiring responsibilities, that he would, in short, be rich, richer than his family now were, as if there were something in the very act of death, the drawing of curtains, the crackling of old testaments and the clearing of lawyers' throats that produced a wealth which had not existed before. And then, of course, last but far from least, there was the mourning apparel and the prospect of appearing in class, the object of sympathetic eyes, with a black tie and armband and a pale, resigned countenance. Michael was even aware, one morning when his aunt reported with tears of excitement a slight improvement in the patient at Bradley Bay, of a small, sharp twinge of something unpleasantly like disappointment.

"I wonder if your mother will want to go on living in that house," Bertie told him at recess. "We lived in a house before Daddy died. Mummy found it too much trouble to run afterwards. Of course, it was a good deal bigger than yours, but even so. I wonder if you couldn't get rooms at the Delphinium. I might ask Ma. She has the manager eating out of her hand." It was this remark that at last opened Michael's eyes to his real situation. Could anyone be so misguided as to think that his mother would ever move to Mrs. Anheuser's hotel? In a single moment the postponed agonies of shame and sorrow broke unbearably over him. He said nothing more as his friend rattled on, but as they turned back to the others to form the procession in which they left the park, he understood at last why it was that his mother hated Bertie. His heart seemed to stand still as he contemplated the enormity of his crime in not understanding it before. If only, if only, he prayed in a sudden passionate whisper, his father could be spared long enough for him to redeem himself! But he knew, as his lips moved, that it was too late. God did not answer such prayers as his.

That night Maury had a relapse and was taken to a hospital in the city by ambulance. Michael fell asleep in his room, exhausted by crying, and was awakened by his mother in the early morning. She looked very thin and wasted, but calm and immeasurably dignified.

"My poor darling," she said taking him in her arms, "it's all over. We'll have to look after each other now."

It was the kindness that overwhelmed him, then as later. His passionate tears were ascribed by all to sorrow for his father. When, two weeks after the funeral, the girls went back to school, Michael begged an additional week. He could not abide the idea of seeing Bertie again and had torn up unread his letters from the Delphinium. When his week was up, and Gertrude, with a touch of her old asperity, told him not to be "slobby" and to remember that his father would have wanted him to go back to school, Michael came down with a fever. After this it was agreed among his mother and aunts that he had better be allowed to finish out the year with a tutor. He was due to go to Averhill in the fall, anyway. Grateful for this concession he worked hard and passed his entrance examinations well. It was only fitting, after all, that he should enter with proper marks the school to which his father had gone. Branford could be classified from now on with Bertie Anheuser and his Hispano as childish things that had been put away. Ahead loomed the Gothic tower of Averhill and a lifetime of reparation.

17

MICHAEL HAD TO FACE the fact, that summer in Bradley Bay after his remarriage, that his attraction to Ginny was different from anything that he had ever experienced. Even in the flush of his early excitement for Flora there had still been the hard little drive within him of what he *ought* to have felt, the unyielding concept of what a young man should go through when confronted by a beautiful woman. And years later, in England with Alida, there had been the same almost obligatory sense that a wartime affair was expected of sailors in wartime. Those had been, of course, his only two women, and not surprisingly, his only two wives. But then there had been the fantasies, the Ingres odalisques that he had looked at as a boy, who returned to envelop him in bold, alabaster arms, the wide-hipped Bouguereau nudes who dragged him, naked, up to an azure sky where winged cherubs puffed at horns. Ginny's uniqueness was just that her figure, as he visualized it, seemed one of these fantasies realized. When he went at noon to the beach club to watch for her, he could even hope that when she did appear, she would be different, that when he saw her, once and for good, as she was, she would cease to fascinate. But this was never the case. Even when she simpered past him with her self-conscious stride and smirk; even when he saw the ladylike manner — oh, *so* ladylike — with which she spoke to the desk clerk, even when he took in, again and again, her silly dignity, her ridiculous dignity, her abominable dignity, he had to concede that the Ginny of his daydreams and the Ginny of the beach club were one and the same. He could only yearn to take her by those round white shoulders and shake her until she dropped her airs of superiority. He had waited all his life for a madness of the blood. Could it be that it came like this?

He knew that she was aware of him. He was sure that the new red bathing suit in which she appeared so demurely at the pool had been purchased with regard to his watching eyes. He could tell, easily enough, by the way she glanced around, elaborately casual, to see if he was still there, that she wanted him to be. But when he nodded to her, she would quickly turn her head away and wiggle one self-conscious toe under the green surface of the disinfected water. Why did he not walk away? He could have. Oh, yes, he still could. There was no failure of will power. Was it not that to walk away might be to crush an impulse that had been forty-six years in the making? It was as if he might have been guilty of a kind of suicide, particularly when there seemed nothing else alive in the cotton-packed box of his existence.

When Alida reminded him that they must decide where they were going on his vacation, he was stricken with dismay at the prospect of leaving Bradley Bay. Yet the perfect excuse came almost unconsciously in the first words he uttered.

"Darling, Ma goes off on her summer visits in August," he said. "I know it's been hard on you having her so close. And your children go to Jimmie at the same time. Why don't you and I stay on here and have our private Bradley Bay vacation?"

"As a matter of fact, there's nothing I'd rather do," she answered in surprise. "But I thought you'd be dying to get out of here. With Flora and Ambrose and all that."

"We've traveled enough. Mexico and Nassau. I'd just as soon stay put this summer."

Ginny came for Saturday night dinner at Alida's sandless, damp-proof, modern beach house, and Michael enjoyed playing the casual, easy host under circumstances that were so new to her. He was scrupulously polite, and she seemed to enjoy herself. But the following week, when Alida was getting ready to drive the children to Jimmie in Maine, he could hardly wait to have her leave.

"It seems so mean to leave you all alone," Alida protested. "I wonder if I couldn't put Ambrose and Julia on a train."

"I wish you could. But they've been looking forward so to the motor trip."

"Will you miss me?"

"Darling, need you ask? I'd go with you like a shot if I didn't have to be at the bank on Monday."

"Maybe we could drive up and fly back."

"But would the plane get off? Could we be sure? You know those Maine fogs."

"Yes, that's true. That's true."

So Alida left, and Michael had the delirium of several days in an empty house. He went to the club on Saturday morning to wait for Ginny, and when she was late, he became as furious as if they had agreed to meet. He hurried up to her the moment she arrived and before he even knew what he was going to say, he heard his voice, tense and low, break into a flow of obscenities. It was a new and startling aspect of himself, as if he were suddenly vomiting up an ancient store of filth that he had never known he was hoarding. Poor Ginny stared at him with eyes that reflected his own fright.

"Oh, Michael, please!"

She hurried away, but the next morning it was the same thing. With an appalling speed it became a habit. It was a new kind of release. He began to think of himself as a sardonic Hamlet abusing a helpless Ophelia, banishing her to a dozen nunneries. They would meet by the pool and pause and talk, smiling as if they were having the most ordinary of beach club conversations. He found a fierce little excitement in the contrast between their demeanor and the nature of what he was telling her.

"Good morning, Ginny," he would say as he sauntered up to her. "You should have been at the Harrises' last night." And then, when they were close enough: "Don't look so smug. You want it as badly as I do."

"Go away, please, Michael."

"It's basic. Every girl wants to make her old lady's man. You've had an eye on me since you were a kid."

"Don't be disgusting."

"Don't pretend you don't love it. How about meeting me down the beach tonight?"

"It's out of the question!"

"Is it? Then why do you squeeze into that red bathing suit every morning? When you know I'm going to be right here? Isn't it to show off that big rear end of yours?"

"Michael, please!"

"Quit kidding yourself."

At this point, she would usually leave him and hurry back to the bathhouse. Sometimes she seemed on the verge of tears. But the next morning, there she would be in the same red bathing suit.

On the last day before Alida's return Ginny did not appear at the club. It was a wet and drizzly day, but he nonetheless expected her, and he was standing by the bar, his back to the pool when he heard a familiar voice behind him.

"But this is where you used to wait for *me*. Remember?"

He turned around, flushed, to stare at Flora. He had not seen her so close all summer. There was more grey in the glossy black of her hair, and she seemed stouter.

"Yes."

"And *now* who do you wait for?"

Her tone was light enough, but her expression was unpleasant, and he did not answer.

"How about a game of backgammon?" she asked. "For auld lang syne?"

He followed her to the board and sat down, starting at once to arrange his men. But just as he became aware that she was not arranging hers, the plump white hand with the familiar rings swept under his eyes and scattered his assembled pieces.

"Of course, I don't *really* want to play, dearie." Her voice was ominous. "I want to talk."

Silently, without looking up, he waited.

"We haven't talked all summer, have we?" the sarcastic voice went on. "But then you must forgive me. I don't believe in friendship after divorce. Frightfully old-fashioned of me, I know. It must be the Cameron blood coming out at last. Give me time. I'll be a dowager yet."

It was true, he thought dully. Flora *would* be a dowager, and a formidable one.

"But today it's different. I want to talk to you as a mother."

His throat went dry as he continued to stare down at the board. Surely, only a child, he reproached himself, should feel such panic.

"I saw you talking to Ginny the other day," the voice relentlessly continued. "I noticed that she seemed troubled. When I asked her about it afterwards, she went red as a beet.

Oh, don't worry, she didn't *tell* me anything." The pause that followed was saturated with disdain. "But let me tell you this, Michael Farish!" The voice rose sharply, and there was relief in the breaking storm. "If you so much as lay a hand on that child I'll ruin you! I'll drive you right out of Bradley Bay! There isn't a respectable house that won't slam its doors in your dirty, wolfish face!"

Was she still talking or was it the roaring in his ears? He stared down the beach at the blue breakers and wondered if this was Michael, the boy who had walked down the dunes to call on Flora Dexter and whose mother had been a Lear of Bonniecrest. He was suddenly overcome with a nostalgia for the very innocence that had been his ancient burden.

"Oh, Flora, Flora."

"Don't 'Flora' me! I was sorry for you when you found out about Danny. I was even sorry for you when you wanted to marry Alida. I knew it was all her doing. Poor Michael, I thought. He meant so well. He tried to do right by everybody. But *this* Michael! This drooling, middle-aged philanderer, sneaking a pinch behind the wide back of his rich wife! At least my faults were honest. But *you!*"

"Go on, Flora. I deserve it."

"Never mind what you deserve! Just concentrate on what you're going to get! If you don't leave that poor girl alone!"

He did not look up until she had gone, and then he had only strength to hurry blindly back to the bar.

For several days he did not go near the beach club. He played golf and tried to content himself with the occasional glimpses that he got of Ginny at dinner parties. Alida, too, was back, and it was harder for him to get away. But what troubled him most was his memory of the outrage in Flora's voice. If it had been only jealousy or a natural indignation at the bad taste of his behavior, he could have understood.

But she seemed to feel more than that; she seemed to feel that Ginny needed to be protected. Was Ginny really a "child," a "poor girl"? Could she be thought of any longer at her age as a helpless virgin, unable to take care of herself? Flora was undoubtedly sincere in believing this; her Spanish blood worked in two ways. But what was Ginny's sex life? Did he shock her? *Could* he?

He received some unpleasant if questionable intelligence on this subject the following Saturday night at Ambrose's. Alida was playing bridge, and Michael, who had watched Ginny as long as he dared and had even danced with her twice, had retired to the bar and was drinking whiskey. There were two young men sitting near him whose conversation he could overhear. He recognized neither, but one, splendid in a red velvet jacket, was being highly sophisticated and knowledgeable about Bradley Bay, while the other, younger and cruder, summed up by his crew cut, put the questions.

"Well, what about it?" the younger one was asking. "What's here tonight?"

"Nothing," the red jacket answered. "Nothing available, that I see."

"Oh, come off it. At a party like this, everything's available."

"Don't be too sure."

"Why would anyone come? Half the girls here are tarts."

"You can't tell. The ones who look the tartiest are from the beach club."

"Who cares where they're from?"

"Well, don't you want to find out if there's a husband? If he's here, if he cares, if he's drunk, that sort of thing?"

"How about Hippy?"

"Who?"

"You know. The one I asked you about. The hip swinger."

"Ginny Dexter? God, man, she must be thirty!"

"I'm not asking for her birth certificate. Will she or won't she?"

"Oh, she will, all right."

"You're sure?"

The red jacket smiled condescendingly. "Of course I'm sure. You know how it is for these spinsters."

"No, I don't. How is it?"

"In a summer place? It's hell. There aren't any bachelors over college age, except for a handful of pansies. So they have to service their friends' husbands. Or go without."

"What do their friends think of that?"

"Oh, they don't mind. If Mrs. Smith is having her little fling, she may want to distract John Smith by dangling Ginny in front of him. Ginny can be counted on to deliver. And it's fair game, too. There's always the possibility of detaching John Smith."

"Okay, pal. Introduce me. Do I need a buildup?"

"A bachelor? My God, she'll swoon!"

They left the bar, and Michael ordered a double scotch. He finished it and ordered another. When he went into the next room to look for Ginny he was swaying. He leaned against the mantelpiece and stared bleakly at the dancing couples until he spotted her. She was walking off the dance floor followed by the young man with the crew cut. He hurried after them and caught her by the arm in the front hall.

"Ginny!"

She turned, startled. "Michael, what is it?"

"Don't leave yet. I've hardly had a word with you."

"But we've danced twice. This gentleman is taking me home. Mr. Terhune, this is Mr. Farish."

"I don't care to meet Mr. Terhune. And if you'd heard him discussing you in the bar, you wouldn't either!"

"Now, just a second!" Mr. Terhune pushed himself forward and faced Michael. "Who the hell do you think you are?"

"I happen to be this young lady's stepfather."

"Oh." Mr. Terhune looked very awkward. "I beg your pardon, sir. I didn't know."

"You ought to have your mouth washed out with soap!"

"But he's not my stepfather!" There was a sudden bewildered anguish in Ginny's tone. "He's not! He and Mummy were divorced last year." Her voice rose to a wail. "He's even married again!"

"Oh, is that so?" Mr. Terhune became very threatening again. "In that case, I'll ask you to get out of our way, Mr. Farish."

"You leave this girl alone!"

"Why don't you go back to the bar, you old lush? It's where you belong!"

Michael slapped him hard across the cheek. A second later he felt a crash in his head, and then he was being helped to his feet. He was aware of Ginny holding one arm and a waiter holding the other. He knew that he must have been knocked down, and after a moment he knew he had been hit in the eye. He looked around wildly for Terhune, but he was gone. Then the hall was full of people, and Ambrose himself was standing over him.

"What the hell do you think you're doing?"

Michael pointed vaguely to the front door. "That man," he murmured. "He was going to take her home."

"Take who home?"

He suddenly heard Ginny's tense whispering in his ear. "He's gone. I'm going home alone. Come and see me later, but for God's sake, shut up!" He turned to her in bewilderment, but she shook her head warningly and hurried out the front door.

"Well, I'll be a ring-tailed son of a bitch!" Ambrose suddenly shouted. He threw back his head and started laughing hysterically. The silence around him was unbroken. He stopped abruptly with a gasp. "Ladies and gentlemen, meet my trust officer!"

There was sporadic, puzzled laughter at this, but it stopped when Alida pushed her way through the crowd. She looked white and grim and took Michael firmly by the elbow.

"Come on. Let's get out of here."

He followed her slowly out to the car, and they drove home in silence.

"Wait for me in the living room," she said tersely as she pulled up before their front door. Michael walked in alone and poured himself a drink at the bar table. He was feeling numb. He noticed in the mirror that he had a large purple eye. Then he heard Alida's voice in the doorway.

"Are you drinking again? Already?"

He said nothing but slumped in a chair. He did not even look up as she came in and stood before him in the center of the huge white carpet.

"Are you so far gone you're not even ashamed?"

He felt her towering over him. "Just about."

"What do you expect to do now?"

"Nothing," he replied with a shrug.

"What do you expect *me* to do?"

"Anything."

He watched the lower part of her dress retreat across the floor. She would pace the room now.

"Well, tell me this," she said. "Will you be ready to leave here tomorrow? And go to Auntie's on the Cape?"

"What for?"

"To get away from this mess. While I think my way through. I've pulled your chestnuts out of the fire once, and maybe I can again. But you'll have to cooperate. How about it? Will you go?"

"You go."

"*I* go! And what'll you do? Stay here and make passes at Ginny Dexter? Not in *this* house, my boy."

"I can move to Ma's."

The dress stopped moving. "What does this mean, Michael? Are you leaving me?"

"You said *you* were going."

"Well, you don't think I'm going to stay here while you scandalize the community by strutting like an old rooster around a girl who's practically your own daughter!"

"I don't know what you intend. I only know what I intend. I intend to stay here."

There was a perplexed silence. "Will you give me your word not to see that girl?" she asked.

"My word is worthless. You know that, Alida."

"Not quite."

"Anyway, I won't give it."

"What do you see in her, anyway?" she cried with sudden violence. "An affected little piece who probably looks upon you as an ogre!"

"Then you have nothing to fear."

"Except your making a fool of yourself!"

"I don't expect you to understand. Or to sympathize."

"Well, I should think not!"

He got up to leave, but, white with anger, she thrust him back in his chair. "Must you be a complete idiot all your life?" she demanded fiercely. "Don't you know what this girl *is* to you?"

"What?"

"Only another chapter in that dreary biography of what you think you *have* to be. Flora was youth. I was maturity. Ginny's your 'dangerous age.' Labels, all of us! Because you couldn't care less!"

"It's not true!" he cried, stung at last. "Ginny's different!"

"Ha! Don't you wish she were!"

"You're wrong!" He was on his feet now. "She's entirely different!"

Alida's face was a vivid clash between her satisfaction at arousing him and her fury at what he had said. She managed to smile pityingly. "You really ought to study your own behavior pattern and snap out of it before it's too late. It's clearly suicidal!"

"Maybe it was. It isn't now."

"Don't fool yourself." Her smile was now frankly a sneer. "I only found out from Daddy last week that it was Flora's boy friend who gave Mrs. Winters that letter. After you had driven him out of the office. *Knowing* he had it."

"What of it?"

"Obviously, you wanted to ruin yourself at the bank. You only went off with me because I was Ambrose's daughter-in-law. And when that didn't work, when Ambrose forgave you, you had to think up something else to destroy yourself with. And you got it, all right. Trust *you!* An affair with your own stepdaughter!"

"You've got it all wrong," he protested stubbornly. "Ginny's different. Ginny and I started way back."

"My dear, you're sick." Alida was cool and condescending now. "You're sick, and you don't know it. Ginny's only the way out of the trap. The trap that you've spent your whole life laying for yourself."

"What trap?"

"The trap of your own success."

"Which *I* laid!" He laughed bitterly. "Which you laid, you mean. Who dragged me back to the bank? Who made me play up to Ambrose? Whose idea was it to come down here this summer and sit on his doorstep?"

"It was the only way to keep you from turning into a beachcomber in Nassau and drinking yourself to death!"

"Having a husband who was president of a bank meant nothing to you, I suppose? Oh, *no!*"

"To *me?*" She stamped her foot in a frenzy. "You think I cared about your miserable little bank? *I,* who divorced the son of the man who owns it! Why, Ambrose would have *given* it to me if I'd asked him!"

"But you didn't want it that way," he retorted. "You wanted to own the bank president. You wanted to carry him around in your pocket and squeeze the life out of him!"

"Life?" It was her turn to laugh bitterly. "*What* life?"

"If there's none left, you know whose fault it is!"

"Get out!" She turned and swept a glass vase with flowers off a table by his feet. Her face was livid. "Get out!"

He stared at the scattered flowers and the dark water stain on the carpet. It was a scene. "Don't make a scene," he said mechanically.

"Get out!"

He went to the french doors that opened on the dunes and turned the handle. As he stepped out he felt the cool breeze in his ears and heard the sudden, close roar of a breaker.

"Get out!" she cried for the fourth time.

As he closed the door and stumbled away across the sand he heard the tinkle of glass behind him. She had thrown something after him through the door.

18

IT WAS A MILE down the beach to Flora's old place, and the air was damp and windy. His shoes bothered him in the sand, and he kicked them off and went on barefoot. He took off his tie, too, and threw it away. When he arrived at the house, he stood for several moments in the faint moonlight, looking up at the familiar weather-beaten white front. There was not a single light on, but as he moved forward again, he saw something move on the terrace, and he heard Ginny's voice.

"Michael! Is that you?"

She hurried down the beach to him, put her hands on his shoulders and turned his face to the moon. "Oh, you poor thing!" she cried. "Look at that eye!"

He reached up and took her hands in his. "Never mind. You're not angry?"

"Angry? Come and sit on the terrace. Do you realize we haven't seen each other once alone? Really alone? All summer?"

"Where's your mother?"

"Gone for the weekend. We're alone!"

The candor of her enthusiasm, after so many weeks of coyness, took his breath away.

"Then I was right," he murmured. "You *do* care!"

"Of course, I care, you dope!"

Her arms were around his neck, and she clung to him. "Come inside where it's warm," he muttered in her hair. "Come in, sweetie."

He felt as he went through the darkened living room what he had wanted to feel in that house more than twenty years before. He felt it as he stumbled up the stairs after her; he felt it as they frenziedly tore at each other's clothes, as they fell on the bed together, struggling in each other's arms. There was no mistaking it now that it was here, no denying that it *could*, after all, happen even to him. Ginny moved her legs rapidly and tore at his back and shoulders with her nails; she cried her gratification with an energy that recalled the tales of the young man in the red velvet evening jacket. But who cared now? He gripped her shoulders violently as he approached a climax that was to make up for everything.

And, then, when it was over, and he fell back, exhausted beside her, she clung to him still.

"Oh, Michael," she sobbed, "it was so true, what you said to me. *All* those things, every one of them! I've wanted you like a mad thing. Don't go back to Alida. Never go back to Alida! Will you promise me?" He tried to sit up, but she forced him back with a cry of terror. "Where are you going? You're not leaving? You're not going back to her?"

"I just thought I'd take a walk on the beach."

"Why? No, don't. Stay with me! *Please*, darling, stay with me!"

He lay still and waited until she should go to sleep, which she soon did, and soundly, with low gasping snores. Then he slipped out from under her arm and dressed hastily in the dark. As he went down the stairs he paused to listen. It was all right. He could still hear her.

Outside on the beach it was even more windy and cold.

A storm was blowing up. The waves were breaking high, but farther out than usual; between them and the beach the shallow water boiled and eddied. He could make out in the half moonlight the sudden crest of white along the top of a rising mass; seconds later came the boom as the great wave broke. There was no one else on the beach as far as he could see, but lights twinkled in some of the big dark shingle piles along the dunes, and once he thought he could catch the distant strain of a jazz orchestra at the beach club. He walked to the edge of the water and then waded over his ankles into the hissing surf. He trudged down the beach for several hundred yards this way, and then stopped and turned to face out at the sea.

He had been with a woman whom he had wanted and who had wanted him. For the first time. There had been no love on Ginny's part; it had been nothing but loneliness and desperation. But that was not the point. To become a man, as other men, to become an animal, as other animals, he had, quite simply, destroyed himself. He had equated manliness with hardness and lust; he had wanted to be a beast, and he had become a beast. Congratulations, Michael! For achieving a lifetime's ambition! The idea that had come to him on the top of the Pyramid of the Sun had now a striking validity. If he had at last achieved the vitality of the living, he had surely earned the right to cease to live.

Standing there in the dark, in the cold water, he reflected with a calm which struck him even then as curious that, having never done anything, he would not have the decision now to put an end to it. That he was quite sure at last he wanted to seemed merely irrelevant. He had come out of himself again, out of his skin, like a snake, and was watching himself, a poor huddled figure, ankle-deep in surf on a deserted beach, waiting for that figure, that other self to wade into the black- and white-streaked water and swim out until it had gone too far to return. Yet it was as if he had no power over that figure, as if there were something indestructible in its very loneliness, its futility, as if it had been placed there as a warning, a kind of aid to navigation, a small black groaning buoy endowed with the agelessness of a bad example. In a sudden spurt of rebellion against the very idea of such a helplessness he took his coat off and threw it behind him on the sand, and then immediately, with growing excitement, tore all his clothes off and stood naked in the indifferent wind. His mind seemed to be turning over like an ancient, throbbing engine, pausing as it reached the top of its arc of revolution and flopping wearily over on the downward pull. Supposing I did, he thought. Supposing I really *did!* He backed out of the surf, exhausted by the very excitement of the idea, and sat down on the wet, yielding sand, trying to picture the news as it would come to Wall Street. He thought of Ambrose, walking in the crowd of commuters in the grey early morning, with the immobile faces around him, the half-nod of the unuttered good morning, and the closer friends moving just a bit closer, with the self-conscious cough, to murmur with a roughness that denied the inference of sentiment: "Shocking news about Michael Farish, wasn't it?" Oh, shocking, shocking, how quick the answering nod, even impatient, the accelerated step to the door of the office building, no further words unless of sports, perfunctory, or unless, yes, the always permissible, the dismissing: "I think people who do that must be a little bit crazy, don't you?" For what would his death be, anyone's death, in the early morning of business things, but an indecency, an irrelevance, a shocking reminder of the approaching end of the day?

If no one cared, did it really happen? Could it happen? He rose now and walked down the sand into the water until it was up to his knees. It was bitingly cold, yet not so cold as he had thought. It would be quite possible to swim out. And he laughed aloud, a small dry sound in the windy night, to think that he would never drown himself, that he would only go through the motions of doing it, as he had gone through the motions of answering every challenge that he had believed life was offering him. He would swim out into the ocean now, warming himself with the vigor of his strokes, and then he would swim slowly and calmly back, making it a symbol of his return to life. And if he swam too far, well, he would have solved the problem, he would have answered the challenge, he would have shown the courage, if only by default. He plunged altogether into the churning water, and the cold was shocking now. Conscious only of the coldness he swam as hard as he could, with long strokes, and he seemed to be shooting through an oddly calm sea. It must have been one of those rare long lulls for he could hear no breakers, nor could he see any dark mounds ahead. When he was tired, he trod water gently, turning slowly about and feeling almost warm. But then he jerked his head around with a shocking, terrified premonition and looked straight up to see looming over him, incredibly high, the white crest of a mammoth breaker. He cried out as the dark cloak swept down on him, crashing over him, whirling him, twisting him, tearing him, roaring in his ears and nerves, until he thought himself dreaming, tossing to and fro on a bed, until he imagined that he would awaken, and his thoughts would coalesce, and he would know where he was and tumble back, exhausted with relief, upon his pillow. Then his head bobbed suddenly above the surface, and he thrashed wildly about, but in the blackness he had no idea where he was headed; every desperate stroke might only be taking him farther out to sea. So he *was* going to drown! He was going to die in this blackness, to become a part of it! In a few more minutes — oh, no! He shouted and screamed until his mouth filled with water, and as he struck out with his arms his mind seemed to slip. Get it over with, he thought frantically as he used up his balance of strength in a desperate crawl, get it over with, the whole fantastic mess! When the second breaker struck him, he had no further energy, and his mouth filled again with water, and when he tried to relax and float he knew that he was going down.

19

GERTRUDE FARISH sat on the porch of her hotel on a morning in late October, a steamer rug about her shoulders, and stared out at the slate-colored, tumbling waves. The beach was deserted except for gulls and the small dark figure of an old man with a stick, poking about among the shells. It was a cold, overcast, dismal day, but the sea was calm. Its long grey swell seemed to heave lazily and then break, half in boredom, into a rash of petulant surf. In a leather box by her chair were stacked the dozens of unanswered letters, blue and white and grey and even pink, their elaborate monograms staring up at her, the shock of their sympathy wobbling through the scratchy, well-bred hands. "Dearest Gertrude, we're thinking of you, *thinking* of you. Is there nothing we can do? When we first heard, we couldn't believe it!" "No, there's nothing you can do, any of you," Gertrude whispered to herself peevishly. She didn't want to be thought of. What good did it do to be *thought* of?

They were all so reticent, so embarrassed. And why? Why should the means of death be so important? Why did one always think of Joan of Arc in the flames and Mary Stuart at the block? Why should Michael have made the whole heritage of the disciplined Lears ridiculous? But there it was. He had. She thought of her mother, dying of cancer, erect and chuckling at the bridge table, of the hours that the coachman had spent polishing the family Victoria, and later the electric; she thought of the laughter, the years of laughter and smiles, an eternity of exercising mouth muscles, until the sound of it seemed to turn into one loud bray and then into the roar of the breakers, closing over the body of one more nervous Lear. Now she would not have to laugh again. She had laughed enough. She looked at her watch fretfully. Why didn't Seymour come? She wanted her lunch.

He was down from Harvard to pick up Michael's things at Alida's house, and he had dutifully proposed to call on her. It was quite proper that he should do so, but she had no desire to see him. As she had told her poor worried daughter, Gwen, when the latter had begged her to stay with her in town, she didn't want to see anyone. What was the point? They were all trying to forget Michael, and they would all succeed. She didn't blame them, but she resented them. And why try to share resentment?

With Alida, for example, grief seemed to have been swallowed in anger. She had acted as one determined to destroy every trace of Michael in her life. She had not only put her house on the market; she had even renounced her share of Michael's estate. When she had called on Gertrude, just before her departure for the city, she had been dry-eyed and sharp and frostily polite.

"You were very handsome about the money, my dear," Gertrude told her. "There was no reason for you to do it. After all, you're Michael's widow."

"Not in my eyes. Had he lived, I would have divorced him. It was all over."

"I think he owed you at least what he left you."

"He owed me nothing. Anyhow, I have plenty of money. Flora and Seymour need it more."

"Well, I know they're very grateful." Gertrude nodded emphatically to cover her embarrassment. What was there to say now? "I wish I understood you better," she ventured. "But, as you say, it's all over. Try to forget the Farishes. I hope you'll marry again and be happy."

"I doubt it," Alida's tone was dry and bitter. "I doubt if I'm made for it. When the children are old enough for boarding school, I can travel with my aunt. We can go round and round the world."

"But you're young, my dear. And I'm sure you have great talents. You should put them to use."

"I'm afraid they're wasted. I've been a terrible fool. When I once get it into my head that something belongs to me, that I'm *entitled* to it, I can't let go. It was that way with Michael. I had to wait and wait until I caught him. And then what could I do with him?" Alida shrugged. "Squeeze him to death!"

"Oh, my dear! Don't say that!"

"Allow me to be melodramatic, Mrs. Farish. I rather enjoy it." Alida rose to take her leave. "If I can't think of myself as ill-used, I can at least imagine myself a demon. Anything's better than the truth. Anything's better than admitting that he just didn't give a damn."

Flora was kinder. She came to see Gertrude several times, and they got on together well. It seemed strange that first her divorce and then Michael's death should have cemented their relationship. But on her last visit she speculated more freely than Gertrude thought fitting on a most distasteful subject. Flora, for all her Cameron blood, had never been quite a lady.

"I've had a terrible time with Ginny," she said. "She hasn't really been herself since the night it happened. You know — moody. Sudden storms of tears. I want to send her on a trip, but she can't find anyone to go with. Michael, you know had been paying some attention to her. Do you suppose they could have met that night?"

"I'd rather not suppose, if you don't mind, Flora."

"But we can't be ostriches, can we?"

"*I* can."

"Well, that's all very well, I suppose, but of course I *am* Ginny's mother."

Gertrude studied her for a long moment. "If there's any question of complications, Flora, I'll be glad to pay."

"Oh, no, it's nothing like that. She's been to a doctor and promised me."

"Then there's nothing more to be said. She'll get over it, I'm sure."

"Oh, yes," Flora shrugged. "She'll get over it."

Ambrose Parr had fled from Bradley Bay with his court the very morning after Michael's death. Gertrude had learned from Gwen that he had given orders that Michael's name was not to be mentioned in his hearing. But, like Canute, he realized that his authority did not extend over the breakers, and the sound of their booming through the windows of Bonniecrest might have been too painful a reminder. The season was over, and Gertrude had Bradley Bay to herself.

When Seymour came at last, he seemed entirely self-possessed. His affectations had been consolidated into a raven-black tie and a wide mourning band. He talked with a new maturity about problems of the estate and what his mother would have to live on. Gertrude listened vaguely, nodding her head, until he placed a worn leather jewel case on the wicker table before her. She stared at it blankly for a moment and then gave a little exclamation.

"But that was Maury's!"

"Of course. Daddy kept his studs in it. Alida left it at the bank for me. Is there anything in it you'd like, Gran? Mummy said I was to ask you."

"No, nothing, dear." But then a thought struck her. When she opened the case, the gold objects seemed to jump out at her: cufflinks, tie clips and pins, watch chains, cigar cutters, knives, an Eversharp pencil and charms, dozens of charms. "Ah, yes, these," she said and picked out a pair of large square cufflinks with tiny rubies. She caught the flash of disappointment across Seymour's face and smiled. "Oh not to keep. Just for a little while. You shall have them back next time you come."

"No, Gran, they're yours, of course."

"My dear, what would a woman my age be doing with such things? I just want to hold them for a bit." She put them up to the thin light. "He got them at Alfeoni's, you know. He used to get all his things like that there. How he adored them! And how mean I always was about it." She put the cufflinks down on the table and gave them a little pat. "Even when he was little I used to say it was sissyish. As if it matters how the small pleasures of life come! And now that I'd be happy to spend my last penny buying him cufflinks, I can't." She smiled dryly. "That's the way life is, isn't it? Or rather that's the way death is."

"Daddy cared a lot about things like that, didn't he? Small things?"

"He was never sure of the big ones."

"Tell me, Gran. It's something that worries me." Seymour leaned way forward and stared at the porch boards between his knees. "Was Daddy a weak man, do you think?"

"It depends." She gazed at the long, level line of a wave that was about to break. "It depends if you think it was weak to do what he did." She shuddered and pulled her blanket more tightly around her. "Personally, I should think it would take a great deal of courage."

"Are you sure he meant to?"

"I'm afraid we have to face that," she said, almost crossly. "It was not like Michael to go for a midnight swim alone. Without a bathing suit."

"But why?" Seymour looked up at her suddenly, and she was shocked to see the anguish in his eyes. "Why did he do it? If he was unhappy with Alida, he could have left her the way he left Mummy! Why did he have to do this to us?"

"What had we done for him?"

"What chance did he give us? He never needed anything! No, Gran, I'm sorry, he was selfish. He was hard and selfish. In my church what he did was a mortal sin."

"Then let your church judge him!" Gertrude was actually trembling with her sudden gust of anger. "Let all of you judge him if you want, but leave me out of it! You add up the score of his last year. I'll take his first forty-five!" She glared at Seymour who looked away, abashed. "He was a good son," she said emphatically. "He was a good husband. He was a good father, as you, of all people ought to know. And a good trust officer, too. So good they'll never be able to replace him!" She paused, breathless with agitation, while Seymour hung his head. She felt a twinge of shame to be so violent with one so young, but before she could control it, her temper had erupted again. "Of course, they'll never know how good he was! He was far too clever at making people think they'd done the job themselves. That's the reward of the perfect diplomat, isn't it? Oblivion!" She contemplated her grandson balefully. "People are so stupid.

They took all he had to offer and never even knew they were taking it. So what, you may say. So it's the way of the world. But I'm old, Seymour. I can reject the world. And I do!"

Seymour looked stricken. "You say he was a good father, Gran," he faltered. "You say I should know that. Maybe I should. I was his only child. But did he ever . . . Well, did he ever really care for me, do you think?"

"He loved you," she said firmly. "He loved you always. And you weren't always so easy to love, my boy!"

"But this last winter. We never saw each other. I suppose I should have, but I was so angry. So resentful. Oh, Gran, I should have, shouldn't I? Oh, Gran, do you think I could have stopped him?" And suddenly he was on his knees by her chair, his head in her lap, shaking convulsively.

"Come, dear. Come now. There was nothing you could have done." But then she stopped; her tone was too dry. The boy's ego, his greed for sympathy, his instant need to turn his father's tragedy into his own, to take even that from Michael, repelled her. But as she sat, rather gingerly stroking his tonicked hair, it came over her that this sobbing young man, for all his exhibitionism, was the only other person who was really affected by Michael's death. And he was forlorn, too, poor Seymour. The evolution from resentment to remorse could be a dreadful one. Flora, of course, would never understand him. For several minutes Gertrude wrestled with herself. Surely at seventy she did not have to take *this* on? But with her, she thought regretfully, self-pity had never been more than a mood, even a luxury, and her hands were already clasping those thin, twitching shoulders.

"Seymour," she said gently, "get up, child. It was in no way your doing. All I'm saying is that if you don't believe in yourself, the world won't, either. But there was *still* a lot to believe in in Michael. Remember that."

"Oh, Gran, I will!" He looked up at her passionately with tearstained eyes. "I want to make it up to him. I want to make it all up! For not believing before!"

"No, child. That's no way to treat the dead. We owe them nothing." She thought of Michael and her husband and shook her head quickly. "Nothing. I want you to come in now. We'll have a drink and lunch, and I'll tell you a lot of happier things. About Bradley Bay in the old days and my family. And how your grandfather and I got married. Oh, Seymour, do you know I've never told you *half* my stories?" He got up with a disconsolate motion, and she took his arm to lead him down the cold, already wintry porch and into the hotel away from the hungry sea.

Auchincloss. Venus in Sparta.

Redwood Library and Athenauem
NEWPORT, R. I.

Selections from the Rules

New fiction is issued for 7 days, new
non-fiction for 14 days, and other books for
28 days with the privilege of renewal.

Books overdue are subject to a fine of 2
cents a day.

All injuries to books and all losses shall
be made good to the satisfaction of the
Librarian.

5 volumes may be taken at a time and
only 5 on 1 share or subscription.